POLLY'S HEART

BY
M. LEE PRESCOTT

Published by Mt. Hope Press

Copyright 2018, M. Lee Prescott

ISBN: 978-0-9982184-4-1

All rights reserved. No part of this publication may be reproduced, stored, or transmitted (auditory, graphic, mechanical, or electronic) without the express written permission of the author, except in the case of brief quotations or excerpts used in critical reviews or articles. Thank you respecting the hard work of this author. To obtain permission to excerpt portions of the text, please contact the author at mleeprescott@gmail.com

http://www.mleeprescott.com/

This book is a work of fiction. Names, characters, places, and events are products of the author's imagination or are used fictitiously. Any resemblance to actual people (alive or deceased), locales, or events is entirely coincidental.

For Abby, Ava, Benjamin and Teddy,
and the world of wonder we share.

CHAPTER 1

Polly Granger stamped her snow-covered boots on the doormat. The warm air of the Cottage was thick with spices, and the heady scent of cinnamon surrounded her. Six inches of snow had accumulated overnight, a rarity in the temperate valley. "Good morning!" she called. "I see you've got everything ready."

It was her co-teacher Lynn's morning to open up the day care. A big woman, Lynn's thick brown hair was tied back in a full, somewhat messy bun. She bustled about the cheerful space, setting up the activities for the day. They were building gingerbread houses with the children in the afternoon, and they used dozens of cinnamon sticks for fencing and various structural supports.

"Hey, Poll," Lynn said, straightening up, charcoal eyes sparkling. "Everything's set except the milk cartons. Gracie's been saving them for us, and I completely forgot to stop on my way in. You okay if I run into town and grab 'em?"

Laughing, Polly pulled off her cap and smoothed her long, ash-blonde hair, alive with static electricity. As Lynn had packed up and flown out of their condo earlier, Polly had reminded her three times about the empty cartons.

"Of course," Polly said as Lynn grabbed her coat and rushed by, a blast of winter air filling the room.

Polly shook her head. *Lynn would forget her head if it wasn't attached.* Her colleague and roommate, Lynn Manguilli had taught her so much in the short time they'd worked together, but her friend was one of the most absentminded people she knew. She hung up her coat, changed from boots to sneakers, and was just heading into the playroom when the door opened again.

"Now what did you forget?" she asked, surprised when she turned to find Kevin Larrabee on the doorstep. "Oh!"

He grinned. "Morning. Sorry to startle you. Didn't Lynn tell you we'd be by today?"

"No, but that's not unusual. Have you come to finish the shelving?"

"Yup."

Polly watched as the tall, broad-shouldered contractor with tousled sandy hair and arresting gray-blue eyes brushed snow from his heavy canvas jacket. They were surrounded by gorgeous men in the Valley, but she thought Kevin Larrabee was in a class by himself. Every time she saw him, the attraction grew, and she felt her heart flutter whenever she found herself in his company. *Watch out, Polly Granger. You're in your fantasy world again, falling for someone who doesn't even know you exist.*

"We had a break at the farm," he said, referring to Saguaro Valley Stables, the thoroughbred breeding and training facility that Ben Morgan Senior and his college buddy Spark Foster were building north of town. Kevin had come to the Valley to build Spark's new Valley home and had never left. He now lived in town, in a small house he'd bought and refurbished. Aside from occasional local jobs, Kevin and his crew worked exclusively for Spark and the Morgans.

As Polly moved about the playroom setting out toys and puzzles, she looked up at him. "How's it coming?"

"We're pushing hard to get the main buildings up and running. Harley and Ruthie's house should be ready by Christmas."

"Really? I hear it's beautiful. The house, I mean."

"Pretty spectacular," he replied as he watched her move about, her slender frame lithe and supple. She was dressed in jeans and a blue turtleneck, her blonde hair in a braid down her back.

As she straightened up, Polly noticed his gaze and blushed. "Is there something I can help you with?"

"No, sorry, I'll stop ogling and get started. Let you get back to work."

As Larrabee disappeared into the storeroom, Polly sighed. She knew he was divorced and had lived in Portland most of his life, but she had no idea if he had friends, a girlfriend, or anyone back home or here in the Valley. She had dated in college, but there had been no one since she'd left Chapel Hill. At Lynn's encouragement, she'd tried online dating and had gone on several dates, mostly with men from Tucson, but no sparks. Back in Rhode Island, her mom was beginning to use the spinster word since both her sisters were married and the oldest, Kirsten, had a new baby. *"I'm twenty-five, Mom!"* Polly would reply, but that usually fell on deaf ears.

"Morning!" a voice called from the entryway. Maggie Morgan stepped in, holding her toddler, Ben Morgan the Third. Her eight-year-old, Emma, followed holding Ben's backpack.

"Hi, Maggie, hi, Emma, hi, Ben!" Polly said, coming to greet them.

"Hi, Polly!" Emma said brightly as her brother buried his head in his mother's shoulder. Both children had brown curls and their father's gorgeous chocolate-brown eyes.

"My father-in-law's coming by in about fifteen minutes to drive Emma to school. I should have asked about this much sooner, but you don't mind of we drop off her like this, do you?" Maggie asked, wrestling her son out of his jacket.

"Of course not! We love having her here any time. In fact, we depend on it. Emma is a huge help. Always. In fact, we're making gingerbread houses this afternoon, and we're hoping Em will be coming here after school."

Emma nodded.

"Terrific. We'll wait till you get here so you can help us and, of course, make a house of your own."

Maggie smiled at Polly, then pointed to her son. "Mr. You-know-who woke up on the wrong side of the bed this morning."

"No worries. We'll cheer him up, won't we, Em?"

"By the way, Polly, thank you so much for your work with Archie," Maggie said, referring to a wild mustang the ranch had recently adopted, one of several they were training for the border patrol program. "Nick says you're a natural."

Maggie managed the ranch's stables now that Harley Langdon was running Saguaro Valley Stables. In truth, she had been the "boss" at the ranch's stables for many years, so it had been a smooth management transition.

Polly smiled. "I don't know about the natural part, but it's good for me too. I've been scared to death of horses my whole life, but Archie's such a love. He makes it easy."

"Before long, you might be riding him."

"Oh boy, don't know about that. That might take a whole lot more courage than I have. Walking him is one thing, but riding? Yikes!"

Kevin's hammering interrupted them, and Maggie turned to her. "Are they still working here?"

"Just finishing up some shelves," Polly said. She gazed from the storeroom and back

"Who?"

"Kevin."

Maggie smiled. "That's nice."

Ben slipped from her arms and headed for the bins full of trucks and cars.

"Better scoot out while he's occupied. Have a great day, Em," Maggie said, bending to hug her daughter. "Grandpa'll be here soon."

CHAPTER 2

By the time Lynn returned, the Cottage was filled with the sounds of laughter and music. Raffi's Christmas CD played softly in the background as Ben Senior, patriarch of the Morgan family, rolled around on the rug with his grandson and Christy Perez, two-year-old daughter of Emilio Perez, who worked on the ranch's organic farm.

Ben Senior's eleven-month-old granddaughter, Lily Dillon, crawled nearby and giggled at their antics, and his eldest grandchild, Emma, was doing a puzzle with five-year-old Toby at a table specially built by Kevin to accommodate Toby's wheelchair. Fara, Christy's five-year-old sister, sat beside them drawing.

"Happy chaos reigns," Lynn said, stowing the bag of milk cartons in the kitchen. "Morning, Mr. Morgan."

"Back at you, darlin', although we gotta break you of this 'Mr. Morgan' business."

Lynn laughed. "I know, sorry. Sometimes it's less confusing with all the Bens around here."

"There is that," he said, giving her a hundred-watt Morgan smile. A charmer like all his sons, the sixty-one-year old was a ruggedly handsome man. Rumors of a heart condition didn't seem to be slowing him down, Lynn mused as she observed the melee on the rug.

"I passed the school bus on my way back," she said, giving him a gentle reminder about Emma.

"Thanks, darlin'. This ole man could stay here all day, but duty calls. Emmie, five minutes, sweetheart!"

"Hey, Ben," Kevin said, stepping back into the room.

"Mornin', son. How're you doin'?"

"Great. I should be finished here soon, then I'm headed over to the farm."

"Wasn't checkin' up on you," Ben said. "Spark and I were thinkin' of headin' up there later this morning. Would the crew like lunch?"

"Are you kiddin'? Of course. Whatever they packed will be bird food if they hear you're bringin' stuff from your kitchens." The senior Morgans and Spark Foster employed two of the finest chefs in the Valley.

"Done deal," Ben said, reaching over to tickle little Ben. "We'll shoot to be there by noon. I'll give Spark a call right after I drop my princess at school."

Spark Foster and Ben Morgan had dreamed of building a thoroughbred breeding and training farm since their college days at Stanford. A widower from Portland Oregon, since the completion of his dream house, Spark had moved to the Valley permanently, and now the two old friends were inseparable.

Spark's daughter, Amy, was a physical therapist in Tucson, married to Jeb Barnes, Maggie Morgan's assistant at the Morgan's Run stables and Toby was their adopted son. Spark had hired a full-time aide, Heather Sanchez, who commuted from Tucson three days a week to work with Toby. They were hoping that in a year or two, Toby could transition to the local elementary school.

Kevin watched as his employer helped Emma gather her things as his grandson hung on his pant leg. Polly gently intervened and picked up the wriggling toddler. "Say bye to Em and Grandpa!" she said.

The toddler frowned. "I want to go with Papa!"

His sister gave him a hug. "You'll have much more fun here, Bennie. And don't forget, when I get back, we're making gingerbread houses. Take a good nap so you won't be grouchy."

They hurried out as Polly diverted his attention, carrying Ben to a bin of trucks,. Puzzle completed, Toby wheeled over.

"Hey, buddy, can I play trucks with you?" he asked, his brown eyes sparkling.

Polly winked at Toby and mouthed *thank you* over Ben's head.

At the storeroom door, Kevin watched, marveling at her easy way with the children. His ex-wife Judith hated children. On their honeymoon, she announced that they wouldn't be having any, *"Period, end of story."* That pronouncement was not what had broken them up, but it hadn't helped.

Polly looked up and met his eyes, and he blushed, knowing he'd been caught ogling. "Everything okay?" she asked softly.

"Great, yup. All set. Gave 'em a coat of primer. I'll come back for the finish coat tomorrow if that's okay?"

"I'm sure that'd be fine. Right, Lynn?"

Lynn smiled. She held Lily, whom she had just changed. "Perfect, great. Thanks Kev," she said, eyeing her friend and the handsome carpenter. "Will we see you tonight at the big wingding?" she asked, referring to the party Spark Foster was hosting for Ruthie Morgan and Harley Langdon. The couple had been married six months earlier by the justice of the peace, but had postponed a celebratory party for so long that the older generation had taken over. Ben and Leonora Morgan, Ruthie's parents, were cohosting.

Kevin grinned, a sheepish expression on his handsome face. "Wingdings are not really my thing, but my bosses would never forgive me if I don't show up."

"Great, save us a dance!" Lynn said merrily.

"Only if you're wearing steel-toed dancing shoes. I've got two left feet, I'm afraid."

"We'll risk it, won't we, Poll?"

"Okay, then. See you later," he said, turning away.

When the door closed behind him, Lynn gathered some books and invited Christy and Fara to come to the rug. As she passed her colleague, she said, "He's a hottie, isn't he?"

"Who?" Polly asked, pulling trucks from the bin and setting them in front of Ben.

"You know who. And, he's hot for you too!"

Polly blushed. "Is not!"

"Is too! Come on, kiddos, who wants to hear about Santa's reindeer?" She settled on the floor. As the children gathered around her, she said, "I predict you'll be a couple by Christmas!"

"Don't be ridiculous," Polly said, gazing up as the door opened again and Heather Sanchez, Toby's therapist, appeared.

CHAPTER 3

"You have truly outdone yourself, dear Spark," Leonora Morgan said, linking arms with their friend, her husband on her other arm.

The tall, handsome Foster, who had often been mistaken for the actor and politician Fred Thompson, smiled down at her. "You look as young as the bride, Nora." And she did. Resplendent in a long, pale, blue-green shimmering gown that flattered every inch of her five- foot-four-inch, slender frame, she waved away the compliment with "Pish, tush! This is my baby's night!"

"She'll always be a bride to me," her husband said, kissing the top of her head.

"That's enough! Don't think I didn't see all the gals' heads turn when you two stepped into the barn. Now, where is my baby girl?"

As Polly and Lynn walked in, Leonora waved. "Hi, ladies, good to see you."

"Don't you put the sun to shame," Spark said as he embraced each of them.

Polly blushed crimson. Reticent by nature, she was still adjusting to the Valley denizens' warm, effusive greetings. She returned Spark's hug, then those of both Morgans. "Thank you, Mr.… Thank you, Spark. This is beautiful. You've created a truly magical place. Have the kids seen it?"

"Not yet," Ben said. "We're enjoying the quiet before the storm."

"Are we early?" Polly asked, noticing that they seemed to be the only guests.

"Not a bit," Spark said. "You're right on time. Now, what can we get you to drink?"

"Thanks, Spark," Lynn said, "but we'll find our way to the bar. You're needed here to greet everyone."

Leonora waved her hand. "Oh, pish tush, let 'em wait on you, sweetie. I can hold down the fort. Now, shoo, both of you, and get these ladies a lovely cocktail."

As they crossed the floor to one of three bars, Polly spied Kevin Larrabee coming in with several of his crew. Lynn spied him at the same time and whistled. "Whoa, he cleans up well, doesn't he? Nothing like a man in a tux."

Polly's heart skipped a beat as she watched him greet Leonora Morgan. *Gorgeous doesn't even begin!*

"Who're you admiring?" Spark asked, turning to her. "Ah, our foreman, one of the most eligible bachelors in the Valley. Kevin's like a son to me."

Ben Senior nodded. "He is a right handsome fella, isn't he?"

"He's from Portland, right?" Lynn asked, knowing the answer.

Spark nodded. "Yup, came down to build my house and never left."

"What about his family?"

If Spark wondered about Lynn's nosiness, he didn't let on. "His folks live outside Portland. Has a couple of siblings scattered around. He's divorced. No kids. I think he and his wife tried to reconcile even after the papers were signed, but I guess it didn't work out. He's a good kid. Bought a house in town, which is terrific news for us. Here we are," he said, winking at the bartender. "What'll you gals have?"

Both asked for Pinot Grigio. Wine in hand, they turned back to the crowd in time to see Ben and Maggie Morgan and their kids' arrival. Baby Ben scrambled out of his father's arms and was off at a gallop. Beth Morgan, Lang Dillon and his parents, Martha and Jaybo Dillon, were right behind them. Beth held their daughter, Lily, and Lang his father's elbow. The elder Dillon had been ailing for quite some time with heart problems and the ravages of life as an alcoholic. Polly waved to Emma, who skipped over to say hello and hug her grandfather. "This is awesome, Papa!"

"Spark's decorators," he said, spinning her around in his arms, her bright red dress a blur of ruffles and sequins.

"Hey, Emmie, you look so pretty!" Polly said as Lynn and the others moved off, Ben Senior and Spark to resume their hosting duties and Lynn to find their place cards.

"Grandma bought this in Prescott," she said, twirling around. "I even had a fitting!"

"Lucky girl," Polly said, smiling at the pretty child. Maggie and Ben Morgan were often referred to as the beautiful couple. They and their offspring reflected that beauty inside and out. All four were dark-haired and Ben and his children, dark-eyed. Maggie's eyes were deep prairie blue. Like women everywhere, Valley women came in all shapes and sizes. Maggie Morgan was all curves, and the dress she wore tonight hugged every one of them.

"Maggie Morgan's a beauty, isn't she?" asked a voice behind her.

"Oh!" Polly said, surprised to find Kevin Larrabee at her side with what appeared to be a gin and tonic in hand.

"Sorry, didn't mean to startle you."

Polly smiled, unnerved by his nearness, every fiber of her being electrified. "Yes, she's spectacular. Her husband's not too shabby either."

He laughed. "Makes us mere mortals look pretty ordinary, doesn't it? With one exception, and she's standing beside me. You look beautiful tonight."

Polly blushed. The little black dress Lynn had convinced her to purchase was worth every penny. Kevin's eyes looked hungry as he gazed at her. "I don't know about that, but I could say the same about you."

Her hand grazed his, and Kevin's libido shot into overdrive. As he searched for a topic of conversation, cheers went up at the entrance to the barn. "Oh boy, it's the couple of the hour."

They spied Harley Langdon and Ruthie Morgan framed in the twinkle lights at the barn's entrance. Eight and a half months pregnant, she looked radiant in a short, off-white lace dress that showcased her lithe, lovely legs, round belly, and glorious cleavage. Her thick red hair was swept up and her freckled face glowed.

Even though Harley looked as if he'd rather be a million miles away, the handsome wrangler was smiling, his arm draped over her shoulders.

"Pregnancy certainly agrees with Ruthie Morgan," Kevin said.

Polly nodded. "She looks so happy."

"Another pupil for your Cottage soon, right?"

"Yup. She claims she's going back to work after a month, but we'll see."

"Longer commute for them once they move to the farm," he said as he looked over to see his crew milling around, looking disoriented. "Would you excuse me? My men look like they've landed in a foreign land."

She laughed. "I know the feeling. This crowd can be a bit intimidating."

"Nothing a few beers won't cure," he said, meeting her eyes. There was a shyness there that had touched his heart from the first moment he had laid eyes on Polly Granger. He hated to leave her side. "You okay?"

"Of course. Go rescue your friends."

"Why don't you come with me? They'd love to meet a friendly, down-to-earth soul."

"Well, I…"

"Come on. It'll be great."

"Well, okay," she said, catching Lynn's eye. Her friend gave her a thumbs-up, which Polly chose to ignore. Gently, he took her arm, and she allowed him to lead her through the crowd. His touch sent shivers up her spine.

"Hey, guys, how's everyone doin'?" Kevin said to the five men clustered by a table piled four feet high with cheeses, breads, crackers, olives, and beautifully cut vegetables, a tower of dips and sauces at the center.

"Great, boss," a tall lanky man said.

"This is Polly. She and her partner run the ranch school."

"Day care," Polly said. "Hello, everyone."

Kevin introduced them all, including Victor, a tall, dark-skinned man who his boss proclaimed to be "The best finish carpenter I've ever met."

"You did beautiful work on the Cottage," she said. "Did you work on this complex as well?"

"Sure did." Victor grinned, revealing several missing teeth. "Biggest project I'd ever been a part of, that is until the super farm came along."

"I hear Harley and Ruthie's house is amazing."

"Pretty cool," Victor said.

They talked for a few minutes before Kevin gazed around at the group and asked, "Do you guys really wanna stand around and eat cheese all night? Where the hell are your drinks? The bar's over there."

They watched as the crew made a beeline to the nearest bar. "I'll pay for that later," he said, chuckling.

"Oh?"

"Vic's missing teeth? Bar fight. Need I say more?"

"Oh dear."

"I'll keep an eye on 'em."

Polly looked around at the crowded barn. "I shouldn't think a little rowdiness would bother this crowd."

"There's rowdiness and there's that crew. Where're you sitting?"

"I think Lynn and I are seated with Ben and Maggie's family, and maybe Lang and Beth? Lynn took our place cards, and as you can see, she's waving."

"I'm sorry to walk away from you, but I'd better figure out where the crew's sitting." On impulse, he reached down and took her hand, giving it a gentle squeeze. "You really do look beautiful," he whispered before letting go.

CHAPTER 4

"I saw that!" Lynn said as she approached the table. "You guys are moving right along, aren't you?"

"Stop it!" Polly said, giving her a swat. "No one is moving anywhere."

"He took your hand. What was that?"

"Honestly, I don't know. I almost fainted. My knees are still wobbling."

"Exactly!" Lynn said, clapping her hands.

"Exactly nothing. I mean, I do find him attractive, but he probably has a million girlfriends."

"Doubt it, but I'll ask around."

"You will do no such thing!"

"Now we've got to find me a man," Lynn said. "You can't have all the fun."

"I do not have a man. Now can we please change the subject?"

"Hey, you two," Beth Morgan said, Lily on her hip as Lang pulled out the highchair for her. Spark had thought of everything, even seating for the children. "What's wrong, Polly? Your face is red as a beet."

"Overheated, I guess." She turned and gave Lynn a look.

"Can Lang get you something?"

"Oh no, I'll be fine. There's water on the table."

As they chatted, two of Beth's siblings took their seats. Drop-dead-gorgeous Robbie Morgan and his fiancée, Hope Seymour, sat to Lynn's right, and Kyle

Morgan sat across from Polly and Beth. The last to arrive were Rose Dillon, Lang's sister, and her new husband, Sam Morgan. Rose and Sam lived and worked in Maryland. Robbie and Hope were living in town in the same condo complex as Polly and Lynn until they decided where to settle down. Kyle was in the process of moving from Boston to assume the job of veterinarian-in-residence at Valley Stables.

"Hey, ladies," Kyle said, "I've been hearing great things about the day care. Okay if I come for a tour while I'm in town?"

"Absolutely, come over anytime," Lynn said.

Polly listened as they chatted, marveling at the easy charm of "the Morgan boys." Sam was quieter, but Kyle and Robbie carried on a lively repartee while the women rolled their eyes as if to say, *there they go again.* Both Sam and Kyle were dark-haired and looked very much like their oldest brother, Ben. Robbie favored his mother, right down to his green eyes and tousled blond hair.

When the group dispersed to visit one of the six buffet tables situated around the barn's perimeter, Polly found herself walking beside Kyle. "I'm headed for the seafood. How about you?" he asked, flashing the Morgan smile.

"Me too. What a treat."

"You're from back East, aren't you?" he asked.

"Yes, Rhode Island," Polly replied as they passed the table where Kevin Larrabee sat with his men and some of the workers from the ranch's produce and livestock farm run by Beth and Ruthie Morgan. She caught Kevin's eye and smiled. He gave her a look that she couldn't quite read as Kyle led her through the crowd.

"Where in Rhode Island? I've spent a fair amount of time there."

"Bristol. Do you know it?"

"Oldest, longest, grandest Fourth of July parade in the country."

She laughed. "Yes, I grew up a block from the parade route, so we always had front-row seats. Have you been?"

"Yup. Buddy of mine keeps a boat in Tiverton, so we docked by the Lobster Pot one year. Great time."

"Well, you were four blocks from our old house. My parents still live in Bristol, but they sold the house and bought a beautiful condo on the water."

"In the old carpet mill?"

"Yes," she said, surprised he knew her hometown so well.

"Bristol has a great waterfront. Must be a big change for you to come from there to here."

"I've lived a couple of other places. North Carolina, Cape Cod."

Kyle handed her a plate. "How do you like the Valley?"

"It's great," she replied as she scanned the long buffet. "Oh my goodness, where to begin?"

There were at least five kinds of fish, prepared in a variety of ways, huge platters of crab legs, sautéed calamari with peppers, bowls of lobster, crab, and conch salads. At the far end, warming trays held seafood Newburg served in flaky puff pastry. As Kyle piled his plate high, Polly selected trout and a scoop of lobster salad and was eyeing the Newburg when he caught up to her.

"Go ahead, you gotta try it. It's a favorite of Spark's and my dad's even though neither should go within a mile of it."

"Maybe just a little?" Polly said as the server deftly settled a full pastry on her plate.

"Enjoy."

Polly looked up, surprised to see Spark's raven-haired chef, Aria Firorelli. "Thank you, I'm sure I will. Everything looks delicious."

"It is," the chef said, eyes now fixed on Nick Parker, one of horse trainers from Morgan's Run stables, who was just behind Polly and Kyle.

"I'd love some salad, but I don't think I can fit anything else on this plate," Polly said to Kyle as they made their way across the room.

"No prob. When we get back to the table, I'll go back and grab some salad for both of us if you like."

Polly marveled at the easy Morgan charm possessed by every member of the large and growing family. As they walked, she asked, "How will it be for you to be back home? Are you excited about your new position?"

"You bet. I love the East Coast, but this is home."

"Will you live out at the farm?"

"At first. They're giving me a couple of rooms in one of the bunkhouses. I may eventually get a place in town. We'll see. You live at the condos where my brother and Hope are, right?"

"Yes. It's great. People are friendly, and it's convenient. You can walk to everything. I love Saguaro. It's a great town."

"Sure is. Okay. What's your pleasure?" he asked as he set down his plate.

"Excuse me?"

"Salad? Veggies?"

"Oh, you don't have to do that. I can—"

"My pleasure."

"Anything's fine. I eat everything, but not too much with all this."

"Be back in five."

"Now you have two admirers," Lynn whispered as she attacked her huge plate of food. She had visited the Southwestern table as well as the long buffet of beef, pork, and chicken.

"Hush!" Polly said as she blushed again. *Kyle Morgan is cute, but he isn't Kevin Larrabee.*

CHAPTER 5

Kevin watched Polly with Kyle. *She's better off with someone her own age, not an old geezer like you,* he thought, turning back to his men, who all had enormous plates of food in front of them.

"Hey, boss, your Ms. Granger is one *fine* woman," Andy, the youngest member of the crew, said. "Think when the dancing starts, she'd dance with me?"

Kevin smiled at the freckle-faced young man with ruddy cheeks and pale blue eyes. In his mid-twenties, Andy had been working for Kevin since he graduated from high school, and he'd followed his boss from Portland. The rest of the guys were local except for Victor, who had been with Kevin for over twenty years. When Spark brought them to the Valley, they'd recruited men from the local communities and now had three full crews employed full-time at Valley Stables. "Never know if you don't ask, buddy."

Following desserts and a few toasts, the band started, and Ruthie and Harley danced a slow reel to Whitney Houston's "I Will Always Love You." After that, the dance floor filled, and, true to his word, Andy approached Polly, who accepted his invitation to dance.

"I have to warn you, I'm not much of a dancer," she said as they strolled onto the dance floor.

"No problem. I'll help you." And help he did. The band played a series of fast rock-and-roll songs, and Andy had her spinning, dipping, and twirling like a pro.

He was an excellent dancer, and Polly gave herself over to his lead, laughing as he spun her here and there.

As Kevin watched the couple's every move, wondering whether he dared ask her to dance, Kyle cut in and swept Polly off, leaving Andy openmouthed in the middle of the floor.

"Better make your move soon, buddy."

Kevin turned to find Kyle's brother Ben beside him.

He shrugged. "Out of my league, I'm afraid."

"Bullshit. Where's that coming from?"

"I'm miles too old for her."

"Bullshit. Forty-two is hardly old. What's ten or so years? Nada."

"More like fifteen. Kyle's more her age. Andy too."

"Yeah, but she isn't sweet on my brother or Andy."

"And how would you know?"

Ben laughed. "Not my observation. I'm clueless. Maggie mentioned something."

"Oh?"

"Guess she's seen you two together."

"Geez, Louise," Kevin said, shaking his head. The Valley pipeline was formidable! "Oh, what the hell," he said and headed onto the dance floor.

"That's the spirit, buddy. Go get 'em!" Ben called as Maggie joined him.

"What are you up to now nosy parker?"

"Nothin', babe," he said, drawing her to him. "Just givin' Larrabee a nudge."

"Poor Kevin. I never should have said anything to you."

"Care to dance, beautiful?"

Maggie wrapped her arms around his neck. "Thought you'd never ask."

*****

A fast song ended as Kevin reached Polly and Kyle. "Can I have the next one?" he asked, meeting her eyes.

"Sure thing," Kyle said, taking Polly's hand and placing it in his.

Eric Clapton's "Wonderful Tonight" began, and he drew her close, letting the music guide his steps. Polly sighed and rested her head against his chest. *Finally,* she thought, feeling safe and warm in his arms.

Kevin scarcely dared breathe as he held her. He could feel himself grow hard and pulled back slightly, not wanting her to feel his arousal.

Too late. She had felt his erection against her belly, and smiled. He wanted her as much as she did him. She gazed up into his beautiful blue eyes.

He met her gaze and smiled. "Thought I'd never get a chance."

"I'm glad you did."

"Look, Polly, there's an attraction here, at least on my end. I realize I'm a bit long in the tooth for a pretty young woman like yourself."

"What makes you say that?"

"Well, I'm forty-two, and you're in your twenties."

"Twenty-five next week, but what does that matter?"

"I'm gonna take a chance here. Polly, would you like to go out sometime? Maybe have dinner, or we could—"

"I'd love to."

Surprised, he gazed down. "You would?"

She nodded.

"Well, great, then. How about tomorrow, or anytime you're free?"

"Tomorrow's great."

"Seven?"

"Perfect."

Once again, he drew her close as the last strains of the song heralded the end of the evening. He was about to offer to drive her home when Lynn approached. "Great party, huh, guys? You ready, Poll? Looks like things are winding down." Pausing, she noticed their expressions. "Shit, I'm interrupting, aren't I?"

"Oh geez," Kevin said, spying the crew staggering en masse toward the bar. "Sorry, ladies. I've gotta corral the gang before there's trouble. See you tomorrow night?" he said to Polly.

She nodded.

He gave her hand a squeeze and hurried off.

"I'm sorry," Lynn said as they watched his retreat. "I should have read the signals. Was he going to drive you home?"

"Not sure. We'll never know, I guess. Anyway, it's fine. We're going out tomorrow," Polly said, smiling.

"Ooh la la!" Lynn said as, arm in arm, they went to say their good nights.

CHAPTER 6

Sunday morning, Polly and Lynn ate breakfast at Gracie's, a diner four blocks from their condo. As they walked back, newspapers in hand, they spied Hope Seymour getting into her truck. Hope waved. "Good morning."

"Enjoying the quiet of Sunday morning?" Lynn asked.

"Not exactly. I'm headed over to the ranch. They've had some bad news. You've met Willow, Harley's daughter, right?"

"Yes, we met her when she was here last summer. She's a sweetie," Polly said. "Is she okay?"

"Willow's okay, but she couldn't come to the party last night because her mom's been failing. Talia died last night."

"Oh, I'm so sorry," Polly said.

"Is there anything we can do?" Lynn asked.

"No. Harley and Ruthie are headed up there now. I don't know who from the family will go up for the funeral, but you know them. I'll bet they'll all want to go to support Willow and Harley."

"Please tell them we're here if they need us to take care of the kids or help out. Anything," Polly said.

"Thanks, I will." Hope slid into the truck and backed out.

Lynn looked at Polly. "Whaddya think? Should we go over too? Or, maybe call the Morgans?"

Polly shrugged. "It's hard to know what to do. We're not family, and I hate to intrude."

"I'll call Leonora. She's the organizer. I'll just tell her we're on call if they need us."

As soon as they got home, Lynn called the Big House. "Oh, sweetheart, thank you for checking in," Leonora said. "The memorial for Talia is Wednesday. All our kids want to go. It would ease their minds greatly if they knew the children would be well cared for. I'll get back to you, okay?"

Lynn rang off. "Funeral's Wednesday. If I had to guess, I'd say we'll have Toby, Ben, Emma, and Lily a bit longer than usual. We'll have to get Emma to and from school, but we can borrow a booster seat, and one of us can go."

"That's Heather's day off, so we'll be short-handed," Polly said. "But, I'm sure we'll manage."

Lynn gazed out the window. "Maybe we can get Sally Pruit. I'll phone Maggie later."

*****

Kevin parked his truck in the condo lot a little before seven and headed up to Polly and Lynn's unit. He was dressed casually in khakis and a blue sport shirt. Polly opened the door. "Hello. Hope I'm dressed okay. We're not going anywhere fancy, are we?"

He grinned and spread his arms wide. "Me, fancy?"

"Well, you were in a tux last night."

"Once in a blue moon. You look terrific, by the way, but then you always do."

Polly was in jeans, a turtleneck, low boots, and a pale gray sweater. Her long hair was loose, falling over her shoulders in soft waves. She wore little makeup, just a hint of blush and lipstick, and her lemony scent lingered as she grabbed a warm jacket.

"All set," she said. "I'm off, Lynn!"

"Have fun!" her roommate called from the bathroom.

"She's in the shower. Just got back from a hike."

"You too?"

"Yes, we took the river trail with Archie. We didn't go far. The snow's packed up. It was beautiful."

"Archie? Should I be jealous?"

Polly laughed. "Archie's a horse. I'll tell you about him later."

"No wonder your cheeks are rosy."

She blushed, and the rosiness crept down her neck. "Where are we going?"

"There's a new place about eight miles down just off the Gila. I haven't been, but I hear it's good."

"Is it Vermillion? Maggie was talking about it last week."

"That's the place. Have they been?"

"She went with her girlfriend, I think."

"Here we are," he said, holding open the truck's door. "Sorry it's the truck. I cleaned it up so you wouldn't be covered in sawdust."

"It's perfect," she said, hopping up.

As they headed out of town toward the Gila Highway, Kevin asked, "How was your day?"

"Quiet except for a trip to the ranch to make arrangements for this week. Do you know Harley's daughter, Willow?"

"Yeah, poor kid, I heard her mom died."

"All the Morgans are going to the service in Flagstaff. We've got the kids. It's pretty much a usual day except they'll be with us a little longer."

"Wish I could help, but we've got all kinds of people coming this week for various projects. I can't very well take off."

"We'll be fine. We've got a local woman coming, and Toby's therapist has agreed to come too. That's plenty of people."

They rode the rest of the drive chatting about Valley Stables and what was happening there. Finally, he turned off the highway into a gravel drive bordered by tall brush on either side.

"This place never ceases to amaze me," he said.

She nodded. "Yes, it's incredible. I came out here thinking I'd be living in the middle of the desert and was so surprised to find it so green."

"That's what an orographic effect'll get you," he said, referring to the unusual cloud formation and abundant moisture that had created this extraordinary valley where a handful of enormous ranches, including Morgan's Run, the Dillons', and a few smaller ones, flourished. While the Valley was largely undiscovered, its three-thousand year-round residents and an equal number of snowbirds, tourists, and wealthy vacationers delighted in its rare, verdant beauty.

"I took a geology course, and we never studied this kind of ecosystem," she said.

"From what I've heard, it's pretty rare. Plus these guys spend big bucks to keep it a secret," he said.

Chapter 7

After turning off the Gila Highway, they drove down the winding drive, grasslands on either side. Vermillion was at the southern edge of the Valley, flat, open spaces interspersed with rolling hills. Finally, they reached a clearing where a large farmhouse, several barns, and numerous outbuildings lay in front of them.

"Wow," she said.

"This is it. Vermillion. It's a farm-to-table restaurant."

He pointed to a long, low barn that looked newer than the others and had recently been painted. A small sign that hung to the side of the double doors read: Vermillion.

Kevin parked, and they strolled toward the barn, looking around at the beautiful countryside. A round, apple-cheeked woman met them inside the door. "Welcome, folks. You must be the Larrabees."

Polly gazed around, surprised to see that every one of the dozen tables was occupied except a small table for two at the far end of the room. Kevin stepped forward. "Yes, I'm Kevin Larrabee, and this is Polly. Some place you've got here."

Polly noticed he didn't correct the woman's assumption about *the Larrabees*.

"We like it," the woman said. "My name's Edna. My husband and I own the place, and one of my daughters'll be serving you."

"Is your husband the cook?" Polly asked.

"Oh, mercy no! We'd never have a customer. No, we have a top-notch chef, Francis Bissett. Imported him from San Francisco. Actually, he wanted to come to the country, so we didn't have to drag him."

"Does he live here?"

"We offered, but he lives in Tucson and commutes. We only serve lunch and dinner, and I do the lunches. They're much simpler, even though Francis prepares a lot of it. Here's your table. Make yourselves at home and I'll send Nancy right over."

"Why Vermillion?" Polly asked, as they sat opposite each other.

"Our clay. It's vermillion yellow. Very unusual. Great for certain crops, poor for others."

Nancy, a slender version of her mother with the same rosy cheeks and bright blue eyes, appeared and handed them menus. "What can I get you to drink?"

"I'd love a white wine," Polly said, "on the dry side, not too sweet. Have you a house wine?"

"Actually, all our wines are from Saguaro Vineyards," she said, referring to the Dillons' winery just south of Morgan's Run. "Although, we do have a California champagne."

"Perfect. I love a sauvignon blanc," she said.

Kevin watched the exchange between the two women, a slight smile on his face. Polly had a quiet warmth that somehow managed to be both sweet and sexy, at least to him. When Nancy turned to him, he was caught off guard. "Sir, what can I get you?"

"Seltzer water with a twist of lime, please," he said.

"I'll be right back," she said, disappearing.

"Oh, I'm sorry. Was it okay that I ordered wine?"

"Of course," he said.

She broke the awkward silence, saying, "This is fascinating. I've never been to a place like this."

He grinned. "Sometime I'll show you Portland. It's a foodie mecca, and there are a bunch of places like this outside the city."

"Portland sounds like a wonderful city. Do you miss it?"

"I miss friends and family, but the Valley's pretty nice too. Who knows? If the work dries up here, I may be forced to relocate. How about you?"

"I'm enjoying it so far, but someday the Morgans' children and grandchildren will grow up and put Lynn and me out of jobs, I'd imagine."

"With the current baby boom, I doubt that'll be anytime soon. Then there'll probably always be new ranch workers' kids."

"That's true," Polly said, smiling as Nancy approached.

Nancy set down their drinks. "Would you like to hear the specials?" she asked.

She described several entrees and appetizers, then said, "Shall I give you a few minutes?"

He looked at Polly. "Whaddya think?"

"I'm going with the trout," she said. "You?"

"Lamb for me. Thanks, Nancy," Kevin said.

"That did sound good," Polly said.

"Are you wanting to change?" Nancy asked.

"Thanks, but I'll stick with my trout," she replied, sipping her wine as Nancy nodded and disappeared.

"Polly, thanks for agreeing to this."

"Thanks for asking."

"I know I'm an old geezer and kind of a hermit. It's rare when I find someone to whom I'm attracted and really want to spend time with."

"I can't speak for the hermit part, but you're hardly an old geezer. I was very pleased that you asked." Afraid to meet his eyes, Polly screwed up her courage. "I might as well warn you. I'm not very experienced. Except for a brief and ultimately tragic relationship in college, I haven't dated much."

"Why not?"

She shrugged. "I think I'm kind of ordinary and plain and most men want glamourous and sexy."

"You're far from ordinary or plain," he said, reaching across to take her hand. *In fact, if this table wasn't between us, I'd pull you into my arms and ravage you right here and now.* "I think you're beautiful."

Polly felt her cheeks grow hot and knew she must be as red as a beet. "Well, it's kind of you to say. Tell me about yourself."

"Not much to tell. I'm one of four kids. Mom's a schoolteacher. Dad owns a hardware store in Beaverton, just outside of Portland. My brother and sister help run it now. My other sister's a nurse in Spokane."

"You didn't want to go into the family business?"

"I thought about it. Worked there all through high school, but I got hired by a builder my first year of college, and I found I liked that better. I'm the youngest, so it wasn't too traumatic for Pops. He has Craig and Elaine to run the store when he retires."

"It's great that it's still in existence. With all the superstore chains, many of the great hardware stores back home have closed."

"It's pretty popular. More like a hardware slash general store. They pride themselves on service. It's a really popular tourist spot, especially during the summer."

"Sounds great."

"I'll take you there someday. I'd love to take you there."

Polly smiled, dropping her gaze as Nancy served their dinners. When she left, he said, "I didn't mean to presume or overstep."

"It's fine," she said, reaching for her fork, unable to meet his eyes.

"No, it's not fine, me presuming like that. You barely know me. If I were you, I'd be running for the hills."

She looked up from her trout. "Well, I have no intention of running for the hills with this delicious meal in front of me. So bon appetit!"

He laughed. "Maybe over dessert, I'll tell you all my dark secrets so you can decide if you need to lace on your running shoes."

They spent the rest of the meal talking about the Valley, the Morgans and Spark Foster, and day-to-day life. "Spark's been super good to me," Kevin said as

Nancy cleared their plates. They opted for warm peach cobbler ala mode. "I've been working for him almost exclusively for almost ten years. He always had a project in Portland, then the estate he's built here, and now this thing with Ben Morgan."

"They're amazing, those two. Both self-made, very wealthy men, and so generous," she said.

"Yeah, they're incredible guys. Ben's wealthy, owns half the Valley and all, but even he's not in Spark's league. Spark's a billionaire, probably many times over. He's got his hand in almost every solar and wind project in the world, and his company's always researching new alternatives to fossil fuels. What those two have in common, though, is ethics, morals, and a love of family and friends. You step into their circle, and you're family for life. He certainly saved my life."

As the sky turned orange and red with the setting sun, Nancy appeared with their cobblers. They had taken her suggestion and were now enjoying coffee and dessert on the deck looking out over the farmlands and the mountains beyond.

CHAPTER 8

As she sipped the excellent coffee, just the way she liked it with thick cream and a hint of sweetness, Polly sighed. "This has been a perfect evening. Thank you."

"No," he said, turning to her. "Thank you. I haven't enjoyed myself like this for a long time."

She sensed an edge to his voice and gazed over, "You okay?"

"Yup."

"I don't want to pry, so don't answer if it's too personal, but you said Spark saved your life?"

"After my divorce. It was really nasty, and I was a mess. Drinking way too much, burning bridges left and right. I was estranged from my family, who'd all but given up on me, and I don't blame them. I was a bastard. I was working on one of Spark's projects at the time. A huge plant just outside Portland. He took me aside one day and read me the riot act. Got me to AA and went to a meeting every day with me for several months until it was a routine I couldn't do without. This was at the same time as his wife, Patsy, was dying. At one point, I was living in their house. She was a saint, by the way. I've never seen two people more in love than those two. He's been like a second dad to me ever since. I love my own father, and we're reconciled now, but Spark is a close second."

Polly listened, the pain in his eyes evident. She wanted to let him know she cared, but she couldn't quite find the words. Finally, she said, "I'm glad he was there for you. He's a very kind man."

"Yes, he is. I want you to know that my drinking… It's my problem. I still go to meetings and haven't had a drop in five years."

"Does it bother you that others drink around you?"

"Not at all. It was tricky at first, but it's fine now. I'm not crazy about drunken bar scenes anymore, but other than that, I'm fine with it. Anyway, enough about my soap opera life. What about you? Any boyfriends lurking in the closet? Deep, dark secrets?"

"Not really. I'm the youngest in my family. I have two sisters and a brother, a great dad and a loving but slightly pushy mom who drives me crazy, always worrying I'll end up a spinster. No boyfriends since college. I had my heart broken by someone I really loved, or thought I did. I've been a little gun shy since then."

"He was an ass."

"Excuse me?"

"Your boyfriend."

"Maybe, but that's in the past. He's married now with two kids. Lives in my old neighborhood. Yet another reason for me to get out of Bristol."

Kevin watched her. Polly's eyes were sad. He wanted to protect her from that pain and any other that might harm her. "You know some of my crew have less than stellar pasts. A couple have been in and out of jail. I could ask if they knew anyone who could rough him up, throw him off the Mount Hope Bridge, whatever."

She laughed. "No, but thanks. I'm over him. Good riddance. Besides, I wouldn't want to leave his kids without a father. How do you know about the Mount Hope Bridge anyway?"

"Let's just say there were several wild rides over that bridge from Newport to Bristol one summer when I was crewing on a sailboat. One of the crew, Roger Hall, came from Bristol, so we'd go over and party at his folks' house."

"Hall?" she said. "That name sounds familiar. Maybe my dad knows him."

"See what I mean? Your dad? I'm *really* old."

Polly threw up her hands. "That's not what I meant at all!"

*****

Lights twinkled along a path that circled the cluster of farm buildings. They walked the length of it, then headed to the truck. As Kevin opened her door, she turned. "Thank you for this."

"My pleasure." He bent and kissed her, softly at first. Then as she responded, his lips parted hers and his tongue delved deep. Kevin felt himself grow hard and pulled her closer.

Polly felt his desire and wrapped her arms around his neck, every fiber of her body wanting him. "Oh, oh," she gasped as he trailed kisses down her slender neck.

"Want to see if they rent rooms?" he asked, his voice husky as he cupped her breasts, caressing and teasing until he could feel her nipples harden. "I'm not sure I can drive home with this boner."

"Hey folks, everything okay?" asked a voice from behind the truck.

They turned, mortified to see Edna waving.

"Yeah, great," Kevin said. "Never better."

"Come back and see us again real soon!" she called brightly, chuckling as she headed toward the main house.

Polly buried her head on his chest, giggling. "Think she knew what we were doing?"

"Absolutely. Must've been something they put in the food. Come on, we'd better get a move on."

The ride back was quiet. Polly had so much she wanted to ask, but the time wasn't right. Despite their passionate embrace, they still barely knew each other. *If he'd asked, I'd have torn my clothes off right there in the Vermillion parking lot. Where did that come from?*

He walked her to the condo door and gave her a chaste kiss. "Would you like to do something again soon?"

"Yes."

"I'll see you at the Cottage, and we'll plan it."

"Night."

"Night." Polly closed the door, leaning against it.

"So?" Lynn said, eying her as she stepped in the door.

Polly smiled. "So, nothing. It was fun. Good night!" *I am definitely not ready to talk about Kevin Larrabee and that kiss.*

CHAPTER 9

Midmorning Monday, they were taking the children outside to play in the Cottage's beautiful new playground, when one of the Larrabee Construction trucks pulled up with Victor driving, one of the other men with him. Victor waved. "Hey, morning. Kev had to be somewhere, so he sent us over to put the final coat on the shelving. Okay if we head in?"

"Help yourself," Lynn said as Polly set Lily in one of the baby swings. Lynn noticed her worried expression and said, "Probably just needed out at the *new* farm. I'll just get the snacks and water bottles."

"I'll go," said Polly. "Can you push Lily?"

"Okay," her colleague said, giving her a quizzical expression.

Once inside, she passed by the tray of snacks and water and went straight to the storeroom. "Got everything you need?" she asked.

The men gazed up, puzzled.

"I mean, did you want water or anything?"

"Thanks, but we'll only be here fifteen minutes. We've gotta work fast and get to the farm."

"Everything okay up there?"

Victor had already turned back to the shelves. "Yup, just busy."

"Is everything okay with Mr. Larrabee?"

"Far as I know," Victor said, staring at her as if she had three heads. "Are you okay, Ms. Granger?"

Polly shook herself. "Yes, of course, sorry. I'll let you work."

"No problem," he said, giving his companion a look as she disappeared.

Stupid, stupid, stupid, she thought as she headed to the door. *What is the matter with you?* Ever since childhood, she had possessed a kind of sixth sense when something awful was about to happen. Her parents took to calling her their little barometer because her behavior so often forecast ill events. Right now, she felt closed in and frightened with no discernable cause or reason.

"Where's the tray?" Lynn asked, interrupting her reverie as she pushed open the gate.

Polly jumped and then gave her head a mock slap. "Oh, sorry! Be right back."

"My absentmindedness must be wearing off on you," Lynn said as they passed the snacks. "You okay?"

"Yes, fine. I just can't shake the feeling that something bad's about to happen."

"To Kevin?"

"I don't know."

"Focus on the kids. That'll take your mind off it." Lynn patted her shoulder. "Bennie wants a boost." She pointed to Ben the Third, who was struggling to scale the jungle gym climbing wall.

"Let's go up by the stairs, Ben, shall we?" Polly said, helping him down.

When they came in from the playground, Polly glanced at her cell on the kitchen counter. There was a text from her mom: *Surprise! Coming to visit! See you Thursday! Looking for a B&B now.*

As Lynn brushed by her carrying Lily, Polly showed her the text. "Mystery solved."

"Thursday?"

"Yes. This is so typical! No warning, no asking if it's a good time. This is all I need right now."

At naptime, she phoned home, and Phyllis Granger answered on the first ring. "Hello, dear!"

"Mom? What's this all about?"

Slight sniff. "I thought you'd be pleased."

"I'm always happy to see you, but it's kind of short notice. Is Dad coming?"

"No, of course not. He's a workaholic like you and your siblings."

"How long do you plan to stay?"

"Maybe a week or two. I thought I'd get out of the cold, do some Christmas shopping, and spend time with my precious baby girl. Maybe even persuade her to come home for the holiday?"

"You know I can't."

"Why not?"

"I have work."

"You mean to tell me that the day care is open Christmas week?"

"We close for a couple of days, but yes, the children's parents depend on us. The ranch and farm don't stop for the holidays."

"Well, that's ridiculous. It's too much for you. How are you, sweetie?"

"Mom…"

"I worry, that's all."

"I'm fine."

"Isn't there a law against people working over the holidays?"

"No. Listen, Mom, I've got to go. We'll talk later. Don't bother with the B&B. You can stay with Lynn and me. We've got plenty of room."

"Are you sure, baby?"

"Yes, but don't even think about pleading for me to come back with you."

"Fine, fine, fine… Have you met any handsome cowboys?"

"Mom, I've gotta go. I'm working. Email your flight info, and I'll pick you up."

"Can't wait, baby."

"Me too. Bye."

Polly groaned as she slipped her cell phone into her pocket. "Just what I need," she muttered, joining the children in the nap room. Lynn was busy setting up the afternoon craft project of pine cone birdfeeders.

"So, it's true?" she whispered.

"'Fraid so. I told her she could stay with us. Is that okay? She can have my room, and I'll sleep on the futon in the office."

"Of course, it's okay. I look forward to meeting her."

"Five minutes is usually just about enough of her."

That afternoon as they were all elbow-deep in peanut butter, pine cones, and birdseeds, Leonora Morgan breezed in. "Hi, ladies, hello my sweet darlings! How is everyone today?"

"Hi, Ganny," Ben said, grinning, his face and hands smeared with peanut butter, seeds in his hair and stuck to his chin. "We're makin' bird nests!"

"So you are, precious!" she said, keeping her distance. "I stopped by to say hi, but I can help if you'd like? Have you an extra apron?"

"On the hook behind the kitchen door," Lynn said. They were used to Leonora's pop-ins. She was usually accompanied by her housekeeper, Carmela, but not today. She hung up her coat and headed for the kitchen.

As Leonora sat beside Lily, who was mostly watching and licking peanut butter off her fingers, she said, "My husband's picking up Emma. I'm just comin' from Cowbelles," she said, referring to a women's charity group based in the Valley. "One of the gals just dropped me off. Thought I'd meet him and go into town for some shopping. Now, Miss Lil, shall Ganny help you make a pine cone?"

Lily gave her a gooey smile.

"Paper towels, ladies?"

Lynn tossed some wetted towels across the table. "Here you go." Then she turned back to Toby, who was working on his fourth pinecone.

"You're a busy boy," Leonora said, smiling at him.

"I'm makin' one for Mama, Papa, Grandpa, Buck, and me."

"Aren't you sweet."

A few minutes later, Emma and Ben Senior stepped in, a blast of cold air in their wake. Emma joined them at the table and grabbed several of the remaining pine cones. "Great, I love these!"

"Hey, gals, this looks like fun. Can an old man help?"

Before Polly or Lynn could answer, Leonora said, "No, you cannot. I'm gonna get cleaned up, and you and I are headed for town."

"Sorry, kids," he said, making a mock sad face.

"Don't worry Grandpa, I'll make you one," Emma said, smiling at him, a smear of peanut butter across her cheek.

"Thanks, darling." He bent to kiss the top of her head.

"I hope my absentminded husband told you about Friday night," Leonora said. "We're having dinner at the big house. Just family and a few friends. We'd love for you both to join us."

Lynn nodded. "Thanks, that'd be great. Can we bring something?"

"Of course not."

"Oh, I'm not sure, sorry," Polly said. "My mom's coming for a visit, and she's arriving Thursday. I really should—"

"Perfect, we'd love to have her," Leonora said, interrupting her. "We'll look forward to meeting her. Around six-ish?"

"Thank you. I'm sure she'd be delighted," Polly said. *She'll probably pee in her pants between ogling that beautiful house and all the "handsome cowboys"!* Absently, she wondered if Kevin was invited.

"Well, ta-ta, sweet peas," Leonora said as her husband helped her into her coat.

"See you tomorrow at two thirty sharp, Emmie," Ben Senior said.

A chorus of "bye-byes" rang out as the elder Morgans departed.

"Another social engagement," Lynn said. "I'm gonna have to beef up my wardrobe for this place. Never been to so many parties in such a short time."

"And you haven't seen Christmas, yet," Emma said, her eyes twinkling. "We have a party almost every night that week!"

CHAPTER 10

After Judith's call, Kevin drove straight to Spark's. He found him in his favorite chair surrounded by the five newspapers he read every day. "Hey, son, good morning. Can we get you somethin' to eat? Coffee?"

"Thanks, I'm all set."

From the look on Kevin's face, Spark could tell something was wrong, very wrong. He gestured to a chair beside him. "What's on your mind?"

"I've had a call. From Judith. Can I just spit it out?"

Spark set his newspaper aside. "You should know by now you're as much a son to me as Buck, so let's have it. Then we can deal."

"I haven't spoken to her in over three years and wasn't planning on ever speaking to her again. You know she moved to Florida, right?"

"I remember somethin' about that."

"That's where her folks are, and her sister. Anyway, out of the blue, she's headed back to Portland and wants me to meet her there. She wants me to meet my son."

"Excuse me?"

"Do you remember that I saw her a few years back? You sent me to Texas to get that lumber, and she flew over and met me? We spent a couple of days together? About a half day of civility, then it was the same old shit that had been happening for years. She got drunk and was screaming and yelling. We did not part well."

"And you never touched a drop. I was proud of you."

Kevin smiled sheepishly. "I might not have touched a drop, but I touched her a little more than I should have. I crossed a stupid line, Spark. A *really* stupid line. I was going through a lonely patch and…well, we did have a brief… I slept with her."

"And she claims the child is the product of that liaison?"

"That's about the size of it. Baby's nearly three. A boy. She named him Jasper."

"How can I help?" Spark said.

"I need to go to Portland. Victor knows the drill and can manage the crew. I'll check in every day and be back as soon as I can."

"I'll phone Fred Butler, my attorney, this morning. He'll be at your disposal. If she's pressing you for money, I'm pretty certain he'll want to ask for a paternity test. Just say the word, and I'll wire whatever you need."

"I'm okay. I've got a fair amount saved."

"Don't let her scam you, son."

"Thanks, Spark. I'll keep you posted and be back as soon as I can."

"Why don't you take the jet? Be much easier. As you know, we have several cars at the airport. I can have one waiting for you."

"I can't ask you to do that."

"Course you can. Get your duds together. I'll call Mickey, have him get the plane ready. I'll also call the garage up there. I'll ask 'em to get one of the company vehicles out for you."

"But—"

"No buts about it. Plane just sits there most of the time. It's good to get it up in the air every week or two. Where're you staying?"

"I'll get a cheap motel, maybe spend a night with my folks."

"Use the condo. It's empty. I'll phone Kiki and ask her to bring in some groceries and make a couple of dinners. You can pick up the key from the doorman."

"Spark, this is too much."

"Nonsense. Now ya better get goin'. What time should I have Mickey standing by?"

"I've got to pack and go out to the farm for the afternoon. Is six thirty too late?"

"He'll be ready to go and will have sandwiches and snacks."

"Thank you, Spark."

"No thanks needed. Good luck, son, and remember, Fred's a call away."

With a heavy heart, Kevin drove home, packed a few things, then headed to the work site. He wanted to phone Polly, but he knew she'd be working. *What the hell am I gonna say to her, anyway? It was bad enough when I was just an old geezer. Now I'm an old geezer with a kid and a manipulative, alcoholic ex-wife.*

*****

After work, Polly stopped at the ranch's farm stand on her way home. It was open Monday, Wednesday, and Friday from two to six at the livestock and produce farm. Ruthie ran most markets with the assistance of several of the farm staff. Today, Polly spied her sitting just inside the barn door, directing traffic. "Hey, Polly," she called, waving and holding her belly as she stood.

"Hi, Ruthie. How are you feeling?"

"Great, I just look like a beached whale. At least it's not too long now. Due date's the week after Christmas, which is why we had the party now. No telling how life will change after the baby."

"Well, you'll have lots of help, and your beautiful new home's almost ready, right?"

"That might be slightly delayed."

"Oh?"

"Kevin was called away unexpectedly. He will probably be gone all week, maybe into next week."

Polly forced a smile while fighting to control her roiling emotions. "He has a very capable crew, and they must be on the finish work now. He told me Victor was the best finish carpenter he knew."

"Yes, but Kevin's the brains of that operation, and he's really particular. Harley doesn't think the guys'll dare make a move without him."

"Surely it's almost done."

"You'd be surprised. It's okay, though. I like Harley's condo. It's cozy. I'd love to have been in before the baby, but the condo sure beats the Big House. My mom's been begging me for months to move in with them."

"Lots of help."

"I know, but then I'd lose my husband. Harley wouldn't last five minutes in my mom's house. You okay, Polly? You look a little pale."

"I'm fine. It's been a busy day."

"That's quite a bunch you've got there."

"It sure is, but they're lots of fun."

Polly filled her basket, paid for the produce and a dozen eggs, and said good night.

"Don't be a stranger!" Ruthie called. "We love company. Come visit while we're still in residence."

"Thanks, Ruthie. Take care."

As she drove down the hill toward the ranch gates, her cell phone rang.

CHAPTER 11

Polly flipped over the phone and saw Kevin's name, so she pulled over to the side of the road. "Hello?"

"Hey, it's me."

"Are you okay?"

"Yes, fine, but I have to go out of town for a few days."

"Is everything all right?"

"I hope so, yes. I want to tell you about it, but I'd rather wait till I return, okay?"

"Of course."

"Sorry about this. I was gonna beg you to have dinner with me tonight. I miss you already."

Miss you too, she thought, but said, "Where are you going?"

"Portland."

"That's a long drive."

"I'm taking Spark's plane, or rather, Spark's plane is taking me."

"That's kind of him."

"Yeah, he's incredibly generous, as we've said before. He also has one of his cars waiting for me and has given me the company condo."

"Wow."

"Yeah. Pretty incredible."

They rang off, and Polly headed home, questions swirling. *Why did he suddenly run off, and why so secretive?*

*****

Days flew by at the Cottage. Wednesday, they had Emma, Ben, and Lily until well after dinner while their parents attended Talia Goldstein's funeral. They took all three to the Big House for dinner, after which Martha Dillon came to fetch Lily.

After Martha departed, Leonora said, "You ladies go home. I'm sure you're exhausted. We'll keep the kids here. We have a crib for Ben, and Emma loves staying overnight. Maggie left clothes and things for them for the morning."

"What time do you expect them?"

"My hubby phoned just before you arrived and said they were on their way home. Should be here by eight thirty or nine."

"Are you sure?" Lynn asked.

"Absolutely. Carmela's here to help me. Now shoo. You've got to be up for work tomorrow, and your mom's arriving too. Night."

*****

As Polly made up the sofa bed in their small study, she called to Lynn, "I think I'll change my sheets too and sleep in here tonight. The sofa bed's pretty comfy, and I might as well get used to it. No telling how long Ms. Thought-I'd-surprise-you will be staying."

"It'll be fine. We work all day, and we'll find things to do."

"It's not that. It's her constant nagging about my finding a husband and getting married. You wait, she'll probably start on you too!"

Lynn came in and leaned against the desk. "How good is she? Maybe she can round up some guys for me. I haven't had much luck."

"Join the club."

"What's up with Kevin?"

"I don't know. He said nothing except that he had to go to Portland. I didn't want to pry."

"You like him, don't you?"

"More than I should," she said, sitting on the now-made sofa bed, giving her friend a glum look. "I hardly know the man. And now, in the event that he actually does come back—"

"Which he's going to."

"If he comes back, he'll have Phyllis all over him, and she's the queen of nosy parkers."

Lynn came to sit beside her and patted her knee. "He will come back, and I'll just bet he is more than capable of handling your mom."

"You haven't met her. Just wait."

"Whaddya say we order takeout from Gracie's and watch a trashy romance movie? I'm sure I can find something on Netflix."

Polly laughed. "Why not. You order, I'll change my sheets, and then do the pickup. That will give you plenty of time to search for a really trashy movie."

"Now you're talkin'!"

CHAPTER 12

Kevin had been in Portland two days and had taken time to visit with his parents and siblings before Judith called to say she was in, two days later than she had told him. His family had never liked Judith, and they had been thrilled when they divorced. They begged him to stay with them in Beaverton, but he declined. He wanted to have the business with Judith as cut-and-dried as possible.

"Well, well, well," she said, wandering around Spark's spectacular condo. Unlike his new home in Saguaro, Spark's condo was sleek and modern. He kept it for his occasional overnights in Portland, when he had late meetings. His son, Buck, who oversaw its furnishing, used it more than anyone, as he shuttled back and forth from his home in Laguna Beach to see friends, meet gallery owners, or deliver commissions. A fairly well-known painter and stained-glass artist, Buck Foster had impeccable taste. "You've certainly come up in the world, babe," Judith added, giving him a disdainful look.

"Belongs to Spark Foster, not me."

She hasn't changed a bit, he thought, watching her strut around, her sweater too tight, jeans painted on, and boots sporting ridiculous, impractical high-heels. Even if slightly rougher around the edges, Judith was still gorgeous, her blonde hair perfectly dyed and coifed. Kevin suspected she had put a lot of effort into her appearance in preparation for this meeting. She'd taken a train into the city from where she was staying with an old college friend, and she hadn't stopped posturing and preening since.

"Ah yes, Daddy Warbucks. Lucky you."

"Judith, we're here. I agreed to meet you. Now, what do you want?"

"You know what I want, sweetcakes," she purred, leaning over the counter dividing the kitchen from the spacious living room, its windows offering incredible views of the harbor.

He sat across from her in one of several upholstered chairs covered in buttery soft leather. "No, I honestly don't."

"Aren't you gonna offer me a drink?"

"Not my house, not my booze. And this is not a social call. I agreed to come. I'm here, so spit it out."

"Let's go to a bar. I'm sure as hell not gonna sit here in your fancy condo chitchatting without a drink. Come on, I know half a dozen places within a block of here." Without a word, she grabbed her purse and marched to the door.

I'll just bet you do, he thought, following. *Please God, make this quick.*

When they had settled at the Pico Pub's empty bar, Kevin with a seltzer water, Judith with a huge margarita, he said, "Well?"

"You're really no fun, Kev, you know that? You used to be a hoot in high school."

"That was a long time ago." *Let her speak and leave it alone.* He was already thinking he should find a meeting right after this. Fortunately, he knew of several in the area, and his sponsor was only a phone call away.

"Aren't you gonna ask me about Jaspie?"

"I kind of thought you'd have him with you."

"Don't be ridiculous. I had no idea what state you'd be in, and I didn't want to upset him."

Kevin took slow, deep breaths. *Don't react.*

When she realized he wasn't going to take the bait, Judith shrugged. "The silent treatment? Okay, well, this is the thing. We have a child together, and we also have a long history together, and I wondered if we might want to give us another chance."

Another deep breath. "That's not gonna happen."

"Even it's best for your son?"

"If, as you say, he's my son, I'd like to meet him."

"If? Do you think I'd schlepp all the way across the fucking country if he wasn't part yours? It hasn't been easy, you know!"

"I'm sorry about that, but why am just hearing about him now? He's almost three."

"'Cause I didn't want to fucking lay eyes on you back then."

"Why now?"

"I just said I thought for Jasper's sake, we should give things another go."

"Well, what's Plan B? 'Cause that's not happening. Have you got help in Florida?"

"My folks, but they're not getting any younger, and they're not all that reliable. I work, so does Ivy, and day care costs a fucking fortune. We're livin' with Ivy," she added, referring to her younger sister, the one member of the Robinson family Kevin could abide. "No way I can afford to live on my own."

"What is it you want from me, Judith? If it's child support, I'm willing to talk about this, provided we have proof he's mine."

"You want a fucking paternity test?" she screamed.

The patrons sitting around them turned to stare, and Kevin began counting in his head, willing himself to stay calm. "Do you want to get something to eat?"

She leaned across the table, hissing, "No, I want you to take fuckin' responsibility for your son, you bastard. Don't you think I can see how smug and satisfied you are in your new life, your wealthy friends, fancy condo, flashy car? Probably got some whore stashed away down in Hicksville."

"Judith, I'm going to pay the check and walk out. If you'd like to eat, there's a place a block from here. I'm happy to talk further when you're sober, but I'm not doing this. Not anymore."

"Typical," she said, gulping the rest of her drink and grabbing her purse.

Kevin threw a twenty on the bar. "Sorry about that."

The bartender gave him a sympathetic look. "Good luck, man."

He found her sitting on a bench a block up the street, smoking a cigarette. "Thought you quit."

"Yeah, like that's gonna fucking happen with my shithole life."

"Let's eat."

"No, thanks. Just take me to the train. We can talk tomorrow."

"Judith, you're in no condition to get back on your own."

"Fuck you, Larrabee! You don't get to say what condition I'm in. Not anymore!"

"No, but I can't leave you at the train like this. Why don't I drive you back?"

"It's an hour away."

"Come on, give me the address, and I'll plug it into Spark's fancy GPS."

Within five minutes, she was passed out, giving him time to think. If Jasper was his son, what was the right thing to do? He knew he couldn't live with Judith. Their season was over. However, he could easily afford to pay child support and would, if the child was his. Was it right to insist on a paternity test? He knew what Spark's attorney would say. He sighed as the lights of the city faded and they headed north.

When they reached Judith's friend Lacey Falco's house, she met them at the door. Kevin carried Judith in.

"Hey, Kev, long time no see. Baby's asleep. Want to come in?"

"Thanks, but I'm gonna take off. Just tell me where to set her down."

"On the sofa's fine. I'll throw a blanket on her later. Don't you want to see him?"

"Will I disturb him?"

Lacey shook her head. "No, he's out like a light. Come on, he's on my bed."

He followed her into the dimly lit room and spied a small form under a blanket in the middle of the bed. Thick blonde curls were matted with sweat, and his thumb lolled at the side of his mouth.

Kevin's eyes softened, and he let out a sigh.

"He's a cutie, isn't he?" she whispered.

"Sure is."

After several minutes, they withdrew, and he said good night to Lacey. "Tell her to phone in the morning. I really would love to meet him when he's awake."

He considered finding a cheap motel nearby instead of driving back to Portland, but then decided the drive would do him good. *A son, a beautiful son, how can I possibly turn my back on him?*

After eleven, when he walked into Spark's condo, it was too late to call Polly. He missed her, much more than he should miss someone he barely knew. As he drifted off to sleep, he wondered what she'd think of this new development.

CHAPTER 13

"Mother, I told you, I have to go back to work. Lynn and Heather are covering so I could pick you up, but I'm going to drop you at the condo and go back. It's not fair to them. There's plenty of sandwich fixings, and we have soups and salad ingredients. Or you can stroll down to Gracie's Diner. The food's fabulous, and she's a peach."

"Eat alone, in a restaurant?"

"People do it every day."

"Not this people! Can't I come to work with you? I could help out."

"You can, if you want, but aren't you tired after the flight?"

"Well…just a little, I 'spose."

"Why don't you unpack and rest this afternoon, and we'll give you a tour either tonight or tomorrow."

Phyllis sniffed. "Oh, you have to work tomorrow too?"

Polly took a deep breath. *Stay calm, don't react.* "Mother, I work every day, and sometimes even on Saturdays and Sundays if they need us."

"Well, that's just plain ridiculous."

"I'm not having this conversation with you now, or any time during your visit. I love what I do and that's that. Period, end of story."

"I just worry, that's all, honey. How are you feeling?"

Polly gave her a look. "You promised you wouldn't."

"Okay, okay, but you wait till you're a mom. Change of subject. Have you met any nice men since you've been here?"

"Many, but they're mostly married. You'll see a bunch of 'em Saturday night. The Morgans have invited us to dinner at the Big House."

"Oh, that sounds like fun. What about the unmarried ones."

Polly debated telling her mom about Kevin but decided against it. She pulled her Subaru into the condo lot. "Here we are. Let's get your bags in, shall we?"

"You didn't answer my question, sweetie."

"Come on, Mom. I've gotta go." Polly grabbed the two bags and led the way to the elevator.

"This looks pretty," Phyllis said, trailing behind. "And right on the river."

Once the bags were in and Polly had showed her around, she gave Phyllis a peck on the cheek. "Here's an extra key. I'll be back by five thirty. I'll call when I'm leaving in case you need anything. There are some real cute shops along Main Street, and the café, bakery, and Gracie's. If you're bored, take a walk. The Daily Scoop across from the town green has the best ice cream in the world. Bye-bye!"

Not waiting for a reply, Polly dashed out, relieved to have somewhere to go. Now to figure out how to dodge her mother's relentless questions for the next week, or however long Phyllis Granger intended to stay. *Thank goodness for Christmas, or she'd probably stay a month!*

As she pulled up in back of the Cottage, Polly's cell phone rang. She considered leaving it in her purse, assuming it was probably her mother, but pulled it out, surprised to see Kevin's name. "Hey," she said, answering.

"Hi. How's it going down there?"

"Oh, just peachy," she said, catching herself. She realized she hadn't told Kevin about her mother's visit, and he was probably wondering at her sarcastic tone. "Sorry, my mom arrived unexpectedly today, and she's already driving me crazy. Otherwise, all's well. Everyone's back from the funeral, kids are their usual adorable selves. I'm just getting back from the airport run, so I can't talk long."

"No problem, just wanted to hear your voice."

He sounded sad.

"How are you? Is everything okay up there?"

"So-so. I'll explain when I get back."

"Will that be soon?"

"Not sure. I'll know more later."

Silence.

Finally, Polly said, "I'm sorry, I really should get inside. Are you sure you're okay."

"Fine, I just miss you. And, I'm more fond of you than I should be considering we've only had one date and I could be your father." *Or someone's father!*

"Please don't start that again," she said. "I already have a father, and he's fifty-six."

"Sorry. I'll let you go."

"Kevin?"

"Yup."

"I'm fond of you too. I hope whatever you're doing up there resolves itself soon."

"Me too. Bye, Poll."

As she headed inside, Polly wondered what was so secretive up in Portland. *Is it time to walk away before I get hurt again?*

*****

Lynn and Polly gave Phyllis Granger the grand tour of downtown Saguaro, ending up at Gracie's for dinner. Since it was dark, they didn't drive out to the ranch, but promised a full tour Saturday morning. As they stepped into the diner, they spied Jeb and Amy Barnes, her dad, Spark Foster, and Toby.

"Hi, Polly! Hi, Lynn!" Toby called, and they went to say hello, introducing Phyllis to all.

"Welcome," Spark said in his warm, robust voice as he grabbed Phyllis in a bear hug. "This your first visit to the Valley?"

"Yes," Phyllis sputtered, surprised at his effusive greeting.

"No place like it on earth. I hope we'll see lots of you while you're here. Your daughter and Lynn are doing a fine job with our precious kids," he said, ruffling Toby's curls.

"That's what I hear. I understand the day care was your brainchild?"

"Most of the credit goes to Leonora Morgan. She and Ben are my dearest friends. We go way back. Ben and I bankrolled the project, but it's really Leonora's baby."

"I'm looking forward to seeing it."

"Nice to meet you," Amy said. "I work in Tucson, and Jeb's in school, so we're all over the place these days, but I'm sure we'll see you again soon."

Jeb nodded. "Maggie Morgan's my boss, and she tells me you all will be at the Big House Saturday night?"

"Yes," Polly said. "It was very kind of them to include us."

Spark grinned. "Better get used to it, darlin'. Once you're here, you're family, and family are included in everything. Now, we'll let you get a table. Enjoy."

As they settled into a booth at the back of the diner, Phyllis couldn't take her eyes off Spark, who was chatting with Gracie, the owner. "What a handsome man. He reminds me of someone."

Lynn and Polly looked at each other but stayed silent. *Better to keep her thinking and guessing*, Polly thought. *Keeps her attention off me and my dating prospects!*

Finally, the tall, gangly Gracie, her wiry gray hair flecked with what appeared to be bread crumbs, came over to take their orders. She also extended a welcome to Phyllis, then disappeared into the kitchen.

"Did you see that dirty apron and her hair?" Phyllis whispered. "Is that sanitary?"

Lynn chuckled. "This is the Wild West, Phyllis."

"I can see that!"

*****

Spark and his group waved as they departed. Jeb held Toby in his arms as his father-in-law held the door. Later, as they asked for the check, Gracie grinned. "You're all set."

"Excuse me?" Phyllis said, wallet in hand.

"A secret admirer has taken care of your dinner. Have a good evening, folks."

Before Phyllis could protest, Gracie vanished.

"What was that?"

"Who knows," Lynn said. "Gracie's been known to comp people, but I suspect Spark did the honors."

Hands on hips, Phyllis looked around. "We can't let him do that."

"He just did, Mother," Polly said.

Lynn laughed. "And he's a billionaire, so he can afford it. Come on, anyone for dessert at the Scoop? Might be cold, but I'd love a cone."

"Well, I never," Phyllis said, shaking her head as her companions grinned at each other.

CHAPTER 14

On his way north, Kevin called Fred Butler. Spark had given him the attorney's cell phone number, and Fred answered on the first ring. "Mr. Larrabee, glad you called. Spark alerted me that you might."

"Did Spark fill you in?"

"He did."

"I'm headed up to meet the child, Jasper, now."

"I hope that goes well."

"Me too. Mr. Butler?"

"Fred, please."

"Fred, I'm wondering what you advise about a paternity test, my responsibilities, and all of it. It's come as a shock. My ex never wanted children."

"I recommend that you do the test."

"I'm not sure she'll allow it. I'm almost afraid to broach the subject. She's very volatile."

"So I understand. Why don't we see how today goes? If she refuses, we'll talk about next steps."

"Thanks so much," Kevin said, and he rang off.

*****

Lacey met him at the front door. "They're out back," she said. "Someone has a headache and is in a foul mood. How much did she drink last night?"

"Only one margarita when I was with her, but I think she'd had more than a few before."

"I love her like a sister," Lacey said, "but she's got a dangerous mix of pharmaceuticals and alcohol going on right now. I'm surprised her sister and her folks let her take Jasper all this way in her condition."

"Not sure anyone has ever been able to stop Judith from doing anything, and we are talking about Belle and Ernie here," Kevin said.

"Yes well…they're useless. No doubt about that. Come on, let's go meet your little boy."

When they stepped out the back door, they spied Jasper, running after a striped soccer ball. His mother sat in a lawn chair, hair in a haphazard ponytail, wearing no makeup and sweats. The day was warm, but the child was bundled in a sweater and fleecy pants.

"Hey, guys, look who's here," Lacey called.

Jasper turned, eyes curious. Judith remained as she was, staring toward the back of the yard. The toddler ran up to Lacey.

"Hey, sweetie," she said. "This is a friend of mine and your mom's."

Kevin squatted. "Hi, Jasper. Nice to meet you." He extended his hand, which the child stared at, then shook.

"Are you here to play with me?" Huge sky-blue eyes studied him. His cherubic face was framed by thick masses of blond curls. A beautiful child with features so like his mother's.

"Sure. Whaddya wanta do, buddy?"

"Chasing."

"Sounds good to me. Let's go."

They spent an hour playing tag, kicking and tossing the ball, and tumbling on the soft, damp grass. Ten minutes after his arrival, Judith disappeared into the house, and Lacey soon followed.

It was almost noon when Lacey reappeared. "Hey, Jaspie. You hungry?"

He nodded.

"What about I take you to McDonalds?"

"Can he come?"

"Kevin and your mom have some business to discuss. Maybe they can join us after lunch at the park?"

"Okay." Jasper followed her into the house, Kevin on their heels.

They found Judith slumped on the couch, watching what appeared to be a soap opera. She grabbed the remote and clicked the television off, smiling at Jasper but making no attempt to rise or embrace him. "Jaspie, you be a good boy for Lacey. Remember, he likes chicken nuggets, no sauce, the apple slices, and milk. Thanks, Lace."

Kevin watched as he took Lacey's hand and they headed out. *Jesus, what kind of a life does he have with her for a mother?*

"So?" she said when the door closed.

"So, this is your show, Judith. You got me here. What did you want?"

"I want you to take some fucking responsibility. That's what I want."

"As I asked you before, why now? Why am I just hearing about Jasper?"

"And…as I told you, I wasn't ready to deal with you before this."

"So? Here I am. What makes it suddenly okay for you to deal with me now?"

"As I said, I'm hoping we can reconcile. Take it slow, but see how things go. For Jaspie's sake. You always wanted kids."

"Yes."

"So?"

"So, if he's mine, I will, of course, help you out, but you and me? We're done."

"How do you know that until we try?"

"Because I've moved on."

"After all our history."

"Because of all our history."

"You loved me once."

"Yes."

"You don't think it's possible again?"

He noticed she had applied makeup, combed her hair, and thrown a scarf around her neck. Judith was beautiful, no doubt about that, but hers was a cold, brittle beauty, not a trace of warmth. "No, I don't," he said quietly.

"There's someone else, isn't there?"

He hesitated, unsure if he wanted to tell her about Polly. Finally, he said, "That's not relevant."

"But there is someone."

"Look, Judith. I don't love you anymore. We had our time, and it's over. We're not good for each other."

"Who is she?"

"She has nothing to do with this."

"I knew it! Poor Jasper is gonna suffer because his daddy has a girlfriend and has turned his back on his family."

Kevin shook his head. He felt as if he'd stepped into an alternate universe. The woman was crazy. "I can't have this conversation with you, Judith. If it's financial support you need, let's talk about that. I'd also like a paternity test."

"Fuck that. Not happening."

"It's a simple swab of his cheek."

"Well, you're not doing it, so fuck off. Go back to your girlfriend and screw you."

"I want to help. Tell me about his day care and the kinds of help you need."

"Let's go meet 'em at the park. Maybe grab some sandwiches on the way?" she said, her tone slightly less frosty.

He spent the afternoon with the two women and Jasper, first at the park, then back at Lacey's. Kevin read him a story, and he took a short nap. Then they played and took a walk around the neighborhood. Lacey invited him to stay for dinner, but he declined. "I gotta head back to Portland, but I wondered if I might come back tomorrow?"

"If you want to see him again, that's your last chance," Judith said. "We fly out early Saturday morning."

"What time would be good?"

"Lacey's gotta work, so I'm thinking maybe Jaspie and I could take the train into Portland?"

"Great. Just tell me the time, and I'll pick you up."

After making arrangements, he hugged Jasper, thanked Lacey, and said goodbye. As soon as he pulled the SUV onto the highway, he called Fred Butler and apprised him of the situation.

Butler listened, then said, "What I suggest is that you do the swabs on the child and yourself and get them to me. Think you could do it without her knowing?"

"Probably."

"The results wouldn't hold up in court, but at least you'd know."

"Okay, then."

Fred Butler gave him his address, and he agreed to swing by on his way home. When he arrived at the condo, he found that Spark's housekeeper had fixed pork tenderloins for his supper along with roasted vegetables and a beautiful salad.

He grabbed his phone, thinking he would call Polly, but then set it back down, not even sure what he would say to her at this point.

Chapter 15

"What the matter, pumpkin?" Phyllis Granger asked, watching her daughter mope around the kitchen. Lynn had left for the Cottage as she was taking the early morning shift. Polly would arrive at nine and let Lynn go earlier in the afternoon, as Phyllis had volunteered to help out.

"Nothing, just tired, I guess."

"That's my point. You know what they told us about you getting overtired."

"I'm fine, Mother. Please don't start."

"Let me fix you something. You want pancakes? French toast? Eggs?"

"Thanks, I'm going to toast a bagel and have some fruit." *What I want is to hear from Kevin, and you can't fix it since I'd rather you know nothing about it!*

"Let me do it!" Phyllis hopped off a kitchen stool and grabbed the fruit bowl.

Surrendering to the inevitable, Polly said, "Great, I'll jump into the shower. Be out in ten minutes."

*****

Kevin met Judith and Jasper's train at noon, and they grabbed sandwiches and headed for the zoo. After lunch, they wandered from exhibit to exhibit, letting Jasper nap. When Judith excused herself to use the bathroom, he slipped the DNA kit out of his backpack and gently swabbed the sleeping toddler's inside cheek.

The day went better than he could have hoped. In contrast to her previous behavior, Judith made an effort to be pleasant and amiable, asking about his work and telling him about her life in Florida. As they pulled into the train station, she said, "I'm sorry we're leaving so soon."

"Yeah, I gotta get back to work anyway. Busy time."

"Maybe a few more days and we could have rekindled the spark?"

He switched off the ignition and looked over at her. "I'm sorry."

"Yeah, well, me too."

"I'll be in touch. I think the best thing would be for my attorney to set up a trust for Jasper. Then I can send monthly support checks. If there are special needs, you can let me know."

She waved her hand dismissively. "Fine, anything's fine. More than I have now."

"Come on, Jasper," he said. As Judith fussed, Kevin unstrapped the car seat. "Don't want you and Mommy to miss your train."

He carried the child and car seat into the terminal. They sat in the waiting area, watching him run back and forth, saying hello to everyone he passed. An open, affectionate child, Jasper had already stolen Kevin's heart. He prayed that Judith's behavior the previous two days was an aberration brought on by seeing him again. He couldn't bear the thought of this sweet little boy living with a drug-and-alcohol-addled mother.

"You're okay livin' at Ivy's?"

She shrugged.

"Did you need support for an apartment or babysitting?"

"My mom has him every day, after day care. We're fine. He stays overnight there once and a while so Ivy and I can have a life."

"Is he close to them?"

"You know my parents. They're no picnic."

"What about hiring a nanny or sitter? I could help with that."

"We're good. Go back to your cushy life. Just send the guilt checks, and I'm sure we'll survive."

"Judith, I'm trying to help. I'm sorry it's not more."

"Fuck you," she whispered before standing. "Come on, Jaspie! I see our train. Say bye to Kevin."

Jasper ran to him, and Kevin scooped him up. "Bye, buddy. Hope I'll see you again soon!"

He handed the child to his mother, then picked up the car seat. "Want me to see if I can help you on with all this?"

"We got here okay, didn't we? I'll take it from here." Without another word, she grabbed the car seat, turned, and disappeared into the train. As the train pulled out, he spied Jasper in the window waving, Judith beside him staring straight ahead.

Well, that's over, he thought as he left the station. *Time to go home.*

He left the DNA kit with Fred Butler and headed to Beaverton to have dinner with his parents. He fielded a number of missed calls from Victor and the crew, and one from Spark. Several times, he considered whether to call Polly but always stopped himself, still unsure of what he'd say or how he felt.

CHAPTER 16

Heartbroken at the silence from Portland, Polly had to admit it was actually comforting and helpful to have her mother there. Phyllis had pitched right in at the Cottage, and the children loved her pretzel-making activity. When Polly and her mom got home Friday evening, Lynn had chili, cornbread, and salad ready for them.

As they sat enjoying the meal, Phyllis said, "What a treat to have someone cook for me! And this is delicious, sweetie. You must give me the recipe. Polly's dad would love it, especially during football season. This would be perfect for our Super Bowl party."

The Grangers hosted a yearly Super Bowl party for twenty or thirty friends and family, depending on who was in town for the game. While Polly was not a football fan, she had always enjoyed the evening and seeing everyone. Most people came decked out in red, white, and blue, even if their favorite team was not playing.

"You guys must be Patriots fans, right?" Lynn asked.

"Diehards," Phyllis said. "You too?"

Lynn laughed. "Bears. I lived in Boston before coming out here, but Chicago's home. Besides, your Patriots have enough fans, don't you think?"

"Never!" Phyllis said, waving her knife and cornbread.

*****

"Come in, come in, welcome!" Leonora Morgan said, opening the door. "You're the first to arrive."

Polly groaned, smiling at their host. "Oh dear, are we too early?"

"Not a bit of it," Ben Senior said, coming from behind his wife to greet them. "And this pretty gal must be your sister."

Always the charmer, Polly thought as her mother blushed. "Oh, so sorry. Ben and Leonora Morgan, this is my mom, Phyllis Granger."

"Delighted!" Leonora said, hugging Phyllis, her tall husband right behind her.

Dazed, Phyllis gazed up at their hosts. "This is so nice of you to include me."

Leonora took her arm and led her into the living room. "Our pleasure. Your sweet daughter is family now, and so are you!" She waved her arm. "As you can see, we're a big group tonight."

"Just the way we like it," Ben Senior said.

A long table set for twelve ran the length of the living room and beyond. In the dining room, an equally long table was visible.

"Drinks are out in the sunporch and also in the study. What can I get you, ladies?" he asked.

"Not to worry," Lynn said. "We'll get our own. You've got to greet your guests, and if I'm not mistaken, that was the doorbell."

Leonora gazed back and forth from them to the front hall, then said, "Thanks, ladies. Help yourself. If you don't find what you want, we have it somewhere." With that, she flew off to greet the crowd at the door.

As they headed for the sunporch, Polly spied a pair from the stables, Nick Parker, one of the wranglers, and the new man, Brendan Statler. She'd met Nick several times but Statler only once, at the party for Ruthie and Harley. Right behind Statler came Kevin Larrabee and a man she didn't recognize. On their heels were Spark and a younger man at his side. Much shorter than Spark, there was something familiar about him, and like most Valley men, he was drop-dead gorgeous, with tousled sandy hair, blue-green eyes, and broad shoulders. As she watched, Aria Firorelli, Spark's chef, grabbed hold of her companion's arm, leaning against him. He appeared amused at her behavior.

"Oh my, there are some cuties," her mother whispered, eying the gang in the hallway. "Are any of them unattached?"

Polly rolled her eyes. "Mother, don't start!" Her stomach was in knots at the sight of Kevin. His eyes scanned the room, coming to rest on hers. He gave her a shy smile before being swept away by Spark and his companion.

What she must think of me? Kevin thought, watching Polly talk with Lynn and a woman he assumed was her mother. There was something almost fragile about her tonight. Everyone was dressed casually in jeans, and she was no exception. She wore a soft mauve sweater and a single silver necklace, and her hair fell loose over her slender shoulders.

"Hey, Poll, Lynn, hi!" Ruthie came up behind them.

"Hello," they both said, smiling at the very pregnant youngest Morgan daughter. Harley Langdon stood beside her, one arm draped over his wife's shoulders, the other over those of a tall, lanky teenager with long flaxen hair and his green eyes.

Langdon grinned, eyes full of pride. "You remember my daughter, Willow."

"Hello," Polly said, shaking her hand. "We were all so sorry about your mom."

"Thank you," she said softly. Although Willow forced a smile, her eyes betrayed her grief. Almost ethereal, Harley's daughter was rail thin.

Polly's heart ached for the beautiful teenager. Willow appeared to have lost at least twenty pounds since they had last seen her. "Willow, Harley, Ruthie, this is my mother, Phyllis Granger."

Phyllis embraced each one of them. "So good to see you. What a beautiful place you have."

"Well, well," Ruthie whispered. "I see Aria's in full attack mode tonight."

"Who's that she's with?" Lynn asked.

"You mean who is she groping? That would be Buck Foster, Spark's son."

At that moment, Maggie and Ben Morgan burst in with their two kids. Emma ran toward the hallway to greet her grandparents, and Ben the third rushed in to hug Polly and Lynn.

"Hey, Bennie!" Polly said, stooping to embrace him just as Kevin appeared at their side.

"Hello," he said, wanting to take her in his arms and kiss away the ache of the past few days.

Polly released Ben, who ran off as his uncle Kyle appeared from upstairs. "Hey, Kevin! You're back?" the youngest Morgan brother asked.

"Yup, this morning," Kevin said, shaking Kyle's outstretched hand.

As Kyle was instantly swept away by siblings and niece and nephew, Polly said, "Kevin Larrabee, this is my mom, Phyllis Granger. Mom, Kevin is the contractor building Valley Stables. Remember, Lynn and I promised to drive you out to see it?"

"Hello, Mr. Larrabee, wonderful to *finally* meet you," Phyllis said, her antennae raised. The flush on her daughter's face coupled with the man's obvious discomfort were not lost on her.

Polly wanted to strangle her mother but took several deep breaths, endeavoring to calm herself. At that moment, a large group descended upon the bar, so Lynn, Polly, and Phyllis drew back to let the others by.

The three wandered into the living room, where Hope Seymour and Robbie Morgan were chatting with his father and brothers. Ben Senior smiled as they approached. "Whaddya think, Phyllis? We're a pretty overwhelming bunch, I'm 'fraid."

"I'm enjoying myself. It's not every day that I find myself surrounded by so many handsome men, and beautiful women too! I promise to learn everyone's name before I depart."

He laughed. "You'll sort things out. Have you met my son Robbie and Hope Seymour, his fiancée?"

"No, hello," she said, extending her hand to each in turn. "Polly tells me you're neighbors?"

Robbie nodded. "Sure are. We'll get you over for drinks while you're here."

Hope smiled at them. "Or maybe dinner? We've noticed that people gather in the back on the riverside for cookouts, but it might be a little nippy to do that now."

Lynn smiled at the couple. "Yes, we went to a couple of get-togethers shortly after we moved in. It's a friendly bunch."

"What are your plans while you're here?" Hope asked Phyllis.

"Helping out with those darling children and seeing more of your beautiful Valley. Polly and Lynn took me to the gallery on Main Street the other day, and I was so impressed by your paintings. I am thrilled to meet such a famous artist."

Hope smiled. "I don't know about the famous part, but thank you for your kind words about the paintings. I'm afraid I've been overshadowed tonight. We've got a genuine West Coast star here. Have you met Buck?"

"Spark's son," Lynn said.

"He's pretty major," Robbie said. "Painting and stained glass. Not in Hope's league, of course," he added, arm circling her waist.

Hope laughed, nudging him. "There you have it—a totally unbiased opinion."

Polly watched the pair, wondering if she'd ever have a man hold her as Robbie held his beautiful blonde fiancée. She scanned the room, but she couldn't locate Kevin.

"What do *you* do?" Phyllis asked, directing her attention to Robbie.

He laughed. "I'm between jobs right now. Finding myself, I guess you could say. It's worked out, 'cause I've been able to help out on the ranch while I plan my next move. Once my sister's baby comes, I'll be full-time at the farm taking Ruthie's place till she's ready to come back."

"We had a lovely drive up there. What an operation."

"Largest organic farm in the southwest," Hope said. "It's amazing."

From the living room, they heard Leonora's voice. "Okay, everyone, welcome again! Grab your drinks, find a place at one of the tables, and head for the buffet. Carmela's got everything laid out on the sideboards, and salads and breads are on the tables."

Lynn leaned close to Phyllis and whispered, "Hold on to your hat, Mama. You're about to experience a Morgan family dinner!"

CHAPTER 17

Polly led her mother toward the buffet. Phyllis was immediately swept up by Spark and Ben Senior, who insisted she sit with the "older folks." Polly waved as her mom was led off, mouth agape as she caught sight of the tables covered with platters of food. There were huge plates of spiced pork tenderloins, fish tacos with Carmela's homemade salsa alongside grilled, stuffed portabellas, pitchers of her special sauce nearby. Interspersed with the platters of meat and fish were colorful rice and bean dishes. The tables both had baskets of warm tortillas and crusty breads as well as several varieties of green salads and Carmela's Southwestern slaw.

"Won't starve here," an unfamiliar voice said as Polly stood alone, wondering how to proceed. "Tom Jacobi." He extended his hand, and she took it.

"Oh, you've met Tommy," Aria said, breezing by with Nick Parker on her arm. She did not stop to chat.

She gave the stranger a shy smile. "Polly Granger. I work at the Cottage, the ranch's day care."

She judged him to be in his early thirties, not much taller than her with lean and craggy face. When he smiled, his features seemed to align, and he was handsome in the wiry way of so many of the Valley cowboys.

"I'm new. Just started a few weeks ago out at Valley Stables."

"Oh, are you a carpenter?"

He laughed. "Not if you want something to actually stay standing. Two left thumbs, I'm afraid. No, I'm Harley's assistant."

"That's great. I'm sure he's thrilled to have you here, especially with the baby coming." At that moment, she spied Kevin in conversation with Harley. He caught her eye and looked almost angry. *Oh dear, wonder what that's about?*

"I'm the one that's thrilled. It's a huge opportunity for me, and how about these guys? Ben Morgan Senior and his college buddy are amazing."

She smiled. "Yes, the kindest, most generous men in the world."

"Shall we?" He indicated the buffet table. His hand touched the small of her back as they made their way to the end of the line.

"Where are you from?" Polly asked as they loaded their plates.

He leaned close and whispered, "Napa. Don't tell anyone, but I met Harley when he came to Hayworth Ranch. You might say I was poached."

Polly wasn't sure what he was talking about but had heard rumors about Harley Langdon's job offer in California. "Uh-oh, was that uncomfortable?"

"Not in the end," he said, his plate now piled with food. "When Harley pulled out, they hired a general manager. Let's just say we didn't see eye to eye, so he was happy to see the back of me."

"Hey, guys, come sit with us," Kyle Morgan called. The new resident veterinarian at Valley Stables, Kyle probably knew Tom best.

As they followed Kyle into the dining room, Lynn caught up with them, her plate loaded. She nodded to Tom, then pulled Polly aside. "Someone's been looking for you," she whispered.

Polly looked down at her friend's plate. "You think you can eat all that?"

"Sure gonna try," Lynn said, turning to Tom. "Lynn Manguilli. I work with Polly."

"Pleased to meet you. Ladies first." He waved them on, following them into the dining room. As they passed Phyllis, she waved, looking a bit overwhelmed seated between Spark and his son at the elder Morgans' table. Also there were Ben, Maggie and their two kids, and Ruthie, Harley, and Willow.

"She'll have plenty to talk about tonight," Polly said to Lynn as she took a seat beside Tom. Lynn scurried to the opposite side of the table and plopped down next to Brendan Statler. Polly smiled at her friend, wondering if she'd get a word in edgewise with Aria on Brendan's other side. Nick Parker sat to Aria's left, looking as if he'd rather be having oral surgery.

Suddenly, Kevin's voice spoke beside her. "This seat taken?" he asked softly.

"Now it is," she said, giving him a shy smile. Polly realized that Tom Jacobi had asked her a question, and she had no idea what he'd said.

CHAPTER 18

Kyle and Aria were prodigious talkers, so their table companions were mostly free to sit back and enjoy the show.

"Are you glad to be home?" Lynn asked Kyle.

"You betcha. Thought I wanted East Coast, but nothing beats the Valley, not to mention Dad and Spark's stables extraordinaire. Almost a shame to put animals in 'em."

"When you gonna give me a tour?" Aria asked, directing her remarks to Tom. "You've been avoiding me all week!"

"We are kind of busy up there," Kyle said, giving Tom a look behind Aria's back.

Polly almost felt sorry for Aria, who didn't seem to be making much progress with Valley men. Tom had told her that he was staying temporarily at Spark's until the manager's house was completed. Avoiding Aria while living in the same house must be tricky, Polly mused. She didn't know the chef well, but the ranch rumor mill had Aria chasing after Nick Parker most of the time. Word was that so far, their resident horse whisperer had managed to deflect her attentions.

As she listened to the conversation, she felt Kevin's hand brush hers under the table. Startled, she grabbed her fork and made sure to keep both hands on the table. Even so, his touch and his nearness meant that every fiber of her being was electrified. She shivered and knew her face was bright red. No one seemed to notice except Lynn, who winked from across the table. This attracted Tom's attention, and he turned to look at her.

Kevin knew he shouldn't pursue her with everything going on, but his body craved her warmth, and he desperately missed her company. Later, as people rose to head for the dessert tables now covered with platters of Carmela's colorful bizcochitos cookies, pumpkin and vanilla flans, tres leches cake, and aromatic Mexican rice pudding, he placed a gentle hand on her arm. "I'd really like to see you. Could we meet for lunch, or a drink or dinner?"

"Things are pretty busy with my mom here. I'm not sure when I'd be free. Tomorrow, Lynn and I are taking Mom museum hopping for the day."

"Monday, then? I'll take anything, even a half hour. Your lunch break?"

She smiled, surprised to see what appeared to be desperation reflected in his eyes. "We eat with the children. Lunch breaks don't exist in day care."

"Please, Polly," he said as she slipped away from his grasp.

"How do you feel about horses?"

"In what way? As a rider?"

"No, but most mornings I walk Archie. Remember I mentioned him the other night at dinner, then never got around to explaining? Archie's one of the adopted mustangs. I told Nick I'd go by Monday morning. It's probably the only time my mother won't be glued to my side."

"You don't think I'll upset Archie's routine?"

"We'll find out, I guess. He's a sweetheart, just skittish."

Like you, he thought, watching her light up talking about the horse. "Tell me where and when, and I'll be there."

"I usually get there around seven. You could meet me at the barn or out on the Loop?"

"Seven at the barn it is. Gonna be cold. They say record lows for the Valley the next two days."

"I'm a New Englander. A little snow and cold doesn't bother me. It's ten below in Rhode Island right now."

"You look really pretty tonight, by the way."

Polly blushed. "Thank you. Not sure if I have room for dessert, but I'm sure gonna try."

When Polly returned to the table, Aria had taken her place, so she joined Lynn and Kyle on the opposite side. Kevin looked like he wanted to crawl under the table and disappear.

"Almost feel sorry for the guy," Lynn whispered. "By the way, better watch out. Your mom's radar is up about 'that handsome Larrabee fellow.' She doesn't miss much, does she?"

Polly rolled her eyes. "You don't know the half of it!"

On the way home, their backseat driver leaned forward. Phyllis made numerous attempts to inquire about Kevin, but Polly successfully deflected her. Finally, she gave up and changed the subject. "That Willow is a lovely girl, isn't she?"

"Sure is," Lynn said.

"Is she coming to live with her father full-time?"

"They're still deciding," Lynn said. "She's taken a leave from college to stay for a while."

"Her grandparents went to Hawaii for the holidays," Phyllis said. "I can't believe they didn't invite her to join them."

"They did," Polly said, "but Willow wanted to be with Harley and Ruthie."

"Harley says Willow is really interested in volunteering at the Cottage," Lynn said.

"Really? That'd be great. We could sure use the extra pair of hands, especially with Gus's two kids, and Ruthie's baby coming sometime in the new year." She referred to Gus Casey, a seasoned trainer, who was one of Valley Stables' newest hires.

"I think that's part of Willow's motivation. She wants to spend time with her new baby sister. What a help it'll be for them to have her here," Lynn said.

Phyllis let out a sigh. "This valley is sure experiencing a baby boom, isn't it? Now, about your Mr. Larrabee."

"We're home!" Lynn said, swinging into the condo lot.

"Thank goodness!" Polly said, hopping out of the car as soon as it stopped.

CHAPTER 19

In the half light of early morning, Nick Parker worked in the stalls and was already half- finished when Polly arrived. In shirt sleeves despite the bitter cold, when he spotted her, he paused and tipped his hat. "Mornin', Poll. You're early."

"I have a friend coming to walk with us this morning, so I wanted to get Archie settled before he arrives."

His warm brown eyes studied her. "You know new people can spook him."

"I know. If he's uneasy, I'll ask my friend to leave."

He grinned. "Don't 'spose your friend would be our friendly neighborhood contractor?"

She nodded. "I don't know if he has any experience around horses."

"And he's building a thoroughbred facility?"

"Hey, Archie," she said, reaching into the adjacent stall to pet the soft brown nose pressed against the bars.

"Halter's on," Nick said. "I'll walk him out." He shrugged into his heavy canvas jacket and turned up the collar.

As she followed man and horse, Polly marveled at the wrangler's gentle, quiet way with the horses, especially Archie. Nick spoke softly as he led the mustang toward the barn doors and into the stable parking area.

She usually walked him down to Emma's Dream, the ranch's summer camp. Then they'd go a short way along the Loop Trail that circled the ranch. Once they left the warmth of the barn and its cozy wood stove, their breath swirled around them in foggy wisps.

Parker turned to her. "Here you go. If he gives you any trouble, remember, just let go. No heroics."

"Will do."

"He's been doing great. Maybe when you get back and he's loosened up, I'll try the saddle. Just rest it on his back."

"That's a big step."

"Have a good walk."

"Thanks, Nick. When Kevin arrives, please point him in the right direction."

He waved over his shoulder. "Will do!"

Archie nickered softly. As they started down the camp road, he nuzzled her side, and Polly leaned against him. "Good boy. This is my favorite time of day, you know."

They had gone about twenty yards when Kevin's truck turned off the ranch drive and headed to the stables. He spotted her and stopped. The screech of the truck's brakes scared the horse, and he reared, giant hooves slashing the air in front of him. Polly stepped back, dropping the lead. Within seconds, Kevin was at her side, placing himself between her and the horse.

"Hey, big guy," he said, hands raised, his voice gentle.

"I'm not sure that's a good idea," she whispered.

Kevin put his right hand on Archie's back, a firm, steady touch. With the other hand, he grabbed hold of the lead, holding it loosely. After several snorts, the horse calmed, its breath creating huge white clouds all around them. "That's it, ole boy," he said, patting Archie's back as he turned to her. "Are you okay?"

She nodded, eyes wide with surprise. "You didn't tell me you were a horse whisperer."

He grinned, that broad, gorgeous smile that made her go weak at the knees. "Hardly, but I do like horses."

"Oh?"

"Worked on a farm in high school."

"I see."

He held out the lead still patting Archie's back. "Ready to take this back?"

They continued down the camp road in silence, Polly soaking in his warmth beside her.

The road ended in an open area, a ring of bunkhouses and camp buildings in front of them. For the past two summers, the verdant, beautiful acres had been home to dozens of handicapped children who came from all over the country to learn to swim, ride, and have a camp experience they would never forget. Maggie Morgan's dream had been made a reality by her generous in-laws. Toby Barnes, Jeb and Amy's adopted son, had been one of Emma's Dream's first campers.

Kevin whistled. "This ranch is an amazing place, isn't it?"

She nodded. "The whole valley is amazing. People look after you in a way they don't back east."

He nodded. "Instant family."

"Yes, it's a little overwhelming for my Yankee mother."

"Looks like Spark, Ben, and Leonora have taken her under their wing."

"Sure have, and I love them for it."

His blue eyes met hers. "Everyone loves those three."

Polly's knees trembled, and she looked away. "We can either walk around the perimeter of the camp or go off that way to the Loop Trail. What do you think?"

"You're the leader."

"Let's go the Loop, then. I know that it's clear, and I'm not sure about the other. This way."

As she turned away, he gently took hold of her arm. "Polly, wait."

Archie nickered, stamping one hoof and nuzzling her shoulder. "Someone wants to get going," she said.

"Not always good to let him lead."

"Maybe, but I—"

He released her. "Sorry… Heck, never mind. It's too frickin' cold to stand around. Thanks for letting me come along."

"My pleasure."

They started off, boots crunching over the snow. "I do want to talk sometime, though. Is that okay?"

"Of course," she replied, her heart fluttering.

CHAPTER 20

As they climbed the Loop Trail, they talked about school, progress on Valley Stables, and her mother's antics. When they returned to the barn, Nick Parker's truck was gone and no one was around. "That's funny," she said, leading Archie back inside to his freshly cleaned stall. "Nick said he wanted to try the saddle on him."

"Maybe something came up."

"I guess." Polly tied Archie, gave him water and food, then a gentle brushing. When he was all settled, they headed out.

As they neared the barn door, Kevin took her gloved hand. "This was really nice."

"Yes," she said softly. "Thanks for coming."

Before she knew what was happening, he drew her close and kissed her softly. She returned the kiss, which deepened.

"Oh, baby, I've missed you," he said, embracing her, his erection tickling her belly.

Polly gasped, then brought her arms up to circle his shoulders and let out a sigh.

"So much to say," he whispered, lips trailing down her neck.

The crunch of tires in the snow startled them, and they looked up to see Nick pulling in. Her already red cheeks flushed scarlet. "Not now, I guess."

Nick rolled down the window. "Hey, guys, want me to back out and come back in ten?"

"Absolutely not!" Polly broke free and hurried toward her car.

After giving the wrangler a look, Kevin followed her. "Polly, hold up."

She opened her car door and turned back. "I've gotta go."

"You free for dinner tonight?"

"Can't. I promised my mom I'd eat with her."

"How about a drink after work? I could meet you somewhere? Please. It's important."

"I 'spose I could ask Lynn to take Mom duty for a short while."

"You name the time and place, and I'll be there."

"Bulldog at five?"

"Perfect."

"What about *your* work? Can they spare you leaving early?"

"The crew'll be fine for a half hour."

He took her hand, but she gently pulled out of his grasp. "I *really* do have to go. It's late."

"Me too."

As Polly pulled out, Nick strolled up. "Have a good walk?"

"Yup, and don't start."

"Wasn't gonna."

Kevin grinned. "Yeah, right."

"Polly's a sweetheart. Hate to see her hurt."

Surprised at Nick's words, he faced him. "Are you her protector now?"

"Nope just a friend."

"Well, I don't intend to hurt her."

"That's what they all say."

"Excuse me?"

Nick shrugged. "I don't know her past, but she seems like a wounded dove. She has an amazing way with horses."

"Maybe the ranch has two horse whisperers?" Kevin said, grinning.

"People who connect with horses are a special breed, that's all. In my experience, it usually means they don't always connect so well with people."

"That your story, cowboy?" Kevin asked, amazed to be having this kind of chat with the normally taciturn wrangler.

"Maybe," Nick said, tipping his hat. "You have a good day now." With that, he disappeared into the barn.

Kevin shook his head and hopped into his truck. *What a week*, he thought, as he headed out to the main road.

*****

"No problem," Lynn said when Polly broached the subject of her drink with Kevin after work. "Phyllis and I'll head over to Gracie's around six thirty, and you can meet us there when you're done."

"Please just say I got tied up here, okay? I'm really not ready for the third degree about Kevin."

"He's crazy about you. You know that, don't you?"

"Stop, right now!" Polly said as the door opened and Ben Morgan came in with his two kids.

"Mornin', ladies. I've got drop-off duty this morning."

"Hey, Bennie, hey Emma, good to see you!" Polly hugged them both as they plunged into the day.

CHAPTER 21

Since she couldn't go home and change without fear of her mother waylaying her, Polly tried to freshen up at the end of the workday as best she could. The front of her sweater was smeared with paint, but she threw on a scarf that partially hid it. As she came out of the bathroom to say goodbye, she felt almost lightheaded. The last of the children had departed, and Lynn was cleaning up and prepping for the next day.

Lynn stared at her. "You okay?"

"Yes, it's been a long day, hasn't it?"

"Pretty usual day, I'd say. You sure you're okay? You look a little pale. Maybe you're coming down with something?"

"No, I'm fine, just the added stress of my mom. Her hovering is wearying."

"Hey, why don't you let me take her out and you go home after the Bulldog? Give you a night off."

Polly smiled at her kind, caring colleague, thinking, as she did most days, how fortune had brought the two of them together. "No, she's only here a few more days. I'm sure I'll survive. Besides, I'm looking forward to one of Gracie's fish specials tonight."

"Okay, but text if you change your mind."

"Will do." Polly grabbed her coat and stepped out into the cold.

*****

Kevin was already seated in a back booth when she walked into the dimly lit saloon, the entry lined with black-and-white photos of local cowboys. She smiled as she passed by a great shot of Maggie Morgan's dad, Ned Williams, by most accounts the best wrangler the Valley had ever produced. Kevin waved, and she nodded, making her way back. She noticed she was the only woman in the bar and was surprised to see eyes following her progress.

When she reached the booth, he stood and took her jacket to hang it on a nearby hook. He quickly turned to give her a peck on the cheek before she sat down.

"Sorry, I didn't have a chance to go home and change. It's been a long, messy day." She pulled the scarf back to reveal the paint stain.

"You look terrific. I've come straight from the farm, and I'm sure I've got you beat in terms of dirt and grime. What would you like to drink? I've got a Desert Amber."

"That sounds perfect."

Kevin waved his glass to Russ Keeler, the owner, who stood behind the bar.

Russ appeared several minutes later with a frosty mug of the local brew. "Here you go. You folks eating?"

"No, just a drink," she said.

Kevin smiled at the burly owner. "Lady can't stay long, but I just might have a Bulldog Burger later. Thanks, Russ."

"Just give me a shout when you're ready."

As Russ disappeared, Polly said, "He's a nice man, isn't he?"

"The best. He's been a good friend to me since I moved to the Valley."

"Someone said he lost his wife recently."

Kevin nodded. "Lizzy's been gone a couple of years. I never met her, but people say she was a sweetheart."

"If he's your friend, maybe sometime we should do something, you, me, Lynn. and Russ?" she said, surprised at her boldness.

"You playing matchmaker now?"

Polly blushed. "No, but Lynn's dying to meet someone. I 'spose Russ doesn't have a lot of free time, though."

"Probably not. Polly, thanks for coming. I know you have to get back to your mom, but I wanted to explain about last week."

"You don't have to."

"Yes, I do. I want to tell you, even if it means you run for the hills."

"Uh-oh… Do I want to hear this?"

Kevin took a deep breath. "Probably not, but here goes. Last week, I heard from my ex-wife, Judith. She was in Portland and asked to see me. Said it was urgent. Said she wanted me to meet my son, Jasper. It was the first I'd ever heard of a child. Judith hates kids. In fact, her desire not to have children was one of the many things that broke us up."

Kevin paused and stared over at her. "Are you okay? You look white as a sheet."

"Yes, just tired, I guess. That must have been quite a shock for you. How old is Jasper?"

"Almost three."

"But you've been divorced for—"

"We had a stupid one-nighter, thinking we might reconcile. One of the dumbest things I've ever done. She claims Jasper was…is… Well, she says he was conceived that night."

"Do you believe her?"

"Honestly, I don't know what to believe. Spark's attorney arranged a DNA paternity test. Results will come tomorrow."

"What's he like?"

"A real cutie."

"So it's been happy news?"

"How could anyone not love a little boy? If he's mine, I'll do what's right."

"Are you telling me that you'll go back to your wife?"

"Hell no, not in a million years! I mean provide financial support for him. I just wanted you to know because, as I'm sure it's obvious, I'm crazy about you. Only now I've got more baggage to go with the old-man part."

Polly covered her eyes, gazing downward.

He reached across and took her hand, which was ice cold. "You're upset."

"No, no, not at all, I just need…sorry… Let me go to the ladies' room, and I'll splash water on my face."

As he watched, Polly stood and swayed. She gripped the table to steady herself, and her eyes began to flutter. Horrified, he jumped up and caught her just before she fell.

Russ rushed over. "Hey, she okay?"

"Clearly not." He cradled her in his arms. "Polly, hey," he said softly, but she was unresponsive. "Call an ambulance," he said, and Russ hurried off.

Kevin checked, relieved to find she was breathing, albeit shallowly. Russ returned with a clean wet towel, which he handed to Kevin. "Ambulance is on its way. This might help revive her."

"Do me a favor, Russ. Go in her purse, find her cell phone, check her contacts, and phone Lynn, her roommate."

Russ found the number and had just reached Lynn when the EMTs arrived. Kevin handed Polly to them and took the phone. "It's Kevin, Lynn. Polly fainted. Ambulance is here. Meet us at Valley Hospital, okay?"

Lynn hung up, and he followed the EMTs outside. As they loaded her in, Kevin said, "I'm riding with her."

"Sorry, man. No room," one of them said.

"Then make room, 'cause I'm coming." Kevin shoved the taller man aside and jumped into the truck beside Polly, still unconscious, an oxygen mask covering her face.

"Heart beat's weak," the shorter man said as his partner slid into the driver's seat. "I'm Guy Ramos, by the way."

As the ambulance raced down the Gila Highway toward Valley Hospital, Kevin's cell phone rang. When he answered, he was surprised to hear Phyllis Granger's voice.

"Hello, dear, it's Polly's mom. We're on our way. Please let them know she has a VSD. They'll know what that is. Tell them her heart has been repaired, but they're always monitoring it."

Kevin looked up at Guy. "This is Polly's mother. She says she has something called VSD."

"Ventricular septal defect," Guy said. "Jesus, is the hole still there?"

"You better talk to her," Kevin said, handing the phone to him as the van pulled up to the emergency room.

Guy listened briefly, saying, "Uh-huh" several times, then he hung up and tossed him the phone. "Ray, tell them we need to get her upstairs ASAP."

Before Kevin knew what was happening, Polly disappeared, surrounded by doctors and nurses. He was left alone in the lobby, unsure of where to go. He was still there ten minutes later when Lynn and Phyllis rushed in.

"Where is she?" Phyllis asked, her voice calm and steady, eyes glistening.

"They took her upstairs, that's all I know," he said. "I'm sorry, I'm sorry."

"It's not your fault," the older woman said, placing her hand on his arm. "She's had this since she was a baby. Comes on in times of stress."

"She *was p*ale," he said.

"Yes, all afternoon," Lynn agreed.

Phyllis shook her head. "She doesn't rest like she should. Come on. Let's find out where she is."

As Lynn and Kevin followed, Phyllis patted his shoulder. "She's gonna be okay."

"I pray you're right."

CHAPTER 22

After learning that Polly was on the fourth floor, Kevin, Phyllis, and Lynn found the waiting room. A short time after they settled in, the doors burst open and in stepped the elder Morgans, Spark Foster, Hope Seymour, and Robbie Morgan.

"What can we do?" Leonora asked. "Who needs food?"

Ben Senior came to sit next to Phyllis, taking her hand. "How're ya holdin' up, Mama?"

Phyllis gazed into his kind blue eyes. "I've been better, but this is life with our Polly. She does this sometimes. She has a heart condition, VSD. She was born with it. What it means is that she had a hole in her heart. She's had several surgeries, and the hole has been closed, but for some reason, she's still vulnerable to these spells, especially if she gets overtired or stressed."

"I know a little about funny hearts," he said, putting his arm around her shoulders. "But my heart's just old."

Spark sat down beside Kevin. "How you doing?"

"Okay. Worried."

Hands on hips, Leonora surveyed the group. "I'll bet no one here's eaten. Robbie, Hope, why don't you come with me? We'll get some food from the cafeteria and bring it back. Any requests?"

Lynn looked up. "Thanks, Leonora. I'm sure anything would be fine."

After the three disappeared, Kevin bent over, hands on his knees, face lowered wondering if the telling of his pathetic story had triggered Polly's episode. Spark sat quietly beside him, hand on his back.

Ten minutes later, a doctor appeared. "Are you Ms. Granger's family?"

As Kevin jumped up, brushing a tear from his eye, Lynn said, "Yes, and this is Polly's mom."

Phyllis stood on shaky legs. "I'm Phyllis Granger."

The tall, thin cardiologist gazed down at her with kind brown eyes. "I'm Dr. Blake. Your daughter's fine. She's resting. I'd like to watch her for an hour or so. If she's okay, you can take her home. I'd recommend bed rest for the next two days and no work for the rest of the week."

"Oh dear… That's never easy," Phyllis said, shaking her head. "Can't keep that girl down for a minute."

Ben Senior rose and approached the pair. "Ben Morgan. You new here, son?"

Blake smiled at him. "Third day, actually, but I assure you, I'm a real doctor. I've heard a lot about you, Mr. Morgan. It's a pleasure to finally meet the legend."

"Don't know about that. And I promise I wasn't questioning your competence. Thanks for looking after our Polly."

"So she's a Morgan, is she?"

"No, she's a Granger," Phyllis said, "but the Morgans have welcomed us into their warm, loving family."

"Lucky you."

The elder Morgan chuckled. "You'll be one of us in no time, Dr. Blake."

The cardiologist nodded, then turned to Phyllis. "Might I ask you to step into the consultation room for a few minutes? I'd like to hear a little bit about your daughter's history."

"Of course."

As Phyllis and Dr. Blake disappeared into a small room at the end of the hall, Kevin exhaled. "Thank God."

Spark patted his shoulder. "She's fine, son. You heard the doc."

He gave the older man a wan smile as the double doors flew open. "We're back," Leonora said, waving several take-out bags and motioning to Robbie and Hope. They had twice as many bags over their arms and a cardboard drinks tray in each hand.

Ben Morgan shook his head. "Whoa, darlin', do they have any food left in the cafeteria?"

Behind her, Robbie grinned. "Only a few scraps."

"Oh, pish tush. Don't be ridiculous." She waved at her son and Hope. "Now lay everything out on the table. We've got sandwiches, salads, lots of sides, and lots of drinks. Help yourselves!"

Robbie looked at Kevin. "Hey, man, you doin' okay? Any word?"

"Doc's with her mom now. She's gonna be fine."

Robbie patted his back. "Big relief."

"Sure is."

"Have something to eat. As you can see, my mom's bought out the place."

The two men grinned as they approached the table.

Suddenly hungry, Kevin grabbed a turkey sandwich.

"Take some chips, honey," Leonora said. "And what'll you have to drink?"

"Thanks, Leonora. This is very kind of you."

"Not like Carmela's, but she and Raoul are having a well-deserved night off, and I didn't want to disturb her."

As he sat back down beside Spark, Kevin gazed around, grateful for his Valley family.

CHAPTER 23

Tuesday morning shortly before sunrise as Kevin prepared for work, his cell phone rang. "Morning," he said, assuming it was Victor or one of the crew.

"Kevin, it's Fred Butler."

"Hey, Fred. I wasn't expecting to hear from you till tonight."

"I'm a morning person."

"Me too," he said.

"The lab technician emailed me late last night."

"Yeah?"

"Jasper is not your biological son."

Kevin's stomach lurched, and his chest tightened. "I was so sure."

"Yes."

"So what now?"

"You have no legal obligation to your ex-wife, so what you do or don't do is your own decision."

"Can I think about this, Fred? I was just headed out to work."

"Of course."

"I'll get back to you soon."

They said goodbye, and he grabbed his backpack. As he drove north, he realized that biology or not, he had already fallen in love with Jasper.

*****

Polly woke, restless and annoyed. Two days in bed with her mother hovering over her. If she didn't go stark raving mad, it would be a miracle. Lynn had assured her they would be fine at the Cottage. Willow was starting work today, and Heather Sanchez had agreed to come for the first few days of her forced confinement. Her mom had already popped her head in first with an enormous breakfast, then various other excuses to hover. Now she was out at the grocery store, though heaven knew why. Leonora Morgan had informed them that she would be dropping off three days of meals.

Polly glanced at her cell phone charging on her bedside table. "Why not?" she said aloud and grabbed it.

Kevin answered on the first ring. "Hey, how are you doing? I didn't want to call and wake you."

Polly loved the sound of his deep voice. "Great, I feel great."

"Following doctor's orders, I hope?" He fought the impulse to turn the truck around and head back to town.

"Yes, but my mother is driving me crazy."

"Surrender may be your only option."

"Yes."

"You gave us a scare."

"It happens sometimes. I'm sure my mom's told you. I'm okay, really. Just sorry I scared you. I should have told you about my heart thing."

"Polly, I was…I'm glad I was there." He was almost afraid to take a breath.

"Me too."

"Are you up to visitors?"

"I'm fine with visitors and anything else. This bed-rest thing is for the birds. I'd love for you to come over."

"After work? Can I bring dinner? I might be able to get away at lunch."

"Dinner would be great, but food is not necessary. I'm pretty sure Leonora's bringing enough to feed an army, and my mom's been cooking nonstop. I wish I could get Lynn to take my mom away."

"I'm happy to bring enough for everyone."

"That's not it. I just want you to myself.

"I like the sound of that. Let me think. I might be able to find your mom an invite she can't refuse."

"Oh?"

"You rest. I'll text later."

As soon as he hung up, Kevin called Spark, who had left several messages asking if he was okay. With Kevin's permission, Spark had spoken to Fred Butler. After discussing the ramifications of the DNA results, Kevin asked Spark for another favor and described what he had in mind.

As soon as he stopped talking, Spark said, "Done. I'll have Phyllis Granger out of that house by five thirty or I'll eat my spanky new Stetson."

Kevin laughed. "I certainly hope that won't be necessary. Thanks, Spark. Should I ask?"

"Nope. Formulatin' the plan now, but I predict it will involve a couple more members of the gray hair brigade."

They rang off, and Kevin texted Polly. He then drove the rest of the way to work with a huge shiteater on his face. It was still there as he greeted the crew.

"Looks like someone got lucky last night," Victor said, eyeing his boss.

"Something like that. Let's hit it, guys."

Chapter 24

"I don't think we should go, honey," Phyllis said, straightening the bed linens. "And you're supposed to be in bed. Doctor Blake said two days of bed rest."

"Mother, stop! I'm going to lie on the sofa the whole time."

"That's what I'm afraid of."

"Mother!"

"Why does he have to come tonight? Why don't we *all* have dinner tomorrow night? I'll cook. Your favorite, linguine Catherine?"

"That would be nice. I'll ask if he's free."

"Good. Should I call him and say you're too tired tonight?"

"No, thank you. He's coming tonight and tomorrow, if he's free."

"Honey, that's not what I meant and—"

"Willow was a godsend today," Lynn said, changing the subject. Polly's mom had been fretting and fussing since she got home, and her roommate was clearly at her wit's end.

"I'm so glad," Polly said, mouthing *thank you* behind her mother's back. "It'll be fun to have her around."

"She's a natural, and the kids love her."

"And Heather can do full days till I get back?"

"Yup, and I asked the bosses, and they, of course, said they'll pay to have her be there full-time as long as we want."

"What about Heather? Is she wanting full-time?" Polly asked, suddenly feeling a little displaced.

"No, but you'll be back soon, so that's not an issue. She has other clients in Tucson, but she says she can move 'em till next week, no problem."

The doorbell rang. "Lynn, would you? I just want to change quickly."

"I'll get it, darling. It'll give Mr. Larrabee and me a chance to chat."

As soon as her mother left the room, Polly turned to her roommate. "Lynn, please! Protect him!"

Lynn grinned. "I'm on it. Go get pretty."

"As if that's gonna happen with this ghostly complexion."

"You look gorgeous.

"Lynn?"

"Yup?"

"Thanks for everything. Covering for me, babysitting Mom, all of it. I'm sure tonight's the last thing you want to do."

"No problem. I love those guys. Happy to do it."

"It's just Spark and Ben Senior. Leonora has a Cowbelles function."

"Even better. Out on the town with the silver foxes? What could be cooler? We might even lasso a handsome cowboy or two."

Polly laughed. "I bet if you asked Ben and Spark, they'd be on the case in a split second."

"I'll keep it in mind."

"Now, please go rescue Kevin from the third degree!"

As Polly dressed, she could hear her mother fussing and Lynn coaxing her toward the door. "Take care, now!" Phyllis called. "Dr. Blake said bed rest, so keep her quiet and don't stay too long."

"Come on, Mama," Lynn said, just before the door closed and quiet prevailed.

"I'll be right out!" she called. Knowing he was out there set her heart to fluttering, and she raised a hand to her chest.

"Take your time!" he called.

CHAPTER 25

Polly ran a brush through her hair and was going to tie it back in her usual ponytail, then decided to leave it down. She hadn't bothered with makeup, and her face was ghostly pale, but otherwise, she looked presentable in a soft blue cashmere sweater and faded blue jeans. She tied an infinity scarf around her neck. The swirling colors brought out the blue in her eyes. Gazing at her reflection in the bedroom mirror, she thought, *This is as good as it gets tonight, girl.*

She found him gazing out the slider at the river. "Hi," she said shyly.

He turned around. "Hi, yourself."

Polly pointed to her cheeks. "Sorry I look like Casper the Friendly Ghost."

"You've never looked lovelier." Kevin crossed the room and took her in his arms. Her scent, ginger and citrus, was intoxicating. Polly melted into his embrace, and their lips found the other's in a deep, lingering kiss.

She sighed, finally feeling warm in his arms. "I'm glad you're here."

Kevin trailed kisses down her slender neck. "Me too. You okay? Want to lie down?"

"Absolutely not," she said. "Despite what my meddlesome mother says, I'm fine. Sorry if she read you the riot act."

"You're lucky to have someone who cares about you like that." Kevin felt his cock growing hard, pressing against his zipper Polly felt it too, but instead of /

drawing back, she nestled closer, loving the feel of him, wanting more, so much more.

"I love feeling you against me," she said, surprised at her boldness.

"Baby, you have no idea. It's going to take every ounce of restraint to keep me in check."

"Then don't." Polly took his hand and turned toward her bedroom.

"Are you sure about this?"

"Surer than I've ever been about anything. In fact, it's essential to my recovery, Dr. Larrabee," she said, arching her eyebrow.

"What happened to Polly Granger, and who's this wanton woman in her place?"

"You bring it out. What else could I say with that rock-hard erection? There's only so much self-restraint in this body of mine. "

After the hospital, Phyllis had insisted on moving into the study and had moved Polly back to her own bed. Kevin paused at the door, remembering Phyllis's warning.

"Hold on, baby. Stop for a sec. I want you so much it's killing me, but maybe we should cool it? Your mom said—"

In answer, Polly reached down, pulled her sweater over her head, and flung it on a nearby chair, revealing a lacy bra and the tops of her perfect round breasts. "Forget my mom. This is me talking. Touch me. Please."

"Oh, baby, I—" He stepped closer, cupping her breasts, kissing her softly, before his lips trailed down her neck to her chest. His fingers teased her nipples to hardness, and Polly moaned, throwing her head back.

"You okay?" he asked, voice ragged with longing.

"The only way I won't be okay is if you stop. I've been waiting for this all day," she murmured, sliding her hand down to caress his penis.

"Oh Jesus," he moaned, taking her in his arms and carrying her to the bed. He stood beside the bed, gazing down at her. "We'll go slow and gentle, right?"

Polly grinned, sitting up and unbuckling his belt, then unbuttoning his jeans to release him. One hand stroked him, the other reached up under his shirt, her light touch caressing his hard, ripped belly. "I certainly hope not. My body is screaming for you."

"Oh, baby, I can't hold on if you do much more of that."

"I'm glad," she said, smiling as she continued to stroke and caress him.

Kevin kissed her lightly, then stepped back out of her reach. He removed jeans and boxers in one fluid motion, then grabbed a condom from his pocket.

"Can I help you out of your jeans?" he asked, hands on her hips. He slipped her jeans down and cast them aside, then took hold of her lacy panties, tugging them slowly down her soft, perfect legs, his fingers and tongue moving up her thighs, caressing and stroking.

Polly arched her back, moaning as she slipped her hands around to unclasp her bra. He threw off his shirt and lay beside her on the bed. "What do you want, sweetie?"

"You, inside of me," she whispered, grasping his erection and rubbing it against her belly.

"You're amazing, Polly Granger," he said, capturing her mouth, their tongues twining and teasing as the kiss deepened. His hands caressed her smooth skin, moving from her perfect breasts to gently spread her thighs. His fingers slipped between her legs, and he groaned, finding her hot and wet.

"You ready, baby?"

"Yes, please," she said, rubbing her hips against him, her hands stroking his hard cock, a rhythmic motion that threatened to take him over the edge.

He kissed her forehead. "I'd never forgive myself if you faint again."

Polly smiled. "Do I look like I'm going to faint?"

"As a matter of fact, you don't. The last few minutes seem to have put some color into your cheeks." He grinned as he turned and reached for the condom, slipping it on, then resting briefly beside her. "You ready, baby?"

"Asked and answered. If you're not inside me soon, I'm going to die, Kevin Larrabee."

Kevin drew close and kissed her as he parted her legs and slipped into her warm depths. First, a tentative thrust, then deeper, more urgent. Polly responded, arching her back, her body begging him to go faster, harder, deeper.

"Oh, oh, oh," she cried. "Don't stop, don't stop!"

In a wild combination of gentle and frenzied, they moved as one. Kevin grasped her beautiful ass, pulling her nearer with each thrust. "Oh, baby," he whispered, finding her blue eyes watching him. As he captured her lips again, they reached a blazing white-hot crescendo that left them breathless and slick with sweat. Polly rested her head against his chest, her body still. For a second, Kevin thought she'd fainted, but when he lifted her chin, she gave him a languid smile. "You okay?" he asked.

"Perfect." She kissed his chest.

"You are perfect," he said huskily.

Mischief in her eyes, she said, "Bet you say that to all the girls."

"Baby, there's never been a girl like you."

Polly began to move against him, loving the feel of him inside her.

"You can't be serious?" he said, feeling himself growing hard.

"Looks like you are," she said, kissing his neck, her tongue tracing an agonizing, slow path to his nipples, which she sucked and teased. All the while, she moved her hips, circling him, squeezing him inside her until he grew fully erect.

"Oh sweetie," he whispered, kissing her as they began the dance again, this time more slowly. Their orgasms were simultaneous and explosive, each releasing long-suppressed emotions and longing. In the aftermath, Kevin said, "What was that?"

Polly smiled at him. "I don't think there are any words." She kissed him softly. "You hungry?"

"For you, but we'd better or your mom'll be suspicious when she returns and wonders what we've been doing."

Polly laughed. "I'm starved. Let's go. But first help me put the bed back the way it was, or she'll really freak out."

As they sat at the counter enjoying Kevin's pasta carbonara and jicama salad and sipping a crisp white wine from Saguaro Vineyards, Polly looked over at him. "Sorry I scared you the other night. Were the Bulldog patrons freaked out?"

Kevin set down his fork and took her hand, noticing that her cheeks were rosy after their lovemaking. "Couldn't tell you. If you haven't already noticed, when you're in the room, everyone else disappears."

"That could be a liability," she said, fingers tracing his palm, then wrist.

He shifted on the stool, feeling his cock grow hard. "Better stop that, or I'll have to ravish you right here on this nice smooth granite."

"Mmm, that sounds interesting." She smiled and withdrew her hand. "This is delicious, by the way."

"My healthier version of the original."

"Oh?"

"Still has the bacon. At least it's ranch bacon, no crap in it, but white miso and brewer's yeast are healthier substitutes for the cheese, eggs, and heavy cream."

"I thought there was something different. I love it. So, you're not only a great cook but an innovative one too?"

He laughed. "Necessity is the mother of invention, or father, in this case. My doc read me the riot act. Told me I was headed for an early heart attack if I didn't clean up my diet. My dad's already had two heart attacks. Runs in the family."

"Well, you're in the right place to eat healthy," she said, lost in the warmth of his gray-blue eyes.

He arched an eyebrow. "I'm supposed to avoid red meat, and it's everywhere here."

"Ben and Maggie Morgan are vegetarians, and they seem to find plenty to eat. At least the meat here is grain fed and pretty healthy. No corn, hormones, and whatever."

Kevin smiled. "I've been known to indulge in a burger or steak from time to time."

"Thank you for tonight, Kevin. The dinner and…well, all of it." Her face flushed crimson as she recalled the prelude to dinner.

He took her hand, gently her knuckles. "Polly, there's so much I want to tell you and—"

"Yoo-hoo! We're home!" Phyllis called as the front door opened.

"We'll find a time soon. Promise," she said softly as she waved to her mom and Lynn.

CHAPTER 26

Friday morning, Polly and Phyllis headed for Tucson and the specialist Dr. Blake recommended. This was supposed to be the day she returned to work, but Dr. Roderiques had an opening, and there was no deterring her mother. Polly was driving, trying to ignore the continuous chatter.

"I wish you'd let me drive, sweetie. I'm sure Dr. Blake wouldn't approve of you being behind the wheel."

One, two, three, don't lose your temper, Polly Granger. She's worried and only wants to help. Polly took a deep breath. "Mama, how many times have we gone through this? I'm fine, and this appointment is completely unnecessary. I only agreed to it for you. Please stop."

"I know, baby, but you're so far away now."

"I have lots of friends and Lynn." She purposely did not mention Kevin, knowing mention of him would lead to another interrogation.

"We just miss you, that's all."

"I know. I miss you too. I'll come back east soon, when I can get away. The Cottage is just getting going, but we have lots of help, so I'm sure Lynn and I will be able to take vacations. I wish someday soon you'd bring Daddy out here."

"You know your father hates to travel. But I've told him we're going to Hawaii for our anniversary next fall, so we'll definitely stop then."

Polly reached over and patted her hand. "See, and I'll come back in a few months so we'll see each other."

"I imagine Kevin takes a bit of your time now too."

Uh-oh, here we go! Polly smiled. "We've just started seeing each other, so no, not too much."

"That's a lot for you, sweetie."

"Mother, you've literally been nagging me to find a man and get married ever since Kitty's wedding."

"Yes, but he seems to have a lot of encumbrances, and besides, he lives out here."

"Which is where I live. And he doesn't have any more encumbrances than the next man."

"Divorced with a child? Then there's the age difference. Why, he could be your father."

"Mother, that's enough. He's a good man, and I love him. There, I've said it. I love him. And who told you about Jasper anyway?"

"Lynn might have mentioned something."

I will have to speak to Lynn later, she thought, *but then who wouldn't crack under Mom's third degree?* "Well, she shouldn't have said anything, *and,* more to the point, you shouldn't be interrogating her about my love life."

As they turned into the clinic parking lot, Phyllis shook her head. "Oh dear, I don't know how this will turn out."

Polly parked the car, then turned to her mother. "Mother, please be happy for me."

"Oh honey, of course I am." Phyllis leaned over and hugged her. "What about the boy?"

"I don't know what will happen there." Polly checked her watch. They were twenty minutes early. She considered for a moment, then took a deep breath. "Can you keep a secret?"

"Of course," Phyllis replied, eyes wide as saucers.

"He had a DNA test done. Jasper isn't his, even though Kevin's ex-wife named him on the birth certificate."

"Oh, my goodness. What's he going to do?"

"I don't think he's decided."

"Well, he certainly has no obligation."

"Legally, maybe, but as I said, Kevin's a good man. He wants to do the right thing for Jasper." As her mother opened her mouth to speak, Polly said, "Come on, let's go find Dr. Roderiques and get this over with."

*****

Martin Roderiques regarded her with kind gray eyes. They were alone. At his request, her mother had stayed in the waiting room. "Everything looks fine, Ms. Granger. That's good news. I know I don't have to tell you that you have a fragility that most people do not."

"Yes, it's always been manageable. I had the hardest time in college."

"Late nights, stress, and not enough rest? That'll do it."

"Yes."

"You've recently taken on a new job. Has that overtaxed you, do you think?"

"Maybe a little, but it's actually been fun."

"Anything else in your life that might have triggered an episode?"

"I've recently started dating a wonderful man, but that's been the opposite of taxing."

"How nice for you. Love is healing, and sexual relations are actually good for the heart, if not out of the ordinary."

Polly blushed. *Sex with Kevin had been far from ordinary!*

"Pardon my bluntness. Your health is my concern. I was referring to stressful sexual practices. I've seen too many patients with *Fifty Shades of Gray* syndrome."

"That's not us, I assure you," Polly replied, certain her face must be the color of a ripe tomato.

"Pregnancy could be dangerous for you."

"I've been told that before. Risky, but not impossible."

"Perhaps. I'd have to do more tests, but from the reports I received from Dr. Blake and what you've told me, I believe there is a procedure that might help and ultimately make your heart more resilient."

"I really don't want more surgery."

"I understand. I will give you some literature about it. It's relatively new, but some patients with your condition have had very good outcomes."

They spoke for several more minutes, then he handed her a folder of materials.

"Thank you," she said.

"My pleasure. Be in touch anytime if you have questions or want to talk further. Liza, my assistant, is also available. Most of all, take care of yourself, Polly."

CHAPTER 27

Crews were everywhere at Saguaro Valley Stables with several projects going on. Kevin's main crew was at Harley and Ruthie's trying to finish up, but he was back and forth, supervising the other crews completing the track and stables. Plumbers and electricians came and went at the bunkhouses and other buildings. In addition to three barns, the stables, and bunkhouses, there was a small office building, a manager's house, and four other cottages, one for Kyle Morgan, the resident veterinarian, two for the head trainers, and one for a yet-to-be-determined purpose that had been designated as a guest house.

As he shuttled from site to site, all Kevin could think about was Polly. He knew she was in Tucson at the doctor's. He would have taken her in a heartbeat if Phyllis hadn't been here. Aside from his love of her company, their lovemaking had left him ravenous for her. Every time he thought of her soft, pink skin and her warmth beside him, his cock hardened and he found himself breathing as if he'd just completed an all-out sprint. Then there was Jasper and what to do about the sweet child with whom he was already in love. Judith had so little, and her family was useless. He decided that at least for now, he would send monthly checks. He had a good deal saved up, and Spark and Ben Morgan were generous employers. Over his protests, they had doubled his bid for the Valley Stables project and would brook no argument about lowering the bid.

"Hey, boss," Victor called as Kevin hopped from the cab of his truck in front of Harley and Ruthie's new house. "We're almost done here. Want us to head over to the manager's house?"

"Is Harley here?"

"Nope. He stopped in this morning and said everything looked great. I think he's at the stables."

"Let me take a look," Kevin said.

The two men headed in, and Kevin nodded to the others, who were cleaning up and collecting their tools. Ruthie, Harley, and her brother, Sam, the family architect, had designed the magnificent contemporary home situated on a rise about a quarter mile from the main stable area. The three-story dwelling had three-hundred-and-sixty-degree views from its windowed walls on all four sides. The open first floor had a massive stone chimney with back-to-back fireplaces in the kitchen and family room. The master bedroom and bath were also on this floor, along with an office area that the couple would share. Three bedrooms and baths were on the second floor, and the third floor was an octagonal living room with a small bar/kitchen, a bath, and a porch that ran all around its perimeter. The octagon room was furnished with custom-built sectional sofas with several built-in chaises. Ruthie predicted that they would be *living up there most of the time, so let's make it mega comfortable!*

Sam Morgan's reputation was growing on the East Coast as well as in the Southwest. Several architectural journals had already contacted them, wanting to feature the home. As they strolled through, Victor whistled. "This is what millions gets you. Think they'll invite us back to party once it's furnished?"

"Can't promise, but knowing the Morgans, it's a pretty safe bet." On the way out, Kevin turned to his foreman. "You go ahead, buddy. I've gotta make a couple of calls, and I'll catch up with you."

"Sure thing," Victor said.

Kevin called Fred Butler and gave him his decision about the support, asking if he could make the arrangements. After they rang off, he called Polly and reached her voice mail. "Hey, baby, it's me. I hope things went well in Tucson. I'd really like to see you. Any chance you're free tonight or tomorrow? Thinking about you."

Understatement of the century, he thought, hanging up. As he started up the truck, he spied Ruthie's antique green pickup headed down the drive. He switched off the engine and stepped from the truck and came to lend a hand as his employer maneuvered her very pregnant body from the truck.

"Thanks, Kev," she said, flashing him a lovely smile.

"My pleasure."

"How's it going?"

"I think we're done. There are a couple of fixtures the electrician needs for the third-floor bathroom. Remember, they sent the wrong ones? And Victor has to get some trim pieces for the octagon room, but otherwise, it's all set. You decided when you're movin' in?"

"Today, if I have my way. The movers are scheduled for noon."

"Really?"

"Absolutely. My fuss-budget husband wants to wait till the baby comes. Thinks it's too much for me, but I want to be in and settled before." She patted her belly.

Kevin grinned. *And I know who'll win that argument.* "Well, it's good to go from our end. I was heading over to the stables. You need me?"

"Would you mind just walking through with me?"

"No problem. Let me text Victor, and I'll come right in."

Kevin grabbed his phone and saw that he had a text from Polly: *All's well. Can't do tonight (Mom duty), but would love to do something tomorrow night.*

He wrote back: *It's a date. Will be in touch to firm up where and what time.*

After texting Victor to let him know he'd be late, he headed into the house. The empty rooms were silent, and he called, "Ruthie," but heard nothing. Figuring she might be using the bathroom, he waited in the kitchen. After ten minutes went by, he called again, walking toward the first-floor bathroom. He found the door ajar and the room empty.

Kevin headed for the stairs and called again. As he reached the landing, he heard a soft moaning from above. Taking the stairs two at a time, he followed the sounds to the third floor, where he found her on the floor, curled in a fetal position, the rug beside her wet, the circle widening. Kevin knelt next to her. "Ruthie, you okay?"

CHAPTER 28

Ruthie gazed up at him, pain shimmering in her glassy blue eyes. "I've been having contractions all morning and now my water broke and they're coming quickly and much worse. I don't think I can move."

"Are you strong enough to put your arm around my shoulders?"

She nodded, draping her arm around him. Kevin cradled her against his chest and stood. In no time, he had her to the truck, where he grabbed his phone and called Harley. "Hey, man, your wife's in labor. Her water's broken. Want me to call an ambulance or take her to Valley myself?"

"Take her. I'm in town. I'll meet you there."

"Are you sure?"

"They told us it'd be hours. You've got plenty of time. See you there."

Kevin settled her in the passenger seat. Ruthie's eyes were closed, and she continued her soft moaning. "Hey, Ruthie, we'll have you to the hospital in no time. Hang on."

As he pulled out of driveway, she began screaming. Ear-splitting screams. "Aah! I can't do this! Help me, help me!"

"Only be a few minutes to the hospital."

He reached over, and she grabbed his hand in a death grip, fingernails digging into his palm. Her face was bright red, and tears streamed down her rosy cheeks. Wild and frightened eyes looked over at him, silently beseeching as she shook her head from side to side. Thirty seconds later, her screams turned to whimpers, and she relaxed her grip on his hand.

"That was awful," she said. "I can't do that again. Really, I can't."

"Sure you can. You're a Morgan."

"Fuck that," she said as another contraction built, and she began screaming and panting. This continued for several contractions. Suddenly, she quieted and said, "There's something between my legs. I think the baby's coming."

"Hold on." Kevin pulled over to the side of the road and hopped out. They were on the Gila Highway, still fifteen miles from Valley Hospital. He opened the passenger door and reached down to recline her seat. "Are you sure you feel something?"

She nodded weakly as the contraction eased down.

"Would it be all right if I checked?"

"Yes, hurry," she said, reaching down to slip out of her panties.

Sure enough, the baby's head was halfway out. "Jesus Christ," he said, watching as another contraction began to overtake her. There would be no going farther until the baby was born.

"Okay, sweetie, let me wash my hands. Hold on if you can."

As she began screaming again, he grabbed hand sanitizer and the clean towel he kept in the truck. As he washed the best he could, he grabbed his cell and called Harley. There was no need to explain what was happening. Ruthie's screams told it all. Kevin gave their location and threw the cell phone aside, applying another glob of hand sanitizer as Ruthie began to breathe more easily, her contractions subsiding.

"Okay, Ruthie, your baby's gotta come out. You ready?"

She nodded weakly.

"On the next contraction, I'm gonna lift you up so you can push." As he spoke, he scooted the towel under her.

As she began groaning, he reached his arm around her back and lifted her slightly. "Now push, sweetie. Push!"

With an ear-splitting shriek, she grunted and pushed until he feared she might burst the blood vessels in her neck. "Oh, oh, oh!"

As Kevin stared, the baby's head emerged, followed by the shoulders. As he gently took hold of the tiny body, a truck screeched to a stop behind them, and Harley appeared. "Hand sanitizer, on the dash, man! Come catch your beautiful daughter."

Several minutes later, the two men stared in amazement at the tiny infant. Harley leaned forward and cradled his wife in his arms, kissing her forehead as Kevin wrapped the baby in the towel.

"Congrats, guys. I think we better get going. Harley, can you hold the baby and Ruthie? I think we need docs now."

As Kevin drove as fast as he dared, he called nine one one and explained the situation. They patched him through to the hospital, and an obstetrician came on, assuring them he'd be standing by at the emergency room door. Dr. Collins said, "Don't 'spose you have any string?"

"Not that's clean," Kevin replied.

They arrived at Valley Emergency Room, and Ruthie and the baby were whisked away on a gurney. Before he followed, Harley turned to Kevin. "I owe you big-time, man. You gonna hang around?"

"Will do."

"Can you call the family and her parents?"

"No worries. Go on," Kevin said, patting his back. "Give the girls a hug for me."

As Harley disappeared, Kevin sat, stunned. Finally, he pulled out his phone.

CHAPTER 29

"You're the Valley hero," Polly said as they sat sipping Pinot Grigio on Kevin's terrace. "I wonder who the next person will be who needs an emergency trip to the hospital."

"Ha-ha. Let's hope no one, ever again," he replied. "You look beautiful tonight, baby. Her cream turtleneck hugged her in all the right places, and her floral scarf in swirling shades of blue picked up the color of her eyes. She wore jeans and clogs, her hair loose, flowing over her shoulders and down her back.

She blushed. "Thank you. I love your home. You have great taste."

Earlier, he had given her a tour of the Arts and Crafts-style bungalow. It had an open floor plan on the first floor, exposed beams, maple flooring, and a new kitchen. A massive stone fireplace sat at one end of the living room, which was furnished with Stickley-style pieces, lots of dark oak and clean lines, a leather sofa and recliner and two matching chairs covered in a Navaho print. A dining room table stood between the living room and kitchen. Two bedrooms and two baths were upstairs. One bedroom was piled with boxes and what he referred to as *"junk I have to sort through."* The second he used as a guest room. The master bedroom was downstairs, furnished with a rustic king-sized four-poster bed covered with a brightly patterned quilt. Kevin had added a master bath with a quarry-tile floor, colorful Mexican tiling, a whirlpool tub, and marble shower.

"It's a work in progress," he said. "This is the first home I've furnished myself with things I like. I'm pretty pleased with it."

"You should be. It's amazing."

So are you, Polly Granger. "You hungry?"

"Not especially, but I know whatever you've made will be terrific. You're the host."

"Is there something you'd rather do?"

"Do you really want to know?"

"I really want to know," he said, his cock already standing at attention.

"Well…that four-poster looks pretty comfortable," she said, smiling shyly. "And I've missed you."

"Me too. Come on." He reached out his hand and drew her up and into his arms, kissing her softly at first. As his tongue parted her lips and the kiss deepened, Polly sighed and folded into his arms. "You okay?" he asked, gazing down.

"Perfect," she said, stroking his neck, her hand moving down to caress his hard cock through the rough denim of his jeans. "I love the feel of you."

"That's good," he said huskily, "'cause just catching sight of you brings it on. Come on, sweetie. That bed's only a year old. It needs christening."

As they moved toward the bedroom, clothes dropped in their wake—boots, shirts, then pants, undergarments until, naked and entwined, they reached the bedroom door. His hands and lips were everywhere as Kevin's fingers found her moist wetness. He drew them in and out as Polly gasped and arched to meet him. Finally, at the bedroom door he grasped her ass and drew her closer, leaning against the door frame. Wrapping her legs around his waist, he plunged inside her. "Too much, baby?"

"Never! Please don't stop. Take me harder, deeper! Oh, oh, oh, Kevin!" All rational thought obliterated, he brought her to an explosive climax, careful to cradle and protect her as he went deeper. His lips and tongue moved from her mouth to take each breast, sucking and teasing. Her orgasm demolished his last ounce of control and Kevin let go, feeling his release deep inside her warm, sweet core.

"Oh Jesus, I love you, baby," he whispered. Holding her ass, he walked to the bed on shaky legs and eased them down as one.

Polly gazed at him with soft eyes. "I love you too. Can we stay like this forever?"

He kissed the tip of her nose. "Won't get an argument outta me."

"Hmm, I like that." She arched her back.

As she began to move rhythmically against him, circling, thrusting, holding him in her warm interior, Kevin felt his cock harden. "Oh, baby, do you know how incredible you are?"

"We fit, don't we?" she said, a shy smile lighting up her face.

"You bet we do, sweetie," he whispered, kissing her, hands moving up and down her body, cupping her breasts, teasing and tickling in ways he knew lit her up.

Their lovemaking was slower this time, deeper, closer, as they held each other's gaze, moving to a tremulous climax. In the aftermath, they lay entwined and sated. Polly trailed soft kisses down his neck to his chest, then back up to his lips.

"You cold, baby?"

"It feels good, the heat against you and the cool on my back."

He rolled slightly and grabbed the opposite edge of the quilt. "Hungry?"

"A little."

"Why don't you stay here and I'll heat things up, then come get you?"

"Mmm." she sighed, kissing him. "Sounds lovely, but I'd rather be with you."

"Let me grab your clothes at least. Hang on."

They let out a simultaneous groan as he slipped out of her. "Be right back, baby," he said, kissing her deeply before standing and making for the doorway.

Polly sighed, watching his tight, gorgeous body walking away from her. As he disappeared, she leaned back, closing her eyes, contented.

Several minutes passed, and she heard the phone ring and Kevin's voice saying, "Hello," then, "What? Jesus Christ!"

The next few minutes seemed an eternity as his voice became louder and shriller.

"When did it happen?

"Who was she with?

"Where's Jasper?

"Okay, okay…I'll get there as soon as I can."

When Kevin returned with their clothes, his face was ashen.

"What is it?" she asked.

"My ex, Judith. She's dead. Died of an overdose last night."

CHAPTER 30

Polly dressed as Kevin phoned the airlines. When he hung up, he said, "I got a flight out at ten thirty tonight."

"I'll drive you."

"That's okay. I can leave the truck."

"I'm happy to take you. Please let me do this for you."

"Of course. Thanks, that would be great."

He crossed the kitchen and drew her into his arms. "It's gonna be okay."

"Do you want to pack and do what you have to do? Shall I put the dinner in the freezer?"

"No, we have time to eat. It's ready. Come on, sit. We might as well enjoy it. No telling how long I'll be gone."

They ate in silence. Neither ate more than a bite or two, Kevin a million miles away. Finally, she reached over and placed her hand on his. "I'm so sorry."

He gave her a wan smile, bringing her hand to his lips. "Thanks, baby. I'm just sorry we don't have the rest of the night. Judith was inevitable. It was never 'if' it would happen, but 'when.'"

"Did they say anything about what happened?"

"No, but I'm sure I'll hear every gory detail from her parents." The thought of seeing Ernie and Belle Robinson again made him feel queasy. In comparison to his own parents, Spark Foster, or the Morgans, the Robinsons were another species. *Reptilian* came to mind.

"Can I do anything while you're away? Water your plants? Take in the mail?"

"Thanks, but the landlord'll do it. I'll call him when I land in Tampa."

"Is that where Judith lived?"

"No, she's been staying with her sister in Coral Reef, but it's right outside of Tampa."

"What about Jasper?"

"He's back and forth between his Aunt Ivy's house and the grandparents. He's fine."

"Poor little thing," she said.

"You've got that right, and you've never met him. Want more fish?"

"No, thanks. Why don't I wash up while you pack? Go on, I'm fine."

He stood, then bent over to kiss the top of her head. "I'm really glad you're here."

"Me too," she said, gently rubbing his forearm.

"Just toss the leftovers. I'll put out the trash when we leave."

*****

They made it to the small Grenville airport by nine fifteen. Polly parked in the open lot and gazed over at him. "Thanks, baby," he said, reaching over to cup her cheek. "I'm going to miss you."

"Me too," she said, covering his hand with her own. "Call me when you arrive?"

"Of course."

They both got out of the car, and he grabbed his bag from the back, then came around to her side and opened his arms. Polly slid into them, burying her face against his shoulder, surprised at the unexpected tears in her eyes.

"Hey, baby. It won't be long. I'll be back before you know it. Promise."

"I know."

"Give me something to remember you by." His voice was husky as he leaned down and captured her lips in a deep, lingering kiss.

Polly held on tight as she returned his kiss. She smiled as she felt his erection against her belly. "We better stop now, or no telling where this might lead."

He looked down at her, his eyes full of love. "If I could make love to you right here in this parking lot, I would. But guess we'd better say goodbye before I embarrass myself walkin' around in there. I do hate to walk away from you, my love."

"I love you," she said, kissing him softly.

"Me too, baby. Take care of yourself. I'll call in the morning."

One last kiss and he was gone, walking resolutely toward the terminal. At the door, he turned and waved. Tears streaked her cheeks as Polly waved back, wondering when she would see him again.

CHAPTER 31

Sunday morning, Lynn, Polly, and Phyllis prepared muffins and a casserole to take to Ruthie and Harley. Ruthie and baby Charlotte had stayed only one night in the hospital and were now home with the entire Morgan clan and friends taking care of them. Lynn had called to ask if they could pop by, and Harley said, "Of course. Love to see you."

As they prepared to leave, Polly's cell phone rang. Seeing Kevin's name, she raised a finger to her companions and stepped inside her bedroom. "Hello?"

"Hey, baby. I made it. How are you?"

"Fine, just missing you. How's everything back there?"

"All's well. Still at the airport waiting for my rental car. Gotta make a bunch of work calls, then I'm heading to Coral Reef. What are you up to?"

"Lynn, Mom, and I are about to pay a short visit to baby Charlotte and her parents."

"So she's finally got a name?"

Polly laughed. "Yes, they decided last night, according to what Harley told Lynn."

"Well, I won't keep you. Say hi to everyone for me. I love you."

"Love you too," Polly whispered, clicking off and half expecting to find her mother on the other side of the door.

When she emerged from the bedroom, she found Phyllis on a stool in the kitchen, chatting with Lynn. "Ready, honey?"

Polly nodded.

"Everything okay in Florida?" Lynn asked.

"He arrived safely. That's all I know."

They each grabbed food and walked the short distance to the adjoining condo building where Ruthie and Harley were still living in his apartment. They were not surprised to find a crowd. Maggie, Ben, and their two children were there, as well as Hope and Robbie.

"Shall we put this in the fridge?" Lynn asked, holding up the casserole as Polly set the basket of muffins on the kitchen counter.

Harley grinned. "Thanks, ladies. I'll take it." He opened the fridge, which was packed. Finally, he managed to find a tiny space in the freezer and shoved it in.

"I see the Morgans have got you well stocked up."

"You have no idea. You should see what's already out at the house. I'll be lucky if I can fit a bottle of Desert Amber in the fridge."

"Hi, Polly! Hi, Lynn," Emma Morgan said, hugging them.

Polly smiled down at the beautiful dark-haired child. "Hi, Em. How's your aunt and your new cousin?"

"Great, come see," she said, taking Polly's hand.

As Emma led them down the hall, Maggie Morgan emerged from the bedroom with Ben in her arms. "Hi, ladies. Ben, can you say hi?"

Her rambunctious son gave a shy wave, then said, "Hi."

"Okay if we say hi?" Lynn said.

"Of course. Ben, Robbie, and Hope are in with her."

They peeked around the corner and spied Ruthie, sitting up, rosy cheeked, and glowing. Willow sat in a nearby rocking chair holding her sister, gazing with love at the tiny bundle. Ben, Robbie, and Hope leaned against the dresser.

Ruthie beamed when she spied them. "Hey, guys! Come in."

"We're only here for a sec. Don't want to tire you out."

"As if. I'm great, Charlotte too."

"What a pretty name," Phyllis said, stepping closer to Willow. "For a very pretty baby!"

"Don't mention that to my mother. She's not happy that I didn't name her for one of the family."

"How did you choose Charlotte?" Lynn asked, nodding hello to the others.

"Harley's favorite aunt's name is Charlotte," Ruthie said. "I haven't met her, but I love the name."

"I'm sure she's thrilled."

"Where's the man of the hour?" Ben Morgan asked. "I assumed he'd be with you."

Polly blanched, unsure of how much to tell them about Kevin's trip. "Haven't you heard? Kevin had to fly back east. His ex-wife, Judith, passed away unexpectedly."

"How awful," Hope said. "I didn't even know he had an ex-wife."

Ben glanced at Polly, then shook his head at his brother's fiancée, clearly hoping to forestall further discussion. "Isn't my niece a beauty?" He crossed the room and took the infant from Willow, then brought her over to meet them.

Charlotte's deep-blue eyes studied her uncle, who cooed and fussed over her. It was no secret that Ben Morgan loved babies and they loved him.

"She's precious," Polly said.

"Of course, she is," Ruthie said. As the youngest Morgan, she was unaccustomed to all the attention being lavished on someone else.

Lynn looked around at the boxes lining the walls. "How's the packing coming?"

Ruthie frowned. "We had the movers all set, but my worrywart husband cancelled them. I am really bummed. I wanted Charlotte to come home to her beautiful nursery."

"Won't be long, Shortcake," Ben said. "Moms have to have a lot of patience."

"As if you'd know. And, since I'm now a mom, you can stop calling me Shortcake!"

"Never happen, little sister. Listen, we gotta get going. You need anything?"

"What do you think? Hurricane Leonora should be bearing down at any minute."

"We can play interference if it gets too bad. Just say the word." He handed the baby back to Willow, then bent to kiss Ruthie's cheek. "Rest up, sis."

After her brother disappeared, Ruthie turned to Polly and Lynn. "Charlotte's looking forward to coming to school."

"Not for a while, right?" Polly said.

"I'm hoping to get back to work in two or three weeks."

"Not if I have anything to say about it," Harley said, stepping into the bedroom.

"Well, you don't," Ruthie said, crossing her arms.

Harley winked at them before going to sit beside his wife. "If I have to chain you to the bed, I will, darlin'."

"We better head out and let you rest," Polly said as they turned toward the door. "We're right around the corner. If you need anything, please call. Take good care and rest."

"Thanks, Poll," Harley said, hugging his wife. "Be right back, babe." He followed Polly and her companions out into the living room, Hope and Robbie on their heels.

Leonora and Ben Morgan now sat with the others, and Ben, Maggie, and the kids were still there. "Hi, ladies, don't you look a picture today?" Ben Senior greeted the three.

Leonora waved at them. "Hi, dears, we're glad you're here. This is kind of a family powwow, but you're family, and we'd love for you to stay. Bethie and Lang are with the Dillons, and who knows where Kyle is, but they're all onboard. Harley darlin', why don't you explain?"

Harley gazed around the room, then cleared his throat. "As you all know, your sister and daughter wanted to be in the house before the baby came."

Ben grinned at his best friend. "Hey, buddy, that's news to me."

Maggie elbowed him. "Hush."

"Anyway, you know I'd lasso the moon for her, but in the meantime, I'd like to make her wish come true. I'd like to get us moved to the farm as soon as possible. Movers and the furniture companies are on hold, ready for the word from us. With your help, we'd like to make the move Tuesday. I want Ruthie to rest tomorrow. Leonora's gotten Ruthie to agree to a day at the Big House Tuesday. She'll come pick Charlotte and Ruthie up early in the morning and keep her there till everything's moved and settled, which is why I need you.

"I can supervise the movers and the furniture guys, but it would be great to have help unpacking the kitchen and all Ruthie's things as well as emptying boxes. I know she'll be pissed 'cause she wants to do it all herself, but it's too much. Those of you who know me know that I don't do well living in chaos."

"It's called OCD," Ben said, receiving another elbow from his wife.

"I'll pick Ruthie and the baby up around eight thirty Tuesday morning," Leonora said.

"And the trucks'll be here at nine," Harley said. "The movers will clear this place out first. I've already had them take all Ruthie's things she had stored at the ranch. So that's it. Is anyone willing to give us a hand?"

"I'm in," Maggie said. "Jeb, Nick, and the others can hold down the fort at the stables."

"Me too," Ben said.

"We'll both be there at nine sharp," Robbie said, his arm draped around Hope's shoulders.

"Kyle, Beth, and Lang are in," Ben Senior said, "and Spark's standing by."

"Wish we could help at the house," Lynn said. "We can certainly keep the kids as long as you need."

Leonora blew her a kiss. "I was hoping you'd say that, honey. Thank you."

"If someone is willing to pick me up, I'd love to help at the house," hyllis said.

"Thanks, darlin'," Ben Senior said. "I'll have Spark collect you in the morning."

They talked a while longer, then dispersed. On the walk back to their condo, Polly said, "Mom, that was really nice, you offering to help on your last day here."

"My pleasure, after all these nice people have done for me and my baby." She put her arm around her daughter's waist, and Polly leaned her head against her shoulder. "He's gonna be fine. He'll be back to you before you know it."

I hope you're right, Polly thought. "Thanks, Mama."

CHAPTER 32

Kevin checked into a motel on the outskirts of Tampa. He threw his bag on the bed, then headed back out for the fifteen-minute drive to Coral Reef. One of the positives of his divorce from Judith was that he would never have to see her parents again. He had supported them throughout the marriage, and cutting them off was sweet closure after years of their nastiness and greed. As he turned into the Lazy L Trailer Park, he pulled over and punched in Polly's number. It went to voice mail, but just hearing her voice cheered him up. *Get in and get out, buddy. Do what you have to do and escape quick!*

He pulled his rented SUV alongside the dilapidated double wide. The Robinsons had moved from Portland to Florida shortly before his divorce was final, so he'd never been to Coral Reef or the Lazy L. The weed-infested front yard was littered with rusted equipment and trash. It looked like a wreck compared to its neighbors' neat lawns, and he wondered if anyone ever complained. His knock was answered by Belle Robinson, her bleached-blonde hair teased a foot high. She wore bright red lipstick, a skintight floral print blouse, shorts, and gold lamé flip-flops.

"Hey, Belle," he said, surprised at how much she'd aged.

"Well, look what the cat dragged in." She stepped aside. "You better come in."

Judith's sister, Ivy, the only sane member of the family, was playing with Jasper in the small backyard, and Ernie Robinson was parked in front of the television watching a talk show.

"Hey, Ernie," he said.

His former father-in-law rose from his recliner and came to shake his hand. "Kevin, you look well."

You do not. "Thanks. I'm really sorry about Judith."

"Go on out. Ivy'll fill you in. Belle and I can't talk about it. We'd appreciate some help with the funeral, though."

"Of course."

"Somethin' to drink?" she asked, waving a glass that held what looked like straight bourbon.

"No, thanks. I'll just head out and say hi to Ivy and Jasper."

"You do that. Your son needs you," she said, plopping down in a chair next to her husband's recliner and lighting a cigarette.

For several minutes, he stood at the back door, watching Judith's younger sister throw a ball for Jasper. He had never understood how Ivy could have grown up relatively normal in this horror show of a home. By the time she was twelve, Judith had turned to drugs and alcohol, but Ivy had managed to stay on the mostly straight and narrow through high school and college. Last he'd heard, she was working as a dental hygienist.

"Hey, Jaspie, look who's here!" his former sister-in-law cried, spying him at the door. "Come on and join us, Kev!"

In denim capris, a bright pink jersey, and sandals, Ivy wore her long, curly red hair tied back in a sloppy ponytail. Cuter than her big sister, she was thin, but had always looked wholesome alongside her anorexic sibling.

"Hi, Ivy. Hi, Jasper!" he called.

To Kevin's surprise, Jasper ran to him and threw his arms around his legs. He lifted the towheaded child and swung him around. "Hi, buddy. Good to see you!"

"Did you come to see Mommy?" he asked, his blue eyes studying Kevin.

We haven't told him yet, Ivy mouthed over Jasper's head. "Hey, sweetie, why don't you run in and ask Grandma to give you two bottles of water for Kevin and me. Okay?"

The child nodded, and Kevin set him down. As Jasper ran for the back door, Kevin embraced Ivy. "Good to see you, sis. Wish it was under better circumstances."

"Leave it to my sister," she said, indicating the picnic table, where they sat opposite each other.

"What the hell happened?"

"When she came back from California, she went straight downhill. Not that she ever needed a reason to party. She actually went out there expecting you to fly into her arms and the two of you would ride off into the sunset together. She and Jasper live with me, as you know, but I can't control her. I moved with them here because she was pregnant and I didn't want the baby ending up with Mom and Dad, or believe me, I'd have stayed in Portland.

"Anyway, it happened two nights ago. She went out with her sleazeball friends. She's been using, and unfortunately, the batch of heroin those idiots bought was mostly fentanyl. They all ended up in the hospital, but only Judy died."

"I so sorry, Ivy."

She shrugged. "Let's be honest, Kev. It was inevitable."

"I feel like a shit that she came back so messed up."

"Don't. She was delusional. You put up with more of her crap than most guys would've."

"What about Jasper?"

"He's okay, but we… I haven't found a way to tell him. His grandparents are useless. Have they hit you up about the funeral?"

He nodded. "I'm happy to help."

"She's being cremated. We're going to spread her ashes at the beach, and Mom wants to keep a little box on the mantel."

"What do you need?"

"It's about three thousand for the cremation, and there's going to be a small memorial at the funeral home. I'm guessing there won't be too many there. Except for her druggie friends and a couple of coworkers, Judy really didn't know many people here. I think her friend Lacey's flying in for it, and I'm sure some of my parents' friends'll come. A couple of my friends'll be there."

"Well, let me know to whom to write the check."

"It's Sunny Acres Funeral Home. I'll get the total. Whatever you do, don't write it to the leeches."

The bitterness in her voice was understandable but still shocking. Again, he thought of his own parents and the family he had in the Valley. "Anything I can do for you?"

"No, thanks. I'm taking Jaspie home pretty soon. Wanta come for supper?" As she spoke, Jasper emerged from the trailer carrying two plastic bottles of water.

"Thanks, that'd be great."

"Where you staying?"

"Motel just outside of Tampa."

Ivy took the bottles, handing one to him, then scooped up her nephew. "Thanks, sweet pea. You're Auntie's big helper. Guess what? Kevin's coming to dinner."

The child peeked under Ivy's arm and gave him a shy smile.

CHAPTER 33

Sadly, Sunny Acres Funeral Home did not live up to its name. It was dark and smelled of mold. The folding chairs in the room labeled "Sanctuary" were rusty, their seats tattered. When he walked in, Kevin's heart sank. He might have been over Judith, but she deserved better than this. At Ivy's suggestion, he had ordered a few floral arrangements, which surrounded a collage of photos of Judith. "Mom and I did that," Ivy said, coming up behind him.

"Nice."

"No, it isn't, but it's the best we could do. I hope you don't mind that we included the wedding photos."

He smiled at her. "Of course not. Where's Jasper?"

"My friend Dottie's watching him."

"What's going to happen to him?"

"That's up to you, Daddy, but beware. Belle and Ernie have no interest in raising him, but they will miss the monthly payments you agreed to."

"What about you?"

"I love him, but I'm not his parent."

Neither am I, Kevin thought, *but there's no way I'm leaving him with Belle and Ernie Robinson.*

The memorial lasted less than fifteen minutes. The funeral director said a few words, Ivy read a poem and shared a few memories of her sister, then the director invited everyone into the next room for refreshments. As they filed out, Belle put on a show of sobbing and hand-wringing.

"Pay no attention to her," Ivy whispered. "It's all an act. She didn't care two hoots about Judy, and if she never saw me again, she wouldn't shed a tear. Watch out, here comes my dad, and he's got his leechy face on."

"Hey, Larrabee, got a minute?"

Kevin turned to face his former father-in-law. "Of course."

Ernie was dressed in a suit that sagged on his stooped frame. What remained of his thinning hair was plastered down in an ineffectual comb-over. "What're your plans?"

"I'll probably head out tomorrow or Wednesday."

"I mean for the kid," he sneered. He raised a gnarled hand, and for a second, Kevin thought he meant to pick his nose. Robinson scratched his head instead. "You're not thinkin' of takin' him away from his grandmother and me, are you?"

"He is my son."

"He's everything to Belle and me. No way he's goin' clear across the country."

"I thought he lived with Ivy?"

"Just till we can get his room fixed up."

"Excuse me?"

"And we're assuming the payments'll continue regular-like, every month?"

"He's my son, Ernie. I'll support him any way that's necessary, but I'm not sure living with you and Belle is what's best for him."

"Well, you'll not get him without a fight."

Kevin took several deep breaths, trying to keep from exploding. "Excuse me, I need some air." As he headed for the SUV, Ivy caught up with him.

"He put the squeeze on you, didn't he?"

"Says they're fixing up Jasper's room at their house."

"Bullshit, of course."

"I think they'll do anything to keep the money flowing."

"Well, don't worry, Jaspie's not going live with them while you're figuring out logistics. I'll get a sitter when I'm at work so they don't get their clutches on him."

"Judith gave me the birth certificate. My attorney has it. My name's on it."

"Better give him a call," she said, patting his arm. "I'm going out with a couple of friends for a quick beer, just one. Wanta come along?"

"Thanks, but I've gotta make some calls."

"Let me know what you decide," she said. "I'll miss him, but he belongs with you."

As soon as he got in the car, he called Fred Butler, who assured him that with his name on the birth certificate, Jasper was legally his, even if he was not his biological father. "Let me get the paperwork ready. I'm assuming you don't have a computer with you?"

"No."

"Just get me a number, and I'll fax everything to the motel in a few hours."

"Thanks, Fred."

"And don't give those people a dime. They have no legal standing. Will the sister keep him safe until tomorrow?"

"She says so."

"Good." Butler rang off, and Kevin called Victor to check on things at the farm. Assured that the crew was in good hands, he started the car and headed for the motel. Once in the room, he phoned Ivy, who was home, Jasper safe with her. He told her what he intended to do, and she promised to keep Jasper with her or her sitter and rang off.

After obtaining the motel fax number and alerting the office manager that documents would be coming for him, he walked across the street, grabbed a takeout burger and fries, and headed back to his room. After eating the greasy mess, he washed up and called Polly.

CHAPTER 34

Monday evening, Polly and Lynn had cooked a special dinner for Phyllis. As they sat enjoying lemon chicken, scalloped potatoes, and a wonderful salad, all courtesy of the ranch gardens, fields, and farm, they chatted about the day and plans for Harley and Ruthie's big move.

"Spark's picking me up at nine," Phyllis said dreamily. "He's a charmer, isn't he? If I didn't love your dad so much, I'd be very tempted."

"Mother!" Polly said, rolling her eyes. "Spark has a lady friend, so no flirting tomorrow!"

"What have you heard from Kevin, honey?"

"Not much. He had dinner with Judith's sister last night, and I believe the funeral was today."

"Tough on him," her mother said. "What a wonderful man to go back there and help out."

"He's doing it for Jasper."

"Have they decided where the child will live?" Phyllis asked.

"He hasn't mentioned it, and I haven't wanted to ask," Polly said, eyes pleading with Lynn to help change the subject.

"You know, Phyllis," Lynn said, "we really should book a spa treatment before you leave. A massage'd feel pretty good after helping the new parents move. We could book one for all three of us, then have dinner at the Lodge for your last night."

"Oh, honey, that sounds divine. Could we?"

"Of course," Polly said. "The only problem is, we won't know what time we'll be done at the Cottage."

"Well, my flight doesn't leave until four tomorrow, so I can sleep late."

"I'll make massage appointments for six," Lynn said. "Then dinner reservations for seven thirty at the Lodge. How does that sound? I can always cancel if needed."

"Sounds perfect," Polly said. "Thanks for thinking of it." Her cell rang, and she hopped up, grabbing it. "I'd like to take this," she said, and her companions nodded, waving her away.

"Hi," she said, "how's it going out there?"

"Funeral's over, thank God."

"Was it awful?"

"A horror show." His voice sounded cold and distant.

"I'm sorry. How long will you be staying?"

"I'm hoping to fly back Wednesday."

"I'm glad. I miss you."

"Polly, I'm bringing Jasper with me."

"Oh." She didn't know what else to say.

"I can't leave him here with his good-for-nothing grandparents."

"I thought he was living with his aunt?"

"He is. She loves him but says she's not ready to raise a child."

"Are you sure about this?" she said.

"No, but it's the right thing to do."

"Of course it is."

"Are you shocked?"

"No, of course not. You're a good, caring man, Kevin Larrabee."

"I'd understand if you want to pull out of our relationship and just be friends."

Shocked, Polly swallowed. "Is that what you want?"

"Of course not, but I already have enough baggage."

"Just get back here, and we'll work things out *together*."

"I hoped you'd say that. I love you."

"Me too."

"What are you up to now?"

"Having dinner with my mom and Lynn."

"Oh, sorry. Go back to your meal. I'll call tomorrow and let you know what's going on."

"Take care," she said, heart heavy as she clicked off.

When she returned to the kitchen, Lynn and Phyllis stared up at her. "So?" her mother said.

"So, he's bringing Jasper back to live with him." She shot her hand up in front of her. "Before you say a thing, that's all I know, and I don't want to discuss it." She sat back at the table, and before Phyllis could say a word, Lynn began discussing plans for the following day.

CHAPTER 35

Tuesday morning, Leonora collected Ruthie and Charlotte, and Operation Secret Move began. Polly and Lynn, along with Willow and Heather Sanchez, had a full house at the Cottage. At noon, Polly stepped into the storeroom and pulled out her cell phone to check messages and found several missed calls and a text from Kevin: *Grandparents have taken Jasper. Police are involved. Not sure when I'll be back.*

As Polly stepped out of the storeroom, Lynn glimpsed her expression. "Bad news?"

"The grandparents have kidnapped Jasper."

"Oh my God, Kevin must be going crazy. Has he called the cops?"

Polly nodded. "Poor little thing. They sound like horrible people."

"He'll find him."

Polly's phone vibrated, and she saw an unfamiliar number. "Okay if I take this?"

"Of course. Take your time."

"Thanks, be out soon," she said, turning away. "Hello?"

"Ms. Granger?"

"Yes?"

"This is Fred Butler. I'm the attorney helping Kevin Larrabee with his custody case."

"Yes, I've just heard from him. He says Jasper's been kidnapped?"

"I'm at the airport about to fly out. Spark Foster has kindly loaned us his corporate jet. Kevin asked me to phone."

"Thank you. That's kind of you. If I may ask, how do things stand?"

"I've had papers served to the Robinsons. The daughter has signed, but the grandparents are trying to extort money from Kevin before they'll sign."

"How awful for him."

"These are not nice people. I believe the papers are what precipitated the kidnapping, but we'll find them. Spark has hired a team of private investigators. They're top-notch."

"What a generous man he is."

"Kevin is like a son to him."

"Yes. Is there anything I can do?"

"Keep in touch with him, if only by text. He needs to hear from friends."

"Of course." She rang off, texted Kevin *I love you*, then went to join the others.

*****

Kevin and Ivy met with Spark's people at the Reef Diner at noon, Tuesday. Too distraught to wonder how Spark had managed to get the investigators on such short notice, Ivy gave the four men photos of her parents and Jasper, then answered their many questions about Ernie and Belle's friends, routines, habits, and hangouts. "We'll find 'em," Jimmy Lopez, the lead investigator, said. "These kinds of people don't have a wide range, particularly when they're short on cash."

When the men left, Kevin turned to her. "Now what? I can't just stand around. Where can we look? Maybe some place you forgot to mention?"

Ivy thought for a few minutes. "Hmm, they have the names and addresses of all their idiot friends, so I don't know. Their social security checks came last Friday, so they probably have a little extra cash, plus they have all the money you sent. Mom loves room service. Maybe we should start checking motels along the beach and in town? Believe it or not, even some of the seediest offer some kind of room service."

They decided to go together. Kevin called Jimmy Lopez and told them about the motels. Jimmy said he'd have one of his guys check the motels in town while they checked the beach. He and Ivy spent the afternoon going from one motel to the next. They started twenty miles north of Coral Reef and worked their way down the coast. First, they'd cruise the parking lot, searching for her parents' car. Then they'd head for the office and show photos of Jasper and his grandparents, just in case Belle and Ernie had parked the car somewhere else. Since the coastline was lined with motels, it was tedious, frustrating work. Every hour, Ivy would phone her parents' neighbors to check to see if Belle and Ernie had returned. While she called, Kevin would shoot a quick text to Polly. It was comforting to know she was there, and her text messages buoyed his spirits.

CHAPTER 36

Maggie picked up Ben and Emma at five thirty. They were the only remaining children."How'd it go?" Lynn asked as Polly gathered Ben's toys.

"Well, we got everything in and put away. The new furniture looks terrific, and Harley's stuff looks great. The man has excellent taste. I'm sure Ruthie will rearrange everything, but I think she'll be pleased."

"So they're completely out of the condo?" Polly asked.

"Yup. Leonora's bringing her home as we speak. Of course, we all wanted to be there to see Ruthie's reaction, but Harley asked that he carry her over the threshold alone. Leonora's agreed to hold baby Charlotte in the driveway so they can walk through it first as a couple. Then Harley'll come and grab the baby. Leonora has promised to drive straight home and leave them alone." Maggie smiled. "This may take a Herculean effort on her part, but she's promised."

"Ruthie's going to be thrilled," Polly said as Lynn chased Ben around the crafts room.

"How are you? Have you heard from Kevin?"

"The baby's grandparents have disappeared with him."

"How horrible."

"Spark has investigators working with the police. I don't know how he does it, but he dispatched Fred Butler on his private jet and supposedly hired the best private detectives in the area."

Maggie patted her arm. "That's what a generous heart and a billion-dollar pocketbook can do. They'll find them." As Emma gave Polly a hug, Maggie asked, "This your mom's last night, right?"

"Yes."

"She worked like a Trojan today. Kept everyone organized and humming."

Polly grinned. "That's Mom. She loves a project. We're taking her to the spa for a massage at six thirty, then a farewell dinner at the Lodge."

"Well, don't let us keep you. Come on, kids. Polly and Lynn have to go." She turned back to Polly. "Spark and your mom left before we did, so she's probably chomping at the bit for her massage. Have fun!" She grabbed Ben and carried him out, Emma following with his backpack.

"See you tomorrow!" Polly called as they closed the door behind them.

Lynn grabbed her backpack. "Let's shake it, partner. I don't want to miss a second of my massage."

*****

In the growing darkness, Kevin turned into the parking lot of the Cozy Harbor Motel. Ivy sat beside him, talking with her parents' neighbors, who confirmed that Ernie and Belle were still not home. When she hung up, she said, "This place looks like them. Sleazy, dark, and crappy, and what do you know, that's their car over by the dumpster."

"Are you sure?"

"Yup."

"Okay, let's be careful. I'm gonna phone Jimmy and Fred and let 'em know where we are. I'll park in back of their car so they can't run off. Then I'll check in at the office, and you watch the parking lot."

A large woman, her hair the color of ripe plums, sat behind the desk. She wore a muumuu, its fabric bright green and swirly. "Howdy. Need a room, hon?" she said.

"No, thanks. I'm looking for these people." He showed her the photos of Ernie and Belle. "Are they here?"

"You a cop?"

"Do they have a small boy with them? Blond toddler."

"Listen, honey, our guests' business is private."

"I'm the child's father."

"So you say."

"Look, if it's money you want…" He pulled out his wallet and handed her sixty dollars.

She snatched it, tucking into the breast pocket of her hideous dress. "They're around. For another sixty, I'll show you personal."

Kevin reached for his wallet just as the lobby door opened and Jimmy Lopez appeared, followed by Fred Butler. "Not another dime," Fred said. He approached the woman. "Are you the owner of this establishment?"

"Who wants to know?"

"Fred Butler, I'm Mr. Larrabee's attorney from Portland, Oregon."

"Whoop-dee-do. I know my rights. You got no legal standing here."

"Actually, he does," Jimmy said as Fred pulled papers from his briefcase.

"This is a court order from Judge Yates here in Florida. Are you familiar with the name?"

"Whaddya think, I'm stupid? Everyone's heard of him."

"Then tell us your name."

"It's Choy. Bobby. Roberta Choy. I own this motel."

Fred stepped closer. "Then, Ms. Choy, you'd better talk fast. The police are five minutes away."

"And they'll arrest your ass if you don't start talking," Jimmy said.

Just then, Ivy burst into the lobby. "I saw 'em! They just crossed the road from that restaurant. They went into a room at the far end."

"Number?" Lopez said.

"Sixteen," Choy said, watching openmouthed as most of the group raced for the door.

Fred snapped his fingers. "Key."

Choy opened a drawer under the counter, then handed him a key, "This is my only master," she said as he snatched it from her meaty paw.

CHAPTER 37

"I bet there's a slider on the beach side," Jimmy said as Fred, Kevin, and Ivy made their way to number sixteen. "I'll go around. Ms. Robinson, do your parents own firearms?"

"My dad has a pistol."

"Then we wait for the cops. They're pulling in now."

"You folks stay back," Jimmy said. "Tell the cops where I am and what's going on."

As he disappeared into the shadows, Kevin called out, "Wait! If there's a possibility of guns, I..."

"We'll handle it," Jimmy whispered from the inky black at the side of the ramshackle building.

Three officers joined them. As Fred filled them in, Ivy stood beside Kevin, waiting. She whispered, "Poor Mom, she's about to be arrested, and the sign in the lobby said that room service is temporarily suspended."

One of the officers moved to the door, and the others waited on either side of it. Suddenly, Kevin stepped in front of the door. "Wait, let me knock. If they think they can get some money out of me, maybe they'll let me in."

"I don't like it," Fred said.

"Too dangerous," Sergeant Larkin said. Shoving Kevin aside, he knocked.

"Who is it?" Belle called.

"Nighttime security, Ma'am."

"We're all set, honey."

"Open up. We've gotta check the windows and back door."

"Go to hell," Ernie shouted just as they heard the crash of glass.

Larkin slipped the key in the lock and threw open the door.

Belle Robinson screamed as she crouched behind the dresser. Her husband and Jasper were nowhere in sight.

"Stand up and get out," Larkin said, motioning her to the door, where his officer pulled her out.

They heard a scuffle, and Jimmy Lopez swung open the bathroom door to discover Ernie Robinson crouched in the shower, his hand covering Jasper's mouth, a pistol at his temple. "Please, Ernie," Kevin called, "you're scaring him."

"Lot you care. Fuck you, Larrabee."

"Ernie please let him go. If you need money, I can help."

Ignoring the officer who tried to hold her back, Ivy pushed by. "Dad, come on. This isn't you. Let Jaspie go, and no one'll get hurt."

"Figures yer on their side," her father muttered. "Fine, take the little brat. He's been nothing but a pain in the butt." He shoved Jasper forward. Lopez pulled him out of reach, and he ran into Ivy's arms.

Both Larkin and Lopez had their weapons pointed at Ernie. "Drop the gun, Robinson," Larkin said.

"Fuck you," Ernie said, tossing the gun, which clattered across the bathroom floor.

Larkin's officers rushed forward and dragged him out to join his wife in the squad car.

As Kevin and Ivy hurried out with Jasper, Ernie called, "You'll pay for this, Larrabee! First you killed my baby, now you're taking the only thing we have left of her."

Fred Butler approached the squad car and peered inside. "No, you'll pay, Mr. Robinson. First with jail time for kidnapping, then a court order forbidding you to have any further contact with Jasper. Ever." As Butler walked away, the officer slammed the car door. Fred gave Larkin copies of Jasper's relevant paperwork and then came to where Ivy and Kevin stood, Jasper now in his father's arms, his face buried in Kevin's chest.

"Thank you, Fred. I don't know how I'll ever repay you and Spark, but I'm sure gonna try."

"You know Spark Foster."

"Yes, I do. He's paying me and my guys a small fortune on his current project, but I'm going to see to it that the next one—and there's always a next one with Spark—is gratis."

Butler laughed. "Good luck with that. Listen, I'm going to head to my hotel. I'll get all the paperwork to my colleagues in Tampa tomorrow morning and meet you at the airport. What time should I schedule the plane?"

"Would two be too early?" Kevin asked.

"Two it is. If there's any problem, I'll call, but otherwise, I'll see you there. Ms. Robinson, it's been a pleasure," he said, shaking her hand.

As the tall, lanky attorney walked away, Ivy turned to him. "Scheduling the plane?"

Kevin smiled at her. "Private jet. Belongs to a friend of mine."

"Boy, you do move in fancy circles."

"Not really, just incredibly lucky. Spark, my friend and employer, is very rich and very generous."

"I'll say."

He put his arm round her shoulder, and they headed to the car. "Let's get this guy to bed." He hesitated, then said, "Your place or mine?"

"All his things are at my place. I'm happy to keep him one more night. You're welcome to stay too." Her eyes suggested more than just watching over her nephew.

CHAPTER 38

After declining Ivy's invitation to spend the night, he set Jasper in his bed and thanked her as she walked him to his car.

Ivy hugged him. "Too much baggage, huh?"

He smiled, gazing down at her. "Something like that."

"You've got someone out there, don't you?"

"I sure hope so."

"I'm glad for you, Kev. Maybe someday I could come for a visit to see you and Jaspie and meet your girl?"

"Of course. Night, Ivy. See you around noon."

"You bet."

*****

When he pulled into his motel lot, it was after ten. Unable to wait a moment longer, he called Polly. Her phone rang, then went to voice mail. He sent a quick text telling her all was well, then headed to his room. He had just stepped into the room when his phone buzzed. He grinned, seeing Polly's name. "Hey."

"Hey, yourself," she said softly. "I'm so relieved."

"Me too. Did I get you from somewhere?"

"I'm having dinner with Mom and Lynn. It's Mom's last night. We've just had massages and are now on the terrace at the Lodge." Polly had kept her phone beside her and had just stepped away from the table.

"Sounds fun. I'll let you go, then."

"I want to hear all about it," she said, loath to hang up, even as her companions stared at her and the server waited to take her order. "How late will you be up?"

"Probably another hour, but no worries. Call tomorrow if you get a chance."

"Will do. I miss you so much," she said. "Night."

"Miss you too, baby. Can't wait to see you."

"Love you."

"Me too," he said, clicking off.

*****

Kevin arrived at Ivy's shortly before noon. She had a small suitcase by the door packed with Jasper's things. "I can ship the few toys that wouldn't fit in his bag, but I packed the important ones."

"Thanks, Ivy."

Jasper hung back, tossing a yarn ball to her cat.

"We talked about Mommy's death, but I'm not sure he understands," Ivy whispered. "He's not sure what's happening now either, but he's excited about the airplane ride."

"It's gonna be an adjustment."

"Yes, but I can tell he's already attached to you. You have that effect on people."

"I love him. As a brand-new clueless father, I'm not sure I'll be up to the task, but I'm sure gonna try."

"You'll do great. And you've got your girlfriend to help you. What's her name, anyway?"

"Polly."

Ivy gave him a wistful look. "She's a lucky woman."

"I'm the lucky one. Take care, Ivy. Thanks for everything, and come visit us anytime. Any chance with Judith and Jasper gone, you'll return to Portland?"

"Probably not. Too many ghosts. It wasn't easy growing up with a father who was one step ahead of the law with all his shady business dealings. I do love the warm weather, and I've made a lot of really good friends here."

"Yes, you have. I enjoyed talking with some of them at the funeral."

"Yeah, they're great."

Kevin handed her an envelope. "All my contact information is in here as well as numbers for my foreman, Victor Gonzalves, and Spark Foster, just in case you can't reach me."

"Honeymoon?"

He laughed. "Wouldn't that be nice? No, mostly because I'm bad about keeping my cell on me when I'm working."

"You're a good man, Kevin Larrabee," she said. "Jasper may not be your flesh and blood, but he's a lucky little boy to have you as his father."

Shocked, he stared at her. "You know?"

"My sister may have been a lot of things, but we loved each other *and* we told each other everything. We were all each other had growing up with Mr. and Mrs. Horror Show."

"Who was he?"

"She didn't tell me his name. Some random guy. Said he was a real loser. Not sure she ever told him."

"Jesus, I hope not. Ivy, I—"

"I won't tell a soul, ever. I promise," she said, fingers to his lips. "Now, let's get the car seat installed."

"No need. I checked *Consumer Reports* last night and stopped and bought one this morning. Give his old one to someone who needs it."

"And you're worried about being a good dad? Come on, let's get my lucky nephew into the car and off to his new life as a cowboy."

She scooped Jasper up and carried him to the car. He began to whimper as she strapped him in, clinging to her. "Sweetie, Kevin's gonna take really good care of you, and I'll come visit soon. Okay?"

He shook his head back and forth, crying now. "I love you, Jaspie," she said, hugging and kissing him before stepping back, tears in her eyes.

"Thanks Ivy," Kevin said, hugging her. "I promise to take really good care of him. We'll send lots of pictures."

"Bye," she said, wiping her eyes. "Call or text when you get there so I know you're both safe."

"Will do," he said, hopping in and starting the car, Jasper's wails heralding their departure.

CHAPTER 39

After a quick McDonalds lunch of french fries and chicken nuggets, which seemed to cheer Jasper up, they arrived at the airport a little before two. Fred Butler was waiting on the tarmac. They boarded, and Fred was able to change their flight plan for a slightly earlier departure. Jasper happily played on the plane and visited the pilot in the cockpit. Finally, it was time to strap him in for takeoff. As they began to move, Kevin looked over at Fred. "Shoot, I was gonna make a couple of phone calls."

"This is Spark Foster's plane, my friend. As soon as we've reaching cruising altitude, use the phone next to your seat to call anyone you want."

Kevin laughed. "Of course. What was I thinking?"

Fifteen minutes into the flight, after watching the clouds below them in awe, Jasper fell asleep. Kevin covered him with a blanket, rose, and headed for the plane's open lounge area to make his calls. Polly answered on the first ring.

"Oh, I'm so glad to hear from you!" she said. They had spoken earlier in the morning, and he'd given her a brief summary of the search and recovery of Jasper.

"Your mom still there?"

Polly pulled her car over to the side of the road. "Just dropped her in Grenville. She insists on being at the airport *very* early."

"Who's covering for you?"

"We've got Heather all week, and Willow, of course. Between the three of them, they can hold down the fort till I get back. I'm gonna owe Lynn big-time after these last few weeks. But never mind me. How are you? When do you take off?"

"In the air as we speak. Polly, I hate to ask, but I have a few favors which I hope won't be too much to ask."

"Of course, anything. Can I pick you up at the airport?"

"Thanks, but Spark's sending a car. The thing is… I… We need a crib and a few supplies. Any chance you have a small bed or cot at the Cottage, just for tonight? I can ask my guys to pick it up and drop it at the house. I'm sure I can figure out how to set it up."

"Done. We'll bring it over. Let me get a paper and pencil, and you can tell me the other things you need."

He listed a few things Ivy had suggested, and Polly added a few that she knew he'd need. Then, almost sheepishly, he asked, "I don't suppose there's room at the Cottage for Jasper?"

She chuckled. "You know Spark. He's already been over and signed him up. Even offered to hire a new teacher."

"I'm really gonna have to do something about him."

Polly chuckled. "No advice about Spark, but of course, we're eager to have Jasper join us."

"Thanks, that means a lot. You can let me know about tuition later."

"That's a simple answer—there is none. The Cottage is totally subsidized by the Morgan-Foster Trust. Do you want Jasper to start tomorrow?"

"No. I'll keep him with me tomorrow and maybe start him Monday?"

"Perfect."

"But if he's not too tired, could I bring him by sometime tomorrow to see the place?"

"We'd love it. I suggest not coming between one and three as that's naptime, but any other time would be fine."

"Maybe around ten? I've gotta make rounds and check on the job sites, but we'll be over."

"We'll be ready," she said softly. "Can't wait."

"Me either. Thanks for getting the supplies and the crib. If you need help, don't be afraid to phone Victor and the guys. There's a house key under a stone to the right of my garage door."

"I'll find it, don't worry. Have a safe flight."

Reluctantly, he rang off. Hearing Polly's voice soothed the ragged edges of the past few days, and he hated to say goodbye. Before returning to his seat, he phoned Victor, who assured him all was going well.

"Everything okay?" Fred said.

Kevin nodded. "Be good to get home. How'd everything go with the attorneys this morning?"

"All set. Because of the gun, Ernie Robinson will do a couple of years, but she'll probably get probation since they're Jasper's grandparents."

"Honestly, I don't care now that they're three thousand miles away."

*****

After work, Polly and Lynn loaded the crib into Lynn's SUV. They then stopped at the pharmacy in town and were headed for Kevin's when Polly said, "Oh, look, Saguaro Dreams is still open. Let's go in."

She referred to a three-story emporium at the far end of Main Street. Along with the grocery store and the farmer's market, SD, as the locals called it, was one of the Valley's largest commercial spaces. It sold all manner of items from penny candy to jewelry, clothing, paintings, sculptures, toys, and gifts. In its third year, SD specialized in the work of local artisans, and their offerings included a number of Hope Seymour's paintings and the work of many Valley artists. Alongside the toy section was a small baby department with unique and lovely quilts and blankets.

Polly headed there and picked up a blue quilt with appliqued squares depicting trucks and cars. "Aw, this is so cute. Look, Lynn!"

"I think that's one of Lorna's quilts," Lynn said, referring to Lorna Perez, mother of Christy and Fara.

"I'm getting it. This too," she said, holding up a pale blue blanket.

"Okay. Then I'll grab a few fun things," Lynn said, selecting a soft, stuffed elephant and a small wooden train set.

One more quick stop at the grocery, and they made it to Kevin's about six fifteen. They found the key and let themselves in. After putting away the food, a rotisserie chicken, some fruit, bread, milk, and a few kinds of toddler snacks, they headed for the bedroom. "He thinks we should set the crib up in here tonight since the other bedrooms are upstairs," Polly said as they unfolded the crib and positioned it in the small alcove to one side of his large bedroom.

As they worked, Lynn gazed around. "Wow, the man has great taste, doesn't he?"

"It's pretty amazing, isn't it? Let's hurry, then I'll give you a quick tour. I don't want to be here when they get home. Better for them to settle in together, just the two of them."

Lynn gave her a look, then shrugged as she tucked in one end of the crib sheet. They arranged the blanket, quilt, and toys and set the supplies Kevin had requested, as well as a few they decided he needed, on a small love seat.

Her hand on a wall switch, Polly looked back as they departed. "Think we should leave a light on in here?"

"You know the man."

"I was thinking of Jasper," she said, deciding that the toddler wouldn't want to come into a dark house. The light stayed on.

They took a quick peek at the upstairs and the backyard. "Amazing to find such a cool place in the middle of town," Lynn said as they headed for the driveway. They left the kitchen and front porch lights on.

"He's done a ton of work on it," Polly said as she slipped the key under the boulder by the garage.

"He's a keeper, Poll. Don't let him slip away."

As Polly followed Lynn to the SUV, she had a premonition of doom, as if things were about the change and not for the better. She hoped it was fatigue.

*****

Spark had a limo waiting for them at the airport. Fred Butler was remaining on the plane, which would take him on to Portland. The two men shook hands on the tarmac, Jasper in Kevin's arms.

"Thanks, Fred. Don't know what I would've done without you, man."

"My pleasure. Good luck to you both."

As they drove into his driveway, Kevin spied the lights on and said a silent thank-you to Polly and Lynn. "Here we are, big guy," he said, looking over to find Jasper sound asleep.

Spark's driver helped with the bags as Kevin carried Jasper into the house. It was after nine, and they'd had food on the plane, so he decided to put the sleeping toddler to bed. He carried him into his bedroom, so grateful to see the care Polly and Lynn had taken over the crib and bedding. Gently, he placed Jasper in bed and covered him with the blanket. After ruffling his curls, he turned out the light, surprised to see that the ladies had also installed a night light in an outlet beside the crib. *How will I ever thank everyone?* he thought, as he headed out to say good night to the driver.

I'm a father, he thought, shaking his head. *Amazing how life can change in the blink of an eye.*

CHAPTER 40

Friday morning, Jasper popped up at five, whimpering. Kevin started to bring him into his bed when he noticed that he was soaked through. Ivy had sent some pull-up nighttime diapers, which she recommended that he use, but in the rush to get home, he'd totally forgotten them.

"Okay, big guy, let's get you changed."

Polly and Lynn had spread a towel on his bedroom love seat and set up a makeshift changing area. After changing him, he carried Jasper back to the bed and covered them both up. This was Kevin's usual rising time, but what did a few minutes matter after the last few crazy days? When they woke again, it was after eight.

Polly and Lynn had strapped a portable toddler seat to one of his kitchen chairs. "Okay, buddy," he said to Jasper, who was still in pajamas. "Let's have some breakfast."

He proceeded to try numerous items to see what the child might like and finally managed to get a banana and half a piece of toast into him. At that point, there was food all over the kitchen floor, and Jasper was screaming to get out of the chair. Kevin unstrapped him before wiping his gooey hands and face. The toddler ran off and hurled himself onto the living room sofa, Kevin following with a washcloth, making ineffectual attempts to clean him off.

"Hey, buddy, slow down!" he said, but Jasper paid no attention. "Fortunately for us, my cleaning lady's coming tomorrow." He made a mental note to change her schedule to once a week instead of twice a month.

"I want Ivy," he cried, flopping to the floor, tears streaming down his round red cheeks.

"I know, buddy, but you're here now. I'm your daddy, and you're gonna live here with me."

"I want Ivy!"

"Hey, buddy, you're gonna love it here. I promise. Wait till you see your school. There are lots of toys and kids."

Kevin decided to get him dressed and visit the Cottage sooner rather than later. He picked him up, and Jasper rested his head on his shoulder. "Okay, buddy," Kevin said, ruffling Jasper's hair. "Let's see what you've got in your suitcase."

They opened his bag, and Jasper discovered a number of his favorite toys. As he began playing with them, Kevin cleared a drawer in his dresser and unpacked the few clothes Ivy had sent. He made a mental note to buy him a few more things soon. *This parenting thing is gonna mean a whole new life*, he thought, watching the toddler throw a ball around the bedroom. Since Jasper was happily occupied, he set out an outfit for him and himself, hopped into the shower for less than a minute, shaved, and dressed. Before dressing Jasper, he shot a quick text to Ivy: *Help! What are his favorite foods! Please send a list, when you can!*

After lots of wriggling and screeching, he managed to wrestle Jasper into his clothes. Coming from Florida, he had no warm jacket. Valley temperatures were below freezing, with predictions of more snow so Kevin put two sweatshirts on him and one of his own knitted caps and hurried out to the car.

"We've gotta get you some warm clothes, buddy," he said as he strapped Jasper into his car seat and threw a blanket over him.

Before they started off, he called Polly. "Hey, good morning," he said, relieved that she'd picked up.

"How's it going?" she asked.

"Oh, it's going. Thanks so much for all the things. You and Lynn are lifesavers. Please let me know how much I owe you."

"Nothing. Consider them Jasper's welcome home gifts. And you can hold on to the crib until you have a chance to get one. We won't need it until Charlotte comes."

"Thanks. Okay if we stop by in about ten minutes?"

"Perfect. We're just finishing circle time. It's too cold to go out, so we'll be having free play and crafts when you get here."

When Kevin walked in, Jasper in his arms, he spied Ben Morgan Senior and Spark, rolling around the floor with their grandchildren and others. "Hey, welcome back!" Spark called.

Kevin helped Jasper out of his double layers as Polly approached. She smiled at Kevin, then turned her attention to his son. "Hi, Jasper!" she said softly. Ben Morgan the third was on her heels, curious about this new little boy.

"I'm Polly, and this is Ben," she said. "Bennie loves trucks. Would you like him to show you where they are?"

Jasper nodded, slipping out of Kevin's grasp.

"Come on!" Ben said, and the two ran off.

Kevin's hand touched hers. He longed to embrace her.

Lynn approached and gave him a hug. "Welcome back. What a beautiful child."

"Thanks. I am so grateful to you and Polly for last night. Everything was perfect."

"It was our pleasure."

"I wish you'd let me reimburse you."

"Absolutely not! We had a ball," Lynn said

Polly moved off to help two-year-old Christy Perez find the doll she wanted.

As he and Lynn chatted, Spark approached and hugged him. "Hey, son, good to have you back. Fine little fella you have there."

"Yes, he is. He's also a handful. Not sure I'm up to the challenge of parenthood," he said as Ben Senior clapped him on the shoulder.

"Sure you are, son! If Spark and this old man can do it, you sure can."

"If you say so, Ben."

The elder Morgan smiled at him. "You're not gonna do this alone, you know. You're with family here."

"Sure are," Spark said. "Whatever you need, just say the word."

"You've already done *more* than enough, Spark."

"Wherever did you get that idea?" Spark said. "Better toss it out too, 'cause we're just getting started. I suspect there's a certain little gal who'll also lend a hand."

Lynn laughed. "I believe you're right, Spark," she said as they all watched Polly playing with Jasper and Ben the third.

CHAPTER 41

Kevin hung back, not sure what he should do. They'd been at the Cottage for almost an hour. He was very late for work, but Jasper was having so much fun that he was reluctant to take him away.

Lynn stood with Polly, observing Kevin watch his child. "Whaddya wanta bet he's afraid to leave? Sounds like they had a rough morning."

Polly nodded. "It's gonna be an adjustment, that's for sure." She strolled over to Kevin and touched his arm. "Wanta leave him for a while or the day? We've got plenty of help, and we'd be happy to have him."

He gave her a weary smile. "Do I look that pathetic?"

"Maybe a little shell-shocked?"

He laughed. "Jesus, Polly, what was I thinking? I'm forty-two years old. What made me think I could take care of a toddler? I must've been crazy."

She patted his arm. "That's fatigue talking. Be kind to yourself and give it time. There's not a right or wrong way. You'll get to know each other, and you'll learn."

"He's homesick. He has no winter clothes. And he rejected everything I offered him for breakfast except a banana."

She grinned. "That's not unusual. Believe it or not, many children thrive on bananas and peanut butter. Did you ask his aunt what he likes?"

"I sent an SOS text."

"We're about to have snack. We'll see if he likes graham crackers."

"He needs so many things, and I don't know the first thing about kids' clothes, where to get 'em, anything. Look at his shoes. They're falling apart, and they're not made for winter, are they?"

"Not really. I'm happy to help with shopping for things tomorrow, if you like. I can ask some of the moms for tips on where to get things. Looks like he needs a coat and boots right away?"

"And mittens."

"We have extras. I'll send some with you when you pick him up. That is, if you'd like to leave him?"

He gave her a grateful smile. "You know it'd be great if I could make a quick trip out to the project."

"He'll be fine Look at him. He's in heaven."

"I could be back around noon? Would that work?"

"Of course. We eat at twelve fifteen. You could stay, if you like."

"Thanks, but I'll grab him, and we'll find something on the way home. Maybe stop at Gracie's."

"Good idea. If you haven't heard from his aunt yet and he won't tell you what he likes, I'd recommend ordering a hot dog and plain hamburger."

"Thanks, Polly. Right now, I'd love to hug you and a whole lot more."

She grinned. "Not in front of the kids." She leaned closer to him. "Me too. Go on now. He'll be fine."

"Think I should tell him I'm leaving?"

"Ordinarily, I'd say yes, but why don't you scoot, and one of us'll tell him in a few minutes, reassuring him that you'll be back very soon."

"Thanks," he said, squeezing her hand.

CHAPTER 42

After checking with Victor and the crews, Kevin headed back to the ranch to collect Jasper. When he walked in, Jasper was painting, Ben at his side. Willow was supervising.

"How's it going?" he asked Lynn, who was prepping for lunch.

"Happy as a clam. We let him know you'd be back soon, and he's been fine."

"Thanks," he said, waving to Polly, who was reading to Christy. He waited until she finished, then walked over. "Good time to take him?"

She gazed over at the two boys. "Let them finish, and Willow will clean them up. We'll be calling everyone to wash their hands for lunch soon."

"Great. He hasn't even noticed me."

"He's been having a ball. Loves the kids."

"I don't think he had much of that in Florida."

"We packed a bag with a few extra clothes, mittens, and an old jacket that'll do until you find a better one."

"Were you serious about tomorrow?"

"Of course. I'd be delighted," she said. "You know, he's been having such a great time with little Ben, I could phone Maggie Morgan and see what they're doing tomorrow. Maybe she'd take him for an hour or two?"

He frowned. "I can't ask them to do that."

"Maggie's a straight shooter. If it's a burden, she'll say so. She might be pleased to have a friend for Ben. If Emma's around, she'll help entertain him too."

"Well, I don't know."

"I can't ask Lynn 'cause she's going hiking with friends. It's either Maggie's or we take you-know-who shopping with us. Have you ever shopped with a toddler?"

"Okay, I surrender! See what you can work out."

"Glad to see a smile."

"Know any good sitters in town? I better start looking now, 'cause I'll probably need 'em!"

"I'll see what I can learn from the other parents, but you could ask Willow. She might be glad of the extra money. I'll text and let you know about Maggie later."

"Thanks. Looks like the hellion is cleaned up, so I'll grab him."

As Kevin headed for Willow and the two boys, Lynn came to stand beside Polly. "I'm about to sound the lunch bell. How's Kevin doing?"

Polly smiled at her partner. "If he survives today, he may have a chance."

*****

After a chaotic lunch at Gracie's Diner, Kevin discovered that Jasper loved hot dogs and hamburgers. As they finished, he ordered one of each to go, figuring that would take care of dinner. He took Jasper out to the ranch in the afternoon, where they found Beth Morgan Dillon in the farm office. She loaned them a golf cart, and he took Jasper out to see the cattle, chickens, pigs, and goats.

Polly texted in the late afternoon to say that Maggie would love to have Jasper in the morning hours as early and as long as needed. After several back-and-forth texts, they arranged for Kevin to pick her up on the way to Maggie and Ben's.

Dinner was a bit more successful than breakfast. After dinner, Kevin ran a bath, which Jasper loved. Along with the extra clothes, Polly had put a few books in the bag. After he got Jasper into pajamas and a nighttime diaper, they read several stories on his bed. At the end of *Curious George Feeds the Animals*, he looked down to find Jasper asleep. Gently, he carried him to his crib and said a silent prayer that he'd sleep until morning.

He switched on the nightlight and left the bedroom door ajar, breathing a sigh of relief. After collapsing into his leather recliner, he grabbed his phone and found a long text from Ivy listing Jasper's favorite foods. At the end, she wrote: *How's it going? Miss Jaspie so much!*

He wrote back assuring her that everything was fine, although he wasn't at all sure that was true.

CHAPTER 43

Around midnight, Jasper woke crying and spent the rest of the night in Kevin's bed. After a successful breakfast of Fruity Os, Kevin found the cartoon channel and a show Jasper seemed to know. Then he quickly showered and dressed himself, then Jasper. Shortly before nine, they drove into Polly's condo complex, where she was waiting on the steps.

"Hi, guys," she said, hopping into the front seat. She wanted to lean to give Kevin a kiss, but something told her Jasper wouldn't like it.

"Morning! Hey, Jasper, say hi to Polly."

"Where's Ben?" the toddler asked.

"We're going to Ben's house, remember, buddy?" Kevin said, winking at Polly. The moment he spied her, Kevin's libido went into overdrive. No woman had ever had this effect on him, and he wasn't sure how he was going to shop with an all-day boner. *Down, boy,* he thought, taking some deep breaths.

Polly turned and smiled at Jasper. "You'll love it at Ben's. Maybe Emma will show you her pony."

"We've been up for many hours," he said. "But is this too early for you on a Saturday?"

She smiled. "Not at all. I walked Archie earlier."

"Oh geez, you've already been to the stables?"

She nodded.

"And here I was thinking *we* were the early birds!"

As the truck climbed the hill to the Morgans' home, Kevin whistled. "Of all the cool Morgan properties, this is by far my favorite."

"It's beautiful, isn't it?" Polly said as Ben the third, Emma, and their father appeared on the porch, waving.

"Hey, guys," Ben called. "Come on in. Maggie had to run to the stables, but I've got two people here who are ready to party!"

Kevin waved. "Morning. You sure this is okay?"

"You bet. We've been waiting for you for hours, haven't we, guys?"

"Yeah, come on, Jasper! We've got lots of toys inside," Emma called.

As Kevin lifted him out of his seat, Jasper clung to him, burying his face in his shoulder. "A little shy, I guess," his father said. "Come on, buddy, this is gonna be fun."

"Got time for coffee?" Ben said.

"Not for me, thanks," Polly said as she followed the group into the house.

"I'm good too, thanks," Kevin said. "This is quite a place."

Ben grinned, the Morgan smile that made women go weak at the knees. "We like it. Sam and I had fun designing it, but Maggie and Emma run the place now. Ben and I are just are just along for the ride, aren't we, buddy?"

Emma proudly gave them a tour, her brother trailing along, chattering beside her. Halfway through, Jasper lifted his head and peered around but was disinclined to leave his father's arms.

"Hey, I've got an idea," Ben said. "Does Jasper like horses?"

This received a shy nod.

"Well, there we go. Em, whaddya say we head out to the barn and you can introduce this big guy to Sunny?"

"Sure!" she said, grabbing a hat, jacket, and mittens.

Polly found Jasper's mittens and hat in his backpack and handed them to Kevin. Ben wrestled his son into his jacket, then grabbed his own jacket. He picked up Ben the third and strolled out beside Kevin and Jasper.

They followed Emma, who skipped her way to the barn and threw open the doors.

"Hey, sweetie," her father called. "You get Sunny, and we'll wait out here. Okay?"

She nodded and disappeared.

"She's such an amazing little girl," Polly said. "So loving and responsible."

"All her mom's doing," he said.

"Does she ride often?" Kevin asked.

"Much as she can. She a good little rider, like her mom."

"What about Ben?" Kevin asked.

"Not yet. Occasionally, he rides with one of us. Maggie's horse is too big, but sometimes we take him on mine or the pony."

When Emma appeared, leading her pony, that did it. Jasper slipped out of his father's arms and headed straight for Sunny. Kevin started to grab him, but Ben said, "No worries. Emma's holding tight, and Sunny's the gentlest horse on the ranch."

"See, Jaspie? You can pet him," Emma said as her brother pushed in to pat the pony.

"Hey, Sun. Hey, boy," little Ben said as the pony nuzzled him.

"If you guys watch you-know-who," Ben said, pointing to his son, "I'll bring out the big guy."

"Of course," Polly said as she and Kevin moved to stand beside the children.

A few minutes later, Ben returned leading the biggest horse Polly had ever seen. She'd heard about Tabasco, but this was the first time she'd laid eyes on the enormous draft horse.

Jasper's mouth hung open.

"That's Bascie!" little Ben said, hopping up and down. They noticed he stayed put and did not approach the chocolate-brown horse with its huge hooves.

"Wow, you weren't kidding about big," Kevin said.

Ben laughed. "He's Maggie's baby. I was scared to death of him at first. He was originally part of the mustang training program, but the border patrol agent that they matched him to wouldn't go near him. Harley, Maggie, and Jeb worked really hard on his training. He's gentle, but he's no pony."

"Do you ride him?" Polly asked, eyes wide. Tabasco appeared to be twice the size of Archie.

Another laugh. "Not if I can help it. I have Rowdy. He's enough horse for me. He's a quarter horse. We keep him at the stables because they sometimes use him for lessons."

Tabasco snorted, throwing back his head. Ben led him into the nearby corral and closed the gate behind him. Tabasco cantered off, stopping every so often to paw the snow.

"Hey, Em, why don't you put Sunny out too. When Mom gets back, I'll take care of the stalls while you guys play."

After she put Sunny into the corral, Emma turned to Jasper. "Hey, Jaspie, wanta go inside and play? Ben's got lots of trucks and fire engines!" Jasper nodded, and off they ran toward the house.

Kevin turned to Ben. "Think we should wait till Maggie gets back?"

"No way. I say get while the getting's good. I'm pretty good with chaos, and we can always turn on a cartoon in an emergency. As you can see, Emma's taken charge, so I predict we'll barely know he's here. She's a great babysitter."

"Thanks, man. Think I should go in and say goodbye?"

"I'd recommend no, let happy kids play, but I'm gonna bet Maggie would say you should. What do you think, Poll?"

"I'm with Maggie," she said.

They headed in, and Kevin knelt beside Jasper, who was pulling trucks and other vehicles out of a huge toy bin in the playroom. "Hey, buddy, I'm going to do some shopping, and I'll be back soon. Okay?" Oblivious, the toddler continued diving into the toy bin.

"There's your answer," Ben said, "and if I'm not mistaken, I just heard Maggie drive in, so we're covered. Good luck!"

"Thanks, I owe you man," Kevin said as they headed for the front door.

"No problem."

They met Maggie on the porch. "Morning!" she said, smiling.

"Thanks for doing this," Kevin said. "Jasper's in heaven."

"We love it. With our crazy schedules, the kids don't get to have friends over very often. They were so excited when we told them last night. Good luck with the shopping. I'm sure you've got a long list."

"Yes, and thanks for all your suggestions," Polly said.

"You know one place I forgot to mention and you really should go there first, is Lulu's. It's a terrific consignment store. Has all sizes, but she specializes in kids' clothes. Like Lang's business, most of Lulu's sales are online since this tiny town doesn't generate enough sales, but she lets the locals roam free in the warehouse. Tell her we sent you. Lulu takes riding lessons from me, and she's madly in love with my husband and most of the other cowboys in the Valley."

"I know that place. It's near Valley Hardware and the Feed and Grain, right?" Polly said.

"That's the one. I'm pretty sure she's open Saturdays. Have fun!"

CHAPTER 44

"Alone at last," he said, smiling over at her as they hopped into the truck. "God, I've missed you."

"Me too," she said, reaching over to squeeze his hand.

"Geez, Polly, am I insane? I'm crazy about Jasper, and I sure as hell couldn't leave him in Florida, but what do I know about kids?"

"You'll learn."

"Well, it better be quick."

She smiled, patting his hand. "You're gonna do great."

"I'd settle for adequate at this point."

"Kevin, that's still fatigue talking. This been really sudden for you, for Jasper, for us. Most people prepare and plan for this kind of life change."

"Thanks for saying 'us,'" he said, shaking his head. "Listen to me. I sound like a spoiled brat."

She laughed. "You're entitled, but only for a limited time."

"Truth is, I was beginning to plan for a very different kind of life change." He looked over at her, his intention unmistakable. "I'm sorry about us."

"We'll have lots of time for *us* once you get Jasper settled in. And remember, you're not doing this alone. You've got lots of help."

They spent the next few hours in a variety of shops, ending up at the town market. As they shopped, each one found ways to brush up against each other, sexual tension building with each touch, the closeness electrifying.

As they headed into the market, Maggie called and asked if they could give Jasper lunch. With the gift of extra time, Kevin and Polly picked up sandwiches at the café and headed to his house to unpack and organize. Polly assured him he could keep the crib for a few more weeks. She also suggested that he get a youth bed with bolsters as Jasper. Since the nearest furniture store was in Tucson, Kevin resolved to either make that trip the next week or order the bed, mattress, and bedding online.

Lulu's had proven to be a treasure trove. They picked up lots of great clothes as well as a brand-new down jacket in Jasper's size with the tags still on. En route to the children's section, Polly had spied many clothing possibilities for herself and resolved to drag Lynn over to look around soon.

They got everything into the house in two loads. When Kevin closed the door behind the last load, he dropped everything, relieved Polly of her bags and swept her into his arms.

"God, I've been waiting a lifetime to do this. Thank you, Maggie and Ben Morgan!"

His lips captured hers, and his hands were everywhere. Her tongue teased his as she hungrily returned the kiss, sighing deeply as she gave herself to him. Outerwear was shed, then sweaters, jeans, and the rest. As they reached the bedroom door, he lifted her gently, carrying her to the bed, laying her in the spot he and his son had vacated only hours earlier.

"Should we do this in sight of the crib?" he asked. His tongue traced a line to her breasts. He sucked and teased each nipple to hardness. In answer, Polly arched her body to meet his. Her passion skyrocketed as his erect cock pressed against her belly. "Oh, Kevin, please, I need you inside me now!"

"Which part of me, baby?" he asked as he moved down to part her legs and slide fingers then tongue into her warm, wet depths. In no time, he had her writhing to an explosive orgasm. He raised his head, pleased to spy her almost beatific expression. "Think you can take any more?"

In answer, Polly began stroking his cock in ways she knew he loved. With the other hand, she wagged a finger at him. "My body needs *this* inside of me, *now*, unless you'd rather my mouth take over?"

Kevin smiled, shaking his head in wonder. "Where the hell did you come from, and what have you done with my demure Polly Granger?"

With one smooth motion, he reared back and took her, gently at first, then harder and more insistent. Polly returned his thrusts with her own, and they moved as one, Kevin holding back as long as he could until they reached blinding mutual climaxes, delirious in their yearning for one another.

As they lay entwined and peaceful, still joined, he whispered, "I love you so much, baby. How the hell are we gonna do this when the crib's five feet away?"

Polly smiled, kissing him sweetly. "For this, we'll find a way. I promise. I did see several bedrooms upstairs."

CHAPTER 45

Sunday dawned gray and overcast. "Not a great day for an outdoor picnic," Polly said as she hopped into the truck. A short time later, Kevin parked near the new bunkhouses.

"Whaddya think? We have lots of open space in the mess hall. It's not yet furnished, but we do have heat."

Polly nodded. "Fine with me. What a lot of progress you've made."

"Thanks for coming out here with us," he said. "I've gotta check on a few things, then we can eat, okay?"

Polly carried the picnic basket, and he held Jasper, who refused to walk. The toddler had been in a mood since waking and had not seemed at all pleased to see Polly. When they stepped into the dining hall, Kevin went to set him down. "You stay here with Polly for a few minutes. Okay, buddy?"

"No!" Jasper screamed, clinging to his jacket collar.

"Hey? What going on? I'll be back in five minutes."

"Let's explore, sweetie," Polly said, holding out her hand.

"No. I want Daddy!"

Kevin shrugged. "He's wants Daddy. Wanta come along?"

Polly studied the child's face. "Why don't you guys go on your own? I'll get everything set up here."

"You sure?"

"Of course. It'll give me a chance to look around."

"Okay. Be back in a few," he said, carrying Jasper out the door.

Polly spread a heavy quilt and several blankets on the floor, then set the basket to the side of it and pulled out sandwiches, drinks, and napkins. She had made chicken salad for Kevin and herself, and a peanut butter and jelly for Jasper, no crusts, white bread, as his aunt had specified. She set small jugs of lemonade and iced tea out with cups and a thermos of ice. Satisfied that all was ready, she strolled the length of the building, peeking into the living quarters, which were spacious and attractive.

Each worker's unit included an open living room with a small kitchenette—refrigerator, microwave, two-burner stove, and cabinet space. A small bedroom and bath were in the rear. Walls were wood-paneled and the floors wide pine boards. In the front of each unit, large windows with attractive sage-green blinds looked out on acres of green fields and the training loops to the east. The bedroom windows faced the mountains in the distance. As she peeked into a small but well- appointed bathroom, she heard the door open.

"Hey, Polly. We're back!"

"Down here!" she called, hurrying to join them. Kevin was helping Jasper with his jacket when she entered the mess hall. "I was snooping."

"Whaddya think?"

"Nicest bunkhouses I've ever seen."

He laughed. "Got a lot of experience with bunkhouses, do you?"

"No, but the units seem really nice."

"Spark and Ben don't do anything halfway."

"That's for sure."

"Sam Morgan and Harley designed them and everything else out here. They're pretty standard-issue bunkhouses, but they didn't cut corners. Authorized us to use top-grade materials."

As they talked, Jasper ran up and down in the empty space. Finally, Kevin called, "Hey buddy, want some lunch? Look what Polly made us!"

The child continued running from one end of the hall to the other.

"Come on, Jasper!" Kevin called. No response. "What do you think? Should we let him run?"

Polly smiled. "If he was at school, we'd get his attention, but you're his dad, and you're the one who needs to establish the rules."

"Come on, I'm begging for advice here," he said, fingers caressing her hand.

"He's having a really good time. Why not give him a few more minutes, then try calling him again?"

"Good plan," he said, taking the sandwich she offered and pouring them both a cup of iced tea. "Delicious, thanks," he added after taking a bite.

Polly gave him one of her soft smiles, the ones that he considered his alone. "You're welcome. He really is adorable, your Jasper."

Kevin grinned, turning to watch the toddler hit the far wall with his outstretched hands. "Yeah, he's pretty cute. Lot of energy."

They sat enjoying their lunch, chatting and watching Jasper until he seemed to be slowing down. As they talked, one or the other of them found a way to make physical contact, a touch of hands, arms, legs. At one point, Polly leaned over for a napkin, and her breasts grazed his outstretched arm. "You're doing that on purpose, aren't you?" he said.

"No," she whispered. "It's just that I feel cold without your touch. My body craves you. It's a physical thing." When he looked over, she was grinning mischievously.

"Physical thing, my eye. Well, I've got a physical thing goin' on under this napkin, so you better watch out, or I'll have to lock Jasper in the closet and make love to you, Polly Granger."

She blushed, moving back to the edge of the blanket. "This is wicked. You'd better call your baby over. He looks like he's getting tired."

"Hey, buddy, come have something to eat," Kevin called.

Jasper ran over and flopped down next to his father.

Polly handed him a sandwich on a small paper plate and a sippy cup of water. He took a long drink, then kicked the plate over. "Yucky."

"Aunt Ivy said you like peanut butter and jelly."

Jasper scowled. "I like Auntie's."

Polly gave Kevin a look and mouthed, *Don't push it* over the child's head, but he ignored her. "This is the same bread, same peanut butter and same jelly as Auntie uses."

"Yucky."

"Jasper, Polly made this specially for you. Now have a bite."

"Yucky, yucky, yucky!"

Kevin's face reddened, and he took a deep breath. "Jasper, say you're sorry, right now."

"Yucky, yucky, yucky! I want to go home."

"We'll go soon, buddy, but I'm sure you're hungry. Just have a little."

"I want Auntie! I want Mommy!"

Polly knelt, beginning to gather their things. "You know what? I think someone's hungry *and* tired."

"I want Mommy! I want Mommy!" he screamed, in full tantrum now. As he kicked out, plates, cups, and food scattered everywhere.

Polly grabbed blankets, quilt, and basket as Kevin attempted to calm Jasper, who flailed arms and legs all the way to the truck. The toddler screamed for his mother and aunt as Kevin wrestled him into his car seat. Once he was strapped in, Kevin smoothed his damp brow and wiped his cheeks. "Okay, buddy, let's go home."

Jasper cried for the five minutes it took to reach the main road, then there was silence. When Kevin looked back, he found Jasper asleep. "Geez, Louise," he said, gazing over at Polly. "What the hell was that?"

Polly smiled. "Welcome to the terrible twos."

"But he's almost three! He'll be stopping this behavior soon, right?"

She smiled at him. "Developmental stages are not hard and fast."

"That's the first time he's mentioned his mom. It's usually Ivy he cries for."

"He's knows about Judith's death, doesn't he?"

"Ivy told him, but I'm not sure it sank in."

"Death is difficult for little ones to comprehend. When toddlers get worked up like that—"

"Tantrum, you mean."

"Whatever… When they're upset, they often say and do things that don't make sense. Poor little thing… So much he doesn't understand and such a major transition for him."

"Thanks for being here," he said, reaching over to squeeze her hand.

"Of course," she said, returning the squeeze.

CHAPTER 46

Kevin drove her home. As she got out of the truck, she said, "Want to come in? Lynn's gone for the day, and Jasper can nap in my bedroom."

"I thought you'd never ask," he said. He stepped out and gently unstrapped his son, who slept soundly on the way inside. Polly covered him with a blanket, and they left the bedroom door ajar before they stepped into the living room.

They sat side by side on the sofa, his arm draped over her shoulders as Polly nestled close beside him. "You know there's nothing I'd rather do than make love to you, don't you?" he asked.

"Mmm," she said, "but maybe not the best timing."

"You're probably right. That's all the little guy needs to see. Though God knows what kind of shit he was exposed to around Judith and her lowlife friends."

Polly looked up and kissed him. A chaste, brief kiss. "He's safe now, with a loving, stable dad. That's what's important."

He kissed the tip of her nose. "You're amazing, you know that, right? Don't you have things you'd rather be doing this afternoon? I mean, you spend all week with kids."

"There's nowhere else I'd rather be and no two people I'd rather be with."

"You know, I could use a nap," he said, drawing her closer.

"Me too," she said, pulling a throw blanket over them. "Maybe a cat nap?"

*****

Kevin felt a tugging on his shirt and woke to find Polly still snuggled against him and Jasper with a pout on his face.

"Hey, buddy."

He gently moved Polly's arm from his chest, and she woke. "Hi, sweetie," she said. "You hungry?"

Kevin stood up, ruffling Jasper's curls. "He's soaking wet. Let me get a change of clothes from the truck.

"No!" Jasper cried, clinging to his leg.

"I'll go," she said. "Is it open?"

He nodded. "Thanks. Come on, buddy, let's get those wet things off." Once Jasper was changed and dressed in dry clothes, Kevin set him down and went to check Polly's bed. "Geez, sweetie, I'm sorry. Your bed's pretty wet. My fault. I forgot to remind him about the potty all morning"

"No worries," she said, one eye on Jasper as she peered into the bedroom. "I'll change it later." She turned back to the living room just in time to see the toddler pick up a crystal vase filled with fresh flowers. "Watch out, sweetie, that's breakable," she said, but he ignored her and hurled the vase and flowers across the tile floor.

The vase shattered, spraying shards of glass everywhere. Water and broken flowers littered the rug and floor. "Jasper, Jesus!" Kevin rushed over to grab him. "Polly, I'm so sorry."

"It's okay," she said, saying a silent goodbye to one of the few things she had from her beloved grandmother. The cut-crystal vase had been in their family since her grandparents' wedding. "Just be careful. There's glass everywhere."

Kevin took Jasper into the kitchen and sat him on a stool. "How can I help?"

"Just keep him in there, and I'll take care of it. Maybe he'll want part of a sandwich now?"

Kevin held Jasper on his stool as Polly cleaned up. He noticed she had gathered the larger pieces of the vase in her dustpan but didn't throw them in the trash as she had with the rest.

By the time Polly put the vacuum and cleaning supplies away, Jasper had eaten both halves of his sandwich and two bananas. Kevin watched her set down the dustpan, her expression sad. "That was something special, wasn't it?"

"It's okay. I'll find a way to save it."

"Geez, Polly, I'm so sorry."

She forced a smile. "It's fine. No worries."

"No, it's not fine. Jasper, say you're sorry to Polly."

The child's lips thrust out in a defiant pout. "No!"

"Jasper...."

"Please, Kevin, don't force it."

"I'll replace it."

"That's okay. It's not the vase, it's the memories."

"Of?"

"I'll tell you later. Let's change the subject, okay?" She turned to the child. "Jasper, great job with your sandwich. Want something else to eat?"

Jasper made a grunting humph sound and cowered against his father.

Kevin stood. "Okay, that's our cue." He wiped Jasper's face with a wet towel. "Thanks for the picnic, Polly. I'm gonna take this guy home and let you have some peace."

"Okay," she said, surprised at his abruptness but also at her own reluctance to encourage them to stay.

"I'll call you tonight," he said, leaning forward to kiss her goodbye as Jasper wriggled and scowled.

When she closed the door behind them, Polly burst into tears. Gazing over at the dustpan, she thought of Granny Jean and Gramps, long gone now. Their wedding photo sat on the bookshelf behind where the vase had stood. Every week of her life, no matter what the season, she had filled it with fresh flowers. It was only a vase, and her memories were as intact and vivid as ever, but still she cried. Sensing that she was in the midst of a sea change, she almost felt seasick.

After a good long cry, she rooted around the kitchen cupboard and found a Mason jar. Gingerly, she dried each broken piece of glass and placed them into the jar. She screwed the lid on tight and set it on the shelf beside her grandparents' wedding photo. "Love you, Granny and Gramps, always," she said aloud, then headed for the bedroom to change her sheets.

By the time Lynn got home, she was feeling better and suggested a walk to Gracie's for dinner. "Fortunately, it's only a block," her friend said as they headed out. "That hike today about killed me."

Polly linked arms with her. "Lean on me if you want, and I'll tell you about my day."

CHAPTER 47

Polly's cell rang shortly after they returned from Gracie's.

"Hey," Kevin said, his voice just above a whisper.

"Hi. How's it going over there?"

"Asleep at last. Polly, I am so sorry. I could see how much that vase meant to you. I promise I will try to make it up to you somehow."

"It's okay, really," she said, and it was, even though she couldn't muster much enthusiasm in her reply. "He's little. That's what kids do."

"Not mine, and he will apologize properly."

"Don't force it, Kevin. Please"

"How are you otherwise?"

"Stuffed. Lynn and I ate at Gracie's. Her pot pies are to die for."

"One of my favorites. Believe it or not, I'm actually partial to the vegetable one."

"Me too."

"Polly, I'm so sorry this has all crashed down on us."

"You need to stop apologizing, Kevin. What's been happening is called life."

"You know I'm crazy about you."

"The feeling's mutual." Her voice sounded weary and sad. Polly loved him desperately, but despite the "life comment," a part of her wondered if they would survive this sea change. "I'm sorry if I sound half-asleep, but I am. I have early duty tomorrow, so I'd better get to bed."

"Of course, sorry. I won't keep you. We'll be there bright and early tomorrow. Are you sure you can handle Hurricane Jasper?"

"We'll be fine. Night."

Kevin said good night and clicked off. *Maybe they can handle him, but what about me?*

*****

When Kevin and Jasper arrived at the Cottage, they found Polly playing with Toby, Christy, and Fara Perez.

"Morning!" he called as Willow followed them in.

"Morning," Polly said. "Hi, Jasper. We're just getting out some toys. Wanta help us?"

Jasper buried his face in Kevin's jacket and clung to him. "Hey, buddy, look. They've got race cars and fire engines."

"And dinosaurs!" Fara said, holding up a Tyrannosaurus rex as her two-year-old sister toddled over with a yellow bulldozer.

Willow hung up her coat, changed out of her boots, came over to the group, and held out her arms. "Hey, Jasper, wanta play with me and Christy?"

Without hesitation, he slid down and took Willow's hand, frowning at Polly as he passed by.

Kevin came and knelt beside her.

"Good night's sleep?" she asked.

"Not particularly. Someone's a bit of a bed hog. I've stowed his extra clothes in his cubby. Where do you want his lunch?"

She pointed to the kitchen. "In the fridge."

When he returned, Jasper was playing on the floor with Willow and Christy. "I'll just say goodbye and take off then, okay?"

She nodded.

"I'd like him to apologize, but I don't want to create a scene on his first day."

"Wise choice," she said, setting puzzles on the table.

"I'm sorry he wasn't friendlier," he said, his hand grazing hers.

"Some people aren't morning people. And what did I say? No more apologizing."

"Sorr… Oops, force of habit." Since he couldn't kiss her goodbye, Kevin squeezed her hand. "Have a great day."

Her fingers caressed his palm for a split second. Polly loved the feel of his rough, calloused hands. "You too."

"Call me if you have any trouble."

"Will do."

*****

And, there wasn't any trouble if she stayed at least ten feet away from Jasper. The minute she got closer or spoke to him, he'd latch on to the nearest adult and hide his face. Lynn noticed the behavior midway through the morning and patted her shoulder.

"Don't take it personally."

Polly gave her a wan smile. "I'm trying."

When Kevin came for pickup shortly before five, Lynn and Willow were with the three remaining children—Christy, Fara, and Jasper. His face registered disappointment when he looked around and didn't see Polly.

"She took the early shift," Lynn said as they watched Willow read to the children. "So that means she gets to head off at three."

"How'd the day go?"

"Great. He took a good nap, played really well with the kids, and ate most of his lunch."

"No tantrums?"

"Not a one, except…" She gave him a look. "Nope, no tantrums."

"What are you not telling me?"

Lynn hesitated, but then said, "He's been a bit standoffish to my co-teacher."

"I was afraid of that."

"He'll come around."

"I hope so. Was Polly upset?"

"Polly's a trouper as well as a wise, kind professional."

"That's not what I asked you."

"It was a hectic day," Lynn said. "We didn't get a chance to talk. Honest."

Kevin felt sure there was more than what Lynn was saying but decided not to press. He collected Jasper's things and then called to him. The child ignored him and continued to play with Willow and the girls. "Come on, buddy. Time to go," he said again. No response.

Lynn strolled over and knelt beside the group. "Hey, Jasper, time to go home." When she received no response, she gently but firmly took one hand, then the other. "Come on, Daddy's waiting, and we're all heading home soon."

For a second, Jasper looked as if he might protest, but then allowed himself to be led forward and helped into his jacket and hat. Lynn winked at Kevin over the child's head. "Have a great night, guys, and I'll see you in the morning."

CHAPTER 48

Jasper loved day care but remained cool and standoffish to Polly. When they arrived each morning, he happily ran to Lynn or Willow but would have nothing to do with their colleague. Polly told herself that things would improve, but as days went by, she wasn't so sure. If she approached him, he screamed. If she spoke to him, he ignored her. If she touched any of his food while serving lunch, he threw a tantrum and refused to eat it. When Lynn tried to talk with him about his behavior, he would curl up in a ball or run to Willow. Finally, they gave up and decided not to push the issue.

Kevin and Polly spoke briefly at dropoff and pickup, but they agreed it was probably best not to get together until he was more settled. Their evening phone conversations were strained and short, neither knowing quite what to say. Polly missed him terribly. As days went by, she grew despondent.

A weekend without him was torture, especially when she heard how much fun he and Jasper had had at Maggie and Ben's. While she was happy for them, she also felt left out. When she wasn't off hiking, Lynn dragged her out to Christmas shopping, and most mornings, she walked Archie. Three days before Christmas, Polly made a decision. As she and Lynn ate dinner, her roommate chattering about the upcoming parties at the Morgans' and Fosters', Polly said, "Would it be too much if I left for five days?"

Lynn stared at her as if she had grown three heads. "When?"

"I checked, and I can get the red-eye tomorrow night. Lang and Beth have taken Lily out for the week starting tomorrow, and Maggie told me that she'd probably keep her two home most of next week since all his siblings will be around. They might even go away after Christmas for a few days."

"You can't run away from this, you know."

"I'm not running away. I just need to go home. Be with my family and have some space for a few days. If you think it's too much for you, I—"

"Stop right there, partner. Of course, we can manage. If this is what you want, go! Phyllis will be over the moon."

Polly smiled. "Are you sure?"

"Absolutely, go pack! How are you getting to the airport?"

"I'll leave my car."

"Not Kevin?"

Polly shook her head.

*****

The next morning when Maggie brought the kids in, Ben the third practically jumped out of her arms to greet his friend. Polly was setting toys out, and she passed Jasper playing on the floor, his back to the door. "Look, Jasper," she said, touching his shoulder. He stiffened and let out a squawk before turning and spying Ben running toward him. Instantly, he brightened and jumped up to hug his buddy.

Maggie smiled at her. "No change in the Mexican standoff?"

"'Fraid not."

"He'll come around," she said, taking Ben's lunchbox to the kitchen. "Leonora's coming for Emma. Should be here in fifteen."

Polly hugged Emma. "We love having our helper."

"I think Ben's picking the kids up this afternoon because my in-laws will be on an airport run. If something changes, one of us will call."

"Busy day?"

"You could say that. We got four new mustangs yesterday. Three more than we expected, but we couldn't say no. Nick and Jeb are out straight, so I'm gonna stay late and help. Tomorrow, I'll corral all my brothers-in-law and maybe my dad to help out. Right before Christmas too. Yikes! Fortunately, we shopped and decorated early."

"How are they, the new horses?"

"Beautiful and very skittish. Come see them. Sorry, I've gotta scoot." Maggie stooped to kiss Emma. "Bye, precious. Tell your brother goodbye, will you?" She turned to Polly. "And I'll see you guys tomorrow or Christmas Eve for sure."

"Lynn yes, me no," Polly said. "I'm flying back east for five days tonight. I cleared it with Ben, Leonora, and Spark."

"I didn't know you were doing that. Your mom'll be so pleased."

"Spur-of-the-moment decision," she said, giving her a sheepish smile.

Maggie opened her arms and hugged her. "It's going to get better. You have a wonderful Christmas. We'll *all* miss you, especially someone I know. Maybe this is just what's needed. Sometimes need a wake-up call, you know? When you get back, if you need someone to talk to, I'm here and so is my wonderful therapist, Haley Alvarez. She literally saved my life."

As Maggie buttoned her jacket, Polly said, "Thanks, Maggie. Merry Christmas to you and your entire family."

CHAPTER 49

As she buckled her seat belt and listened to the pilot's announcements, Polly realized that in the rush of packing, she had forgotten to call Kevin. Remembering Maggie's words, she leaned back and closed her eyes. *Maybe a break will do us both good.*

Her brother Bob picked her up at the airport with her niece and nephew in the backseat. A chorus of "Hi, Aunt Polly!" greeted her as she slipped into the SUV beside her brother.

"Hi, guys," she said as she leaned over and kissed Bob. "Good to see you all!"

Bob's blue eyes studied her. "Mom's beside herself at this sudden and completely unexpected event. You okay?"

"Yes, just needed to get out of Dodge for a few days. Plus, I wanted to see all my awesome, amazing nieces and nephews!" She winked at Cara, nine, and Stu, eight.

"Well, get ready for the third degree. Mom's convinced there's been a major crisis and you're moving back for good."

"Oh Lord," Polly said. "And I have to face her with only an hour's sleep?"

*****

"What do you mean she's gone?" Kevin said as Jasper ran off to join the other children. He was staring at Lynn as if she'd sprouted horns.

Lynn looked away and bent down to help Fara reach a bin of dolls. "Spur-of-the-moment decision."

Kevin scratched his head. "I guess. What about Christmas?"

"She was missing her family, particularly her siblings and their kids. I think she wanted to spend the holiday with them. "

"When's she coming back?"

"Couple of days after Christmas. Didn't she tell you?"

He shook his head. "It's been a tough week."

"For her too. Now that Jasper's settled in, it's probably time to address his behavior toward her. We haven't pushed it 'cause she insisted we not, but it's gone on long enough. He can't keep doin' what he's doin' and come here. It's not fair to her, the other kids, or the rest of us."

"I know. I'm gonna talk to him."

Lynn stared at the handsome contractor. Kevin looked as if he might burst into tears. She patted his shoulder. "It's gonna work out. You'll see."

"She didn't mention a thing about going east."

"It's been a really hectic week. I'm sure she'll call when she's settled in."

"Hope so. Well, have a good day."

"You too," Lynn said, waving as he closed the door. She wondered if she should shoot Polly a quick text to suggest that she call and put Romeo out of his misery, but then decided that a little time and distance might spur *him* into action.

*****

When Kevin drove up beside the new stables, Harley was talking to several of the farm's newest employees, two wranglers who had moved to the Valley from New Mexico. "Hey, buddy, morning!" Harley called. "You've met Greg and Whip, right?"

Kevin nodded. "Hey, guys, mornin'. The bunkhouses should be up and running by the new year."

"No prob, man," Whip said, grinning. "We're pretty comfortable over at the ranch." The two men were sharing one of the Morgan's Run cabins and receiving regular meals from the Big House.

Kevin laughed. "I bet you are. Those Morgans are some hosts. "With his long blond hair and beard, Whip reminded Kevin of Wild Bill Hickok.

"Foster's not too shabby either," his short, wiry partner said, shoving his well-worn Stetson up to reveal a line of dirt across his brow.

Kevin wondered what the two wranglers had been doing this early in the morning to get so dirty. He turned to Harley. "How's it lookin'?"

"Great. Got a minute to walk through the barn with me?" Calling the state-of-the-art stables a barn was like calling the Grand Canyon a hole in the ground.

"Sure," Kevin said, following him inside as Greg and Whip headed for the corrals.

They strolled slowly, Harley pointing to several items that needed attention. Halfway along, he stopped. "You okay, man? You seem a tad distracted."

Kevin looked over to find Harley's eyebrow raised. What the hell, he decided, and proceeded to relate the events of the past week. When he finished, he said, "So that's my pathetic life at the moment."

"I hear you. It's a jolt to the system to find out you have a kid you never knew existed, especially a little guy who doesn't sleep. If it makes you feel any better, there's not much sleep goin' on at my house right now either."

"Sleeplessness I can handle. It's this shit with him and Polly that's rough. I mean, I'm crazy about Jasper, don't get me wrong."

"And you're crazy about her too, if I'm not mistaken?"

Kevin nodded. "Completely gaga. I'm going nuts. I've barely seen her this past week, and now she's flown the coop back to Rhode Island for Christmas."

"Want my advice?"

"Anything, please. I'm drowning here."

"There's a great therapist in town, Haley Alvarez. She's helped a bunch of us get our heads back on straight. If she can help a clueless cowboy like me, she might have some ideas to get the little guy to warm up to Polly, or at least be civil."

"Not sure a three-year-old knows the meaning of civil, but I'll try anything. Don't 'spose you've got her number?"

Harley pulled out his phone. "Got her on speed dial."

Kevin noted the number. "Thanks, man."

"Call her."

"I will. And Harley?"

"Yup?"

"I was listening. I'll get the guys over to knock out some of this today and the rest tomorrow."

The minute he slid into the truck, Kevin dialed Haley's number. It went straight to voice mail, and he left a message.

CHAPTER 50

Kevin and Jasper pulled into Harley and Ruthie's at nine in the morning. His appointment with Haley Alverez was at ten, but he wanted to be early so Jasper could settle in. He had hired Willow to accompany them because Haley had suggested it might be useful for her to meet Jasper. He was debating whether to leave Jasper in his car seat while he got Willow, but Harley opened the door and waved. "Got time for coffee?"

He carried Jasper in and set him down in the beautiful quarry-tiled entry. The house truly was a work of art, a comfortable, homey work of art. He gazed through to the open living area, where Ruthie sat nursing Charlotte. "Come in, come in," she called. "Willow'll be right down."

"Coffee, buddy?" Harley said again. "And what would this big guy like?"

"We're good, thanks," Kevin said. "If I have any more coffee this morning, I won't be able to utter a coherent word to Ms. Alverez."

Harley grinned. "First time seeing a shrink?"

"She's not a shrink!" his wife said. "Don't listen to him, Kev. Haley's terrific, and she won't care two hoots if you're high on caffeine. Hey, Jasper, come meet Charlotte."

Kevin and Harley watched Jasper approach the infant, who had now detached from the breast and lay calm, sated, and peaceful in her arms, milk dribbling from her cherubic mouth.

"She's a beauty," Kevin said.

"Like her mom," Harley said, sliding in beside mother and child, kissing his wife's cheek. It was a rare side of the taciturn, self-contained wrangler that people seldom saw, but when he was around Ruthie, and now Charlotte, Harley Langdon turned to mush.

"She's grown so much," Kevin said as Jasper reached out and patted the baby's head. "Careful, buddy!"

"All good, man. Charlotte has a hard head like her mom." This statement got Harley a poke in the ribs. "Here's my other girl," he said as Willow came down the stairs.

Her pale eyes lit up. "Good morning! Hi, Jaspie!"

Harley's older daughter was tall and slender, her flaxen hair tied back in a long braid. She wore jeans, a pale green fleece, and Uggs. Kevin had never seen her mother, but he certainly saw traces of her dad in the lovely seventeen-year-old.

Jasper ran to her, and Willow picked him up and twirled. *Wish that was the greeting he'd give Polly,* Kevin thought, watching the two. As if reading his mind, Harley said, "Haley'll have some ideas for you."

While Willow and Jasper played hide-and-seek, they talked about the house and how much they were enjoying it. "I begged Mom to have Christmas Eve here so everyone could see it, but you know Leonora. Maybe New Year's Day," Ruthie said. "I mean, I'm fine now, for goodness' sake. Going back to work in a few weeks, I hope."

Harley made a face but wisely remained silent. As Jasper ran through the room, Kevin said, "Come on, buddy, we've gotta go."

"No!" the toddler said, ignoring him as he looked for a hiding place.

"Willow's comin' with us," he said, grabbing Jasper and putting on his coat. "See? She's getting her jacket too." This announcement seemed to placate him. Jacket on, he hurried to Willow's side, and she took his hand.

"Good luck, man," Harley said as he walked him to the door.

Kevin watched Willow lead Jasper down the front walk. "Thanks, I'll need it. Your daughter's amazing, isn't she?"

"All her mother's doing. Talia was an extraordinary person."

"How's Willow doin' with that?"

"She has her moments, but being here helps, and she's crazy about her baby sister. Loves working with Polly and Lynn."

"Well, see you tonight, I guess."

Harley grinned. "Yup, hold on to your hat. There's nothing quite like a Morgan Christmas Eve."

"You're right about that," Kevin said, having experienced his first the previous year.

CHAPTER 51

When they stepped into Haley Alverez's plant-filled waiting room furnished in muted greens and blues, Kevin shook his head, wondering what this peaceful space would look like when Jasper got through with it. He turned to Willow, who was holding Jasper's hand. "Did you bring your cell?"

She nodded.

"Why don't you guys go over to the park? I'll text if and when she might like to meet Jasper."

As the door closed behind them, the inner door opened, and a short, plump woman in jeans and a flowing top in swirling shades of purple appeared. She wore wool socks in the same marled grays as the curly hair falling over her shoulders to her waist. She was shoeless, a warm smile on her face. "You must be Kevin?"

"Yes, hello," he said, crossing the room to shake her outstretched hand. "Shall I take off my boots?"

"Thanks for asking, but there's no need unless that would make you feel more comfortable. I'm Haley. Welcome." She gave him a firm handshake, then stepped aside. "Come in."

They each took one of the deep upholstered chairs positioned opposite one another. "Can I get you something? Tea? Water?"

"Thanks, I'm good. And, thanks for seeing me on such short notice."

"My pleasure. I was going to take the day off to shop, but this is much better. How can I help?"

It was on the tip of his tongue to apologize for taking her away from her shopping and interrupting her day off, but, encouraged by her warm, genuine smile, he launched into a recitation of the events of the past few weeks. She listened without comment until finally he said, "So, that's where we are. I'm crazy about Polly and want her in my life, but my son won't go near her."

"Why do *you* think that is?"

"Jealousy, maybe?"

"Sounds like Jasper's been through a lot. Does Polly look like anyone from Florida, do you think? Remind him of a traumatic situation or person perhaps?"

"Not that I know of. As I said, his mother was an alcoholic and a drug user, so who knows the kinds of people he was exposed to. Judith claims she stayed clean when she was pregnant, but her sister said she pretty much fell apart after Jasper's birth."

"And they were living with the sister?"

"Ivy, yes, most of the time. Although my former in-laws cared for him a fair amount, I think. They are and always have been major train wrecks."

"Must have been very traumatic when they abducted him."

"Yes."

"All these experiences make their mark. There may well be some work a child therapist could do with him down the road. For now you, Jasper and Polly must attend to the present. His behavior toward Polly, your dear friend and his caregiver, is neither appropriate or acceptable."

"I agree."

"So, it is up to *you* to communicate that to Jasper. Shall we give it a try here first?"

Kevin nodded, then pulled out his cell phone and texted Willow.

*****

Kevin held Jasper on his lap. Haley had said, "Hello," then waited quietly for them to get settled. Finally, she said, "So, Jasper, you had a long plane ride, didn't you?"

The child nodded, then put his thumb in his mouth.

"And you're living with your dad now."

Another nod.

"Do you know what happened to your Mommy?"

"She's in heaven."

The conversation continued with Haley gently probing his past, leading up to meeting his dad and moving to the Valley. They had already been there for well over an hour, but Haley assured them she had plenty of time. They were talking about his friends at the Cottage, especially Ben the third, when Haley said, "What about the grown-ups at the Cottage? Who takes care of you?"

"Willow and Lynn, and Ether."

"He means Heather," Kevin said softly.

"What about Polly? Doesn't Polly take care of you?"

He nodded.

"Remember when you said Ben was your friend?"

Another nod. He was now hiding under Kevin's arm.

"Polly's Daddy's friend. Do you know that?"

Jasper shook his head.

"Grown-ups have friends too. Daddy has something to tell you about Polly."

Kevin swallowed hard, then said the words he had rehearsed with Haley. "I love you, Jasper. You know that, don't you, buddy?"

No response.

"I love Polly too."

Jasper grunted, slipping out of his lap and onto the floor.

"You and I are a family, and I'm hoping Polly will be part of our family too someday."

"No!" Jasper began kicking his feet and flailing his arms.

"Jasper, that's enough," he said quietly.

Wailing now, the toddler inched across the floor.

Haley looked at Kevin, then the child. "Let's let Jasper have a few minutes to himself, and you and I can talk, okay?"

They turned away and continued to chat, as they'd planned, paying no attention to Jasper. The child kept coming to his father's feet, continuing to kick and cry. Kevin would pick him up and carry him to the opposite end of the room. "You stay here, buddy. When you stop crying and kicking, you can come back."

Occasionally, Haley would say, "Jasper, are you ready to come back with Daddy and me?" but the wailing continued. Thirty minutes later, the crying had turned into a whimper, and Jasper was curled up near the radiator. Haley nodded to Kevin, and he rose and brought his son back to sit on his lap.

"I'm so glad you're back," Haley said. "It was so good to meet you. Maybe I'll see you again soon?"

Kevin took him out and left him with Willow, then returned to the inner office. They chatted for a few minutes then he rose to leave. "It is my suggestion that you follow this procedure when you and Polly are together with you removing him. It is also my suggestion that Polly do this at day care as best she can."

They made another appointment, and he said goodbye, feeling calmer than he had since Jasper had arrived in the Valley.

CHAPTER 52

Christmas Eve, Perris Granger watched his baby girl as Polly chatted with her siblings and played with her nieces and nephews. "Good to have her home, Mama," he said, squeezing Phyllis's shoulder as they sat side by side on the sofa.

"Sure is. Our baby's hurting."

"You think?"

"I know. Something's happened with that boyfriend of hers. I just know it. I have half a mind to call Leonora Morgan and see what she knows."

"Oh no you don't. I love you more than life itself, honey, but I forbid you to interfere."

"Then will you talk to her, please? She listens to you."

"We'll see."

As her parents talked, Polly sat with her sister Kitty. Kitty's three-year-old twin boys rolled around the floor nearby. Two years older than Polly, Kitty was seven months pregnant. Unlike their oldest sister Margot, with her auburn hair and hourglass figure, Kitty resembled Polly with her light hair and eyes. Growing up, the sisters had sometimes been mistaken for twins when they were younger. Kitty's husband, Dale, was a pediatrician.

"Whaddya want to bet Mom's chewing Dad's ear off wondering why you came home," Kitty said.

Polly smiled. "Oh yes. I'm anticipating the third degree myself."

"So…why *are* you here, sis? I mean, don't get me wrong, it's terrific having you home, but it was a bit of a shocker to all of us."

"And it's terrific to be here," Polly said. "I'm really glad I came."

Kitty gave her a look. "You haven't answered my question."

"You really want to know?"

"I really want to know," her sister said as she reached out and grabbed one of the twins before he could crash headlong into a card table covered with platters of food. "Chip, no! Where's your dad? Go find him now!" She hugged her son, and he ran off toward the kitchen. "Be lucky you're footloose and fancy-free, sister dear. Now let's hear it."

"Well, I thought the footloose-and-fancy-free part of my life might be nearing an end, which I was happy about. Then things got complicated." She gave Kitty a quick summary of events up to the present.

When Polly stopped talking, she gazed over and found her sister smiling. "It's called life, sweetie. You *finally* have one, and you're just going to have to deal."

"That's easier said than done."

"Maybe so, but it's worth it."

She nodded.

"A forty-two-year-old hunky bachelor gets a kid dumped in his lap. Wow, he must be in shock. What's he had the kid, a week or two?"

"Yes. He's in shock."

"He'll get used it. That's parenting. But that business of Jasper recoiling from you? That's bullshit. Typical toddler naughtiness. Daddy Dearest needs to put a stop to it. Pronto."

"If he can."

Suddenly distracted, Kitty looked across the room just as Dale Junior knocked over a glass of red wine. "Oh shit! Red wine on Mom's new rug. I gotta get the hellions home. Where the hell is my husband?"

As if on cue, Dale Senior appeared at the kitchen door. Kitty waved him over, extending her hand to him. "Help me up, hon. We've gotta go before the kids destroy the house."

After everyone departed with hugs and kisses and "see you in the mornings," Polly helped her parents clean up. As Phyllis knelt, trying to deal with the red wine stain on the rug, Polly and her dad washed dishes, or rather, he washed and she dried. "Anything you want to talk about, baby?" he asked, handing her a large platter.

Polly gave him a weary smile. "It's good to be home, Dad. That's what I want to talk about. I've missed you."

"Me too, you," he said.

"Mom's probably told you that I've been seeing someone?"

"A little."

Polly laughed. "Or as much as she knows. Well, it's gotten a bit complicated since the arrival of his almost-three-year-old son, Jasper, whom he didn't know existed. Jasper throws a major tantrum if I come within ten feet of him." She went on to tell her father more of the situation. Every so often, she looked over her shoulder to see if Phyllis was listening, but her mother appeared to be engrossed in her carpet cleaning.

Later, after all the dishes were put away, Polly hugged him. "Thanks for listening."

"My pleasure, baby. I'm pretty sure from what you said that things'll blow over. I'd like to meet your Mr. Larrabee."

"And you will, someday soon. It'd be great if you could come to Saguaro."

"You know me. I'm a diehard homebody."

Polly smiled. "Night, Dad. And, feel free to tell Mom whatever you want, but mostly *please* tell her not to worry."

"Tell me what, sweetie?" Phyllis said, catching them at the stairs.

Perris Granger grinned as his arm circled his wife's shoulders. "Nothing, honey. Did you get the spot out?"

She pushed him away. "Yes, I did, no thanks to you two conspirators. Now let's get up to bed, and you can tell me every detail!"

*****

Polly washed up and slipped into bed, loving the scent of her mom's freshly laundered sheets. Even in the dead of winter, Phyllis hung the sheets outside on the line to dry. Polly took a deep breath and reached for her cell phone.

Kevin answered on the first ring. "Hey."

"Hey, yourself. Happy Christmas Eve."

"Same to you. How's your family?"

"They're great. It's good to see everyone. I'm sorry to miss what would have been my first ranch Christmas. How was the Morgans' Christmas Eve? Did you guys have fun?"

"Crazy, noisy, over-the-top party. Jasper was in heaven. I spent most of the night runnin' after him, tryin' to make sure he didn't break anything."

Polly chuckled. "It was a similar scene here."

There's no scene like the Morgans' house on Christmas, he thought, but said, "So how are you?"

"Kevin, I'm so sorry I didn't call before I left."

"It's okay."

"No, it's not. I acted like a petulant child."

"I think I'm livin' with someone who fits that description."

"But he's allowed to be petulant. He *is* a child."

"Well, he's not allowed to be rude to you. I'm working on that, by the way. I saw a therapist today."

"Oh?"

"He and I both went. Willow came so some of the time I could speak with her alone. I'll tell you all about it when you get back. She was helpful."

"I'm glad. Does she have time for me?"

"I love you."

"I can feel the smile in your voice," she said. "I love you too."

"We're gonna get through this."

"That's what people keep telling me."

"When're you comin' back?"

"Tuesday. Will you be at Spark's tomorrow?"

"Oh yeah. How bout you?"

"We're all going to my oldest sister Margot's house for brunch and presents."

"Merry Christmas, my love."

Now she could hear sadness in his voice. "You, too," she said softly. "Night."

"Night."

CHAPTER 53

Polly flew back the Tuesday after Christmas. As she gazed out at the clouds below her, she realized how glad she was that she'd come home. Even if the motivation had been escapism, it had been really nice to spend time with her parents and Kitty, Margot, Bob, and their families. Talking through her situation with Kitty had been so helpful. She now had a tentative plan, at least for Jasper's behavior at day care. She was a professional educator. She knew what needed to happen. When the three of them were together? That was another story. That was personal. Her love for Kevin and her genuine caring for his son meant that her skin was thinner there.

It was twilight when the plane taxied to a stop at the small Grenville airport. Kevin had offered to have Willow babysit so he could pick her up, but Polly declined since her car was waiting in the lot. When she got home at nine thirty, she found Lynn watching a mushy, romantic movie.

Polly grinned. "Hey, is that one I haven't seen?"

Lynn rose and came to hug her. "At this point, I'm not sure if I've seen it. They all kind of blend together. Welcome home, partner. We've missed you."

"And I've missed *you*. How'd yesterday go?"

"A bit of holiday withdrawal, but we only had four—Jasper, Christy, Fara, and Toby. The rest are home, maybe for most of the week. Heather and Willow were there, but Heather's going skiing with her new boyfriend till after New Year's, so

I'm glad you're back. Our newest arrival has been testing the limits of acceptable three-year-old behavior."

"Oh dear. What now?"

"Let's just say your little Jasper is feeling his oats. Nothing we can't handle. By the way, I'll take early arrival tomorrow. You unpack and unwind. Want a glass of wine?"

Polly rarely drank in the evening, but she heard herself say, "Yes, love one," as she wheeled her suitcase into her bedroom.

*****

Movie in the background, Polly and Lynn chatted, devising a strategy for dealing with Jasper's behavior toward Polly should it arise. Finally, Polly said, "That's it for me, or I'll be useless tomorrow." She unpacked, washed up, and was just slipping into bed when her cell rang.

"Hey, sorry to call so late," Kevin said. "Just needed to hear your voice. I was actually going to satisfy myself by hearing your voice mail speaking in case you'd gone to bed."

Polly laughed. "Oh dear... I'm glad you got me."

"How was your flight?"

"Smooth. How's everything over at your house?"

"Okay if you don't count the four tantrums we had before bedtime. I'm thinking of moving my office upstairs and making the current office into his room. This sleeping in the same room isn't working out."

"Probably a good idea." Polly wanted to offer to help, but she held back.

"I can't wait to see you."

"Lynn's taking early arrival tomorrow, so I probably won't see you until pickup."

"You free for dinner any day this week?"

"Do you think that's wise?"

"Yes if we're gonna lick this. I thought we could cook for you."

"Why don't we see how tomorrow goes," she said.

"Okay…if that's what you want?"

"Now this jet-lagged person has got to get some sleep."

"Of course. See you tomorrow. Love you."

"Me too."

CHAPTER 54

By the time Polly arrived, Jasper was immersed in a block-building project with Toby and Willow. Lynn had just gotten the Perez sisters settled with some puzzles and she was prepping for the morning craft. Polly hung up her coat and came to assist her. She waved and called hello to everyone. All the children except Jasper waved and cried their hellos.

Christy ran to her. "Poll Poll!" she cried, hugging her knees.

Polly bent and picked up the toddler. "Hey, Christy. I missed you. Did you have a good Christmas?"

"Santa brought her a new baby," Fara said.

"How about you big sister?" Polly said, kneeling beside her, holding Christy in her lap.

"I got boots and a new riding hat. Daddy says I can take lessons."

"On the ranch?"

Fara shook her head. "My Uncle Miguel has two horses and a pony. He's gonna teach me."

Polly smiled at the beaming child. "Oh, honey, that's so exciting!"

"Me too!" Christy said, jumping up to retrieve a hobby horse from the toy bin.

Fara leaned toward Polly and whispered, "Not big enough," then joined her sister. Each with a hobby horse now, they whooped as they galloped around the sofas in the front room.

Polly joined Lynn, placing yarn, paper plates, and glue on the craft table. "Such sweeties," she said. "You know, I never asked last night. How were your holidays? Was it fun at the Morgans and Fosters?"

"I've never seen anything like it. Over-the-top doesn't even begin to describe it."

Polly laughed. "They do know how to throw a party. Any handsome bachelors?"

"There were a few, but they seemed occupied. Not that he's my type, but Aria really has her claws into Nick Parker."

"Oh dear," Polly said.

"There were a couple of strangers at Spark's on Christmas afternoon, new hires at Valley Stables. Pretty cute, but I never got over to meet them."

"Next time," Polly said, patting her arm. "We all set?"

"Yup," Lynn replied. "And I think *you* ought to call them in and see what Mr. Mind-of-His-Own does."

"Here goes," Polly said, approaching Toby, Jasper, and Willow. "Hey, we've got the craft project all set up. Who wants to try it?"

Toby brightened. Crafts were his favorite time of day. As the oldest child this week, he often ended up helping the little ones. "Come on, Jasp, let's go."

Jasper frowned at Polly, then followed, hanging on to the side of Toby's wheelchair. They were making masks out of paper plates, yarn, and scraps of paper. The activity was open-ended, and if a mask had ten eyes and no mouth, that was just fine. Polly circulated, helping the children with each stage of the project, while Lynn sat with Christy and Jasper, opening glue sticks and assisting as needed. As the activity wound down, by prior arrangement, Lynn said to her two, "I'm gonna get snack ready. Polly will help you finish up."

"No!" Jasper said, throwing his mask across the table. It grazed the side of Toby's head. Polly took his hand. "Jasper, that is not acceptable behavior. Let's take a few minutes for you to cool down." As she attempted to lead him into the front room where the sofas served as time-out spaces, Jasper went limp, flopped to the floor, then started kicking and screaming. Careful to avoid his feet, she lifted him and carried him to a sofa, then set him down. He immediately slipped to the floor and resumed his kicking and flailing.

"You take a few minutes, Jasper. When you're ready, come back and join us."

"You're a poopy head!"

Calmly, Polly said, "We don't use bathroom words here, Jasper. Lynn, Willow, and I will be with the other kids. Let us know when you're ready to come back."

"Poopy head! Poopy head! Poopy head!"

Polly left the room, rejoining the others. The children stared at her, clearly shocked by Jasper's behavior. As snack went on, Jasper slowly calmed and was now whimpering, curled in a ball beside the sofa. Every five minutes, Polly would go in and ask if he was ready to join them. At first, she received a scream, then grunts, but no more name-calling. Finally, a half hour later, as the other children finished their snacks, he followed her in and sat beside Toby. With a pout on his face, Jasper drank his milk and ate his tiny graham cracker bunnies.

Lynn patted her shoulder. "This is a start of what I predict will be a lengthy campaign."

Polly gave her a tired smile. "Are we up to the task, do you think?"

Lynn chuckled. "I'm mixing metaphors, but Rome wasn't built in a day, partner."

*****

They were on the playground when Kevin came to pick up Jasper. The snow had melted and it was unseasonably warm, so the children had abandoned jackets and hats. Polly was pushing Christy on the swing. When Kevin spied her, his heart flipped and his chest constricted. He wanted nothing more than to take her in his arms and shut out the world.

"Daddy!" Jasper called, jumping from the monkey bars and running to him.

Lynn watched and shook her head. "Jasper, remember the rule about jumping from that high!"

"That kind of day?" he asked, scooping the toddler up in his arms.

"We've had our ups and downs. Polly can fill you in. He misses his buddy Ben."

"Oh? He's not here?"

"Maggie and Ben took the kids to Tahoe for the week."

Jasper wriggled down and ran to sit in a riding fire truck. Fara asked for sidewalk chalk, and Lynn excused herself. Kevin strolled over to the swings just as Polly was helping Christy down.

"Hi," she said, smiling as Christy ran off to get a riding toy.

"Hi yourself. How was the day?"

"We had one episode, but all and all, it was okay."

She told him about the tantrum, and he shook his head. "Polly, I'm sorry."

"Don't be. He's tiny, but there's a strong will there."

He took her hand, fingers caressing her palm. "I've missed you, baby."

"Me too," she said, returned his caress.

"Don't suppose you'd like to brave dinner tonight?"

"I've got to stay till the girls go home, so I won't be free till five thirty, and I promised to get down to walk Archie today. With me away and now Maggie, Nick and Brendan are swamped. Archie needs that constant attention to make progress."

"A late dinner?"

She wanted to see him desperately, but she was bone-tired and fearful of another tantrum. "Not for your guy. He took no nap today."

"I could put him to bed, then you and I could eat?"

She withdrew her hand. "Can I take a raincheck?"

"Of course. How about tomorrow?"

"That sounds better."

"Better take my little hellion home before my cock gets any harder," he whispered, hips grazing hers as he headed for the careening fire truck. "Come on, Jasper, time to go!"

Every inch of her body on fire, Polly watched Willow assist Kevin in gathering Jasper's belongings.

Lynn came to stand beside her. "Damn, that man gets better looking every time I see him."

Polly smiled. "You head out. I just saw Jeb's truck pull in. I'm fine here with the girls."

"Thanks, I'm stopping at the market. You need anything?"

"Can't think of a thing at the moment, but if I do, I'll text."

CHAPTER 55

As she walked Archie back to the barn, Polly heard a woman's voice, raised and angry. Aria Firorelli. "But when?" she cried.

Polly led Archie into the barn. Nick and Aria were at the opposite end of the barn, near the parking lot.

"Give me a break, Aria. We're out straight here."

"That's always your excuse."

"Hey, Polly," he said, coming to greet her.

"Typical!" Aria said, throwing up her hands and stomping toward her car.

Nick rolled his eyes and gave Polly a look. "Sorry about that. Here, I'll take him."

"Everything okay?" she asked.

"From my perspective, yes. Aria wants something I can't give her. I mean, she's beautiful and talented, but I'm just not… She's not… I don't know. Anything I say will sound like a cliché, but to use one, she's just not my type."

"And you're hers?"

He laughed. "Who knows? Aria has many types."

"Maybe she's just lonely."

"She is. I mean, Spark's terrific and her apartment's really cool, but she's out there by herself most of the time. Somehow, she's convinced that I can solve that for her. The loneliness, I mean."

"If you don't mind my asking, who is your type? Do you have a girlfriend?"

"Nope. Had someone at home, but that imploded, which was one of the reasons I ended up here."

"Do you still communicate with her?"

"He's moved on," he said, smiling at her. "I'm gay, Polly."

"Does Aria know?"

"Yup."

"Then why does she keep pushing for a relationship?"

"She thinks she can cure me."

"Oh dear."

"You can say that again."

"Well, maybe she'll turn her eye to one of the new people at Valley Stables. Most of those guys are single."

He smiled. "One can hope."

"Well, I guess I'd better get going. Can I help out in any way before I go?"

"Thanks, I've got this. Take care. And, Polly?"

She turned. "Yes?"

"It's not a secret, my being gay. I mean, I haven't put a sign in the general store, but Maggie, Jeb, and Harley know. I'm sure most of the Morgans too. I'm not in a relationship at the moment, but maybe someday."

"I hope so," she said, "although speaking from recent experience, relationships are wonderful things, but they do turn your life upside down and inside out."

"Yup."

"Night," she said, waving as she turned toward the door.

CHAPTER 56

Thursday, Jasper had three tantrums at day care. Polly was not at all sure that dinner was a good idea, but Kevin insisted. She stopped at the bakery for cookies and a small berry tart, then walked the short distance to his house.

"Hey, welcome. Come in," he said, swinging open the door. "Look who's here, buddy! Come say hi to Polly."

The toddler ignored him and continued playing with his cars and trucks in the toy area Kevin had set up in the corner of the living room.

"Jasper, come here now."

No response.

"Don't push it, please," Polly said. "As I told you, this was a rough day, and he didn't take a nap. He's probably exhausted. What's the progress on the bedroom project?"

"This weekend, if I have time."

"You might want to wait a bit longer till things settle down. Might be an easier transition."

"Maybe. What can I get you? Wine? Beer? Seltzer?"

"I'd ordinarily say seltzer, but I'd love a glass of wine. Doesn't matter, red or white. Whatever you've got open."

"This is pretty good," he said, producing a bottle of cabernet sauvignon. "Spark gave it to me, so it probably cost a fortune."

She accepted the wine and sat at the counter, watching him remove a bubbling lasagna from the oven and toss a green salad. Out of the corner of her eye, she observed Jasper, who seemed absorbed with his play. *Poor little thing*, she thought. Despite all his naughty behavior, her heart went out to the tiny child who had been through so much.

"So are you and Jasper going to Spark's New Year's party?" she asked.

"For a short time. I understand all the kids go for supper at least. I'd be inclined to skip it, but Maggie, Ben, and family will be back, and Jasper's dying to see his buddy."

She nodded. "They are such good friends in such a short time. It's actually unusual to see friendships in kids that young. Twos and threes tend to parallel play."

"I don't think he's ever had a buddy. I suspect his foul humor this week at day care is partially 'cause he's missing Bennie. What about you? Are you going to Spark's?"

She smiled. "If it were up to me, I'd stay home and watch a silly movie, but my roommate's ready to party."

"Looking for Mr. Right, is she?" he asked, filling their plates and bringing them and the salad to the table.

"I think she'd settle for Mr. Let's-Do-Something-Once-and-a-While."

"Everything's ready. Shall we?"

"It looks amazing."

Kevin pulled out Jasper's new highchair. "Not sure how you-know-who will do at the dining room table, but we'll give it a try. Jasper, dinner's ready. Let's wash those hands."

Polly waited to sit until they returned from the bathroom. Kevin sat Jasper in his chair at the end of the table. His and Polly's places were set on either side. He had chopped up lasagna and some hamburger for Jasper. There was also a little bowl of corn and a sippy cup at his place.

"Okay, buddy, let's eat!"

Jasper picked up his spoon and was about to scoop up some corn when he saw Polly sitting down beside him. No sooner did she set down her wine than he reached out and knocked it over.

"Oops," she said, trying to make light of the child's deliberate move.

"Jasper!" Kevin said, just as the bowl of corn flew across the table, lasagna and hamburger following it.

Unlike his previous tantrums, all the food throwing was done in complete silence. Finally, Jasper, who was not strapped into his chair, slipped down and ran back to his toys. Kevin shot across the room and picked him up. "We do not throw food in this house," he said calmly.

Jasper wriggled and squirmed, but his father held fast. "Now, you come back and say you're sorry to Polly."

Polly was still sitting when Kevin came to stand in front of her. "Jasper?" he said, warning in his voice as he set him down. "What do you say to Polly?"

"She's a poopy head! Hate her!" With those words, he ran screaming from the room and slammed the bedroom door.

"Oh God, I'm so sorry!" he said, his face stricken.

Polly stood. "I think I should go. This may have been pushing too many things too fast."

"No, please stay. I'll talk to him."

She patted his wrist. "Right now, I think you better check to see what he's doing in there. Have you child-proofed your bathroom?"

"Oh geez!" he said, running into the bedroom. Polly heard wailing, then the crashing of several hard objects.

She found a dustpan and cleaned up the floor, then cleared the plates and wiped the table. The melee was still going on when she finished. She wanted to help but also knew this was something Kevin needed to do alone as Jasper's parent. They certainly didn't need Jasper's teacher in the middle of it. She wrote a note" "Hope all settles down. See you tomorrow. Love, P," then slipped out the door.

CHAPTER 57

Friday morning, Polly had her hands full with orientation for four-year-old Dulcie Casey and her baby brother, Cal. Their dad, Gus, dropped them off earlier than expected, and Lynn was not yet in. A single parent, Gus was one of the assistant trainers at Valley Stables. It was his first day at work, and he didn't want to be late.

Spark Foster brought Toby and stayed to help, but things were hopping when Jasper and Kevin arrived. After putting Jasper's things away, Kevin found her in the kitchen with Cal on her hip. "Hey, good morning. Can we talk?"

"Does it look like I can talk?" she asked, her voice uncharacteristically shrill.

"I'm sorry about last night."

"Don't be."

"Where'd this little guy come from?"

"Gus Casey's. He and Dulcie are here till noon to get oriented. They start the day after New Year's. Excuse me." She pushed past and called to Toby to help Jasper find some toys.

"Polly, please, I'm going crazy here."

The baby began fussing, and Polly grabbed a bottle from the fridge. "Look, I've got to feed him. It's okay. Really. I'll see you tomorrow night at Spark's. Maybe there'll be a few minutes then. I just can't do this right now."

She turned away, leaving him alone in the kitchen, where Spark found him. "Hey, son, you okay? You look like you just lost your best friend."

"I might have," he said glumly.

"Give it time, son. Give it time."

"That's what everyone keeps telling me."

"'Cause it's true. Now indulge an old man and have a cup of coffee at the café with me."

As Kevin and Spark departed, Lynn and Willow came in laden with bags and boxes."Thank goodness," Polly said as Loren Perez and her girls followed them.

*****

Against her better judgment, Polly allowed Lynn to drag her to Gabriela's the morning of New Year's Eve. "Come on," she begged. "It'll be fun, and we deserve something snazzy for Spark's big shindig."

"I'm not feeling snazzy at the moment, and besides, Gabriela's is very expensive!"

Her roommate prevailed, and shortly before noon, they stepped into the popular dress shop, its owner eccentric but blessed with impeccable taste and an acute eye for which one of her many unique creations would perfectly suit a client. "Mornin', ladies," a voice called from behind the counter. Seconds later, Gabriela popped her head up. "Dropped an earring. Can't find it or my glasses." She wore a loose, crinkly top in a pale shade of lavender over black leggings. Her waist-length auburn hair was tied back by a scarf. Intense violet eyes studied each one of them in turn. "How can I help?"

Lynn stepped forward. "We're both looking for a cocktail dress. We've got a fancy party tonight."

"Lemme guess—the Fosters' New Year's Eve party," Gabriela said. "Lots of ladies have been in the past few days. Social event of the weekend in the Valley."

"That's the one," Lynn said. "Are you going?"

"I was invited, but I'm off to Tucson to spend New Year's Eve with friends. I'm Gabriela, by the way."

"I'm Lynn."

"Polly. Hello."

"Okay then, let's get you some fancy duds for a fancy party."

Without bothering to inquire as to their sizes, she began whizzing around the shop, grabbing dresses and accessories, which she then separated and hung in the two dressing rooms. "Okay, Polly on the right, Lynn on the left. See what you think. If I'm way off base, we'll start from scratch. Sound good?"

Polly first slipped into a peach dress with long sleeves and a flouncy skirt. It fit her perfectly and was flattering, but she wasn't sold. She waited with Gabriela eyeing her until Lynn came out in a diaphanous chestnut top and flowing black slacks. She looked radiant as she gazed at herself in the full-length mirrors.

"You look beautiful," Polly said.

"It's not bad, is it?"

"Not bad?" Gabriela said. "That outfit was made for you, honey. Gold necklace, earrings, and strappy heels, and it'll be perfect."

"I'm more of a silver person," Lynn said.

"So am I, dear, but trust me, that outfit and your dark eyes need gold. Let me grab a few things. Don't panic. They're not real gold, just high-quality costume jewelry."

Polly twirled, regarding herself in one of the mirrors. "What do you think of this, Lynn… I mean ladies?"

"Cute," Lynn answered, still distracted by her own perfect outfit.

"Hmm," Gabriela said, regarding her as she grabbed accessories and shoes for Lynn. "Let's see the others."

Polly modeled two more dresses, a white, then a pale shimmery blue. They fit and received a thumbs-up from Lynn, who was still accessorizing, but Gabriela wasn't convinced. Finally, Polly slipped into a shimmery silver sheath that hugged her slim figure as if it had been custom made for her. The skirt flared ever so slightly at the hem. When she looked in the mirror, Polly gasped. For a second, she didn't recognize herself.

Lynn stopped what she was doing and whistled. "Oh boy, Kevin Larrabee won't know what hit him!"

Gabriela clapped her hands. "That's the one. You, my dear, need silver, but just a touch. And these shoes, I believe?" She held up a pair of gray pumps with four-inch heels.

"Oh gee. I'm not sure I can walk in those," Polly said.

"Sure you can. They're incredibly comfortable. Slip 'em on."

Polly was amazed to find that Gabriella was right. Despite the ridiculously high heels, they were comfortable, and they looked fabulous with the dress. Gabriella began waving necklaces and earrings in front of her until Polly said, "Thanks, but I have lots of silver pieces, and I know just what I'll wear with it."

"Simple, sweetie. You really don't need any adornment. You look glorious."

"I can do simple," Polly said, smiling as she turned and gazed in the mirror.

Halfway down the block, they began breathing normally after the sticker shock at the cash register. "I should take these back," Polly said, holding up the bag with the shoes, dress, and a beautiful shawl Gabriela had insisted she needed. "These prices are fine for the Morgans, but yikes!"

"You only live once," Lynn said, waving her bag back and forth.

"That's what I'm worried about. Being able to live the next few months now that my credit card is probably maxed out."

"Come on, let's go to Gracie's for lunch to celebrate," Lynn said.

"Okay, but after this, I won't be able to afford to eat out again for months," Polly said, following her into the diner. "It better be a light lunch, or I'll never fit into this dress."

CHAPTER 58

Spark's barn was aglow when Kevin arrived with Jasper. Before they got out of the truck, he sat beside the toddler and told him if he wasn't good, they couldn't stay. Jasper nodded solemnly before he was liberated from his car seat. At the barn door, Kevin said, "Remember, buddy. You be a good boy, or we're outta here."

The first people they spied were Maggie, Ben, and their kids talking with Spark and Buck Foster. "Bennie!" Jasper cried, wriggling down and running to meet his friend. The two boys hugged each other and ran toward the food tables.

"Don't worry," Jeb Barnes said, coming to stand beside him, Toby in his arms. "These things are crazy. No one cares if the kids tear up the place, do they, Tobe?" His son smiled as Amy arrived with his wheelchair. Jeb settled him into the motorized chair, and he was off to join the melee.

Amy laughed. "You were here last year, weren't you?"

Kevin nodded. "Yup, but not with a wild toddler in tow."

"He's adorable," Amy said. "I'm sorry we haven't seen more of you guys. How's it going?"

"Pretty good. I consider it a good day if he has fewer than three tantrums."

"Aww... Must have been so hard for him to lose his mom, then come all the way across the country," she said.

"Yeah. He's settling in, but it's been a bumpy road. Thank God for Bennie. He's crazy about him."

"Things any better at day care?" Jeb asked, then noticed Kevin's surprised expression. He grinned. "Sorry, our little spy gives us a complete rundown of every minute of every day."

"Things are actually better at least with the acting out around Polly, but days with no naps are rough."

"Speaking of Polly," Jeb said, eyes wide as he gazed toward the entry. "Wow, our schoolteachers clean up well, don't they?"

Kevin turned, and his mouth dropped open. Lynn looked glamourous and sexy, but Polly shimmered. Her hair was pulled back with silver combs, flowing, long, and loose, and her dress hugged every inch of her. *And oh those legs!* Kevin couldn't take his eyes off her.

"She does look lovely," Amy said, watching Kevin. "Jeb, let's go say hello, shall we? I'll just bet that's one of Gabriela's creations."

As they headed to the entrance where Polly and Lynn stood talking to Kyle and Robbie Morgan, she caught sight of Kevin, handsome in a dark navy suit, red tie, and blue shirt. He was staring at her as if he'd seen a ghost.

The crowd thickened, and she lost sight of him. Children ran everywhere and waitstaff passed drinks and all kinds of appetizers. There were bars set up at opposite ends of the barn as well. Lynn pushed her along, making the rounds, and Polly searched in vain for Kevin. Finally, as they stood chatting with Tom Jacobi and several of the men from Valley Stables, Lynn looked at her friend.

Much as she hated to tear herself away from the handsome newcomers, Lynn grabbed Polly's arm. "Come on, you're in agony. Let's find him and get this over with."

"What are you talking about?"

"You know damn well what I'm talking about. You've been on edge for days, you're not sleeping, and a certain blue-eyed builder looked ready to eat you up just now."

"Don't be ridiculous."

"There he is," Lynn said as Kevin tried to corral Jasper. "Come on."

Not waiting for a reply, she grabbed Polly's arm and yanked her along. When they reached him, Kevin held Jasper in a vise grip and was lecturing him about running as his little friend Bennie jumped up and down beside them.

"Hey, Kev, hey, Jasper," Lynn said. "I'm gonna take charge now. Jaspie, I'm your babysitter 'cause your dad has some business to take care of. Okay?"

Jasper looked at her like she'd invited him to fly to the moon.

"You wanta keep playing with Bennie?" Lynn asked.

He nodded.

"Okay, then be good, 'cause I'm watching. Scoot!" The boys ran off, and she turned to Polly and Kevin. "And you two. Go. Take a walk, whatever. Just please work this out. No more moping around. Now shoo!"

"You sure?" he asked.

"Get out of this barn. Now!"

They walked to the side door and stepped out. The weather had warmed up, but the night was still chilly. "I'm not sure this was a good idea," she said, pulling her shawl around her shoulders.

"Did you bring a coat? I can get it."

"No."

"How 'bout my jacket?"

"I'm okay for now, thanks."

"I've got an idea," he said, taking her hand and leading her around the barn to the back of the house. He tried the sunporch door, and it yielded.

CHAPTER 59

"Oh, that feels better," Polly said, stepping into the heated, glass-walled room.

He closed the door behind them. The room was darkened, but soft light fell on them from the lanterns outside. "You look beautiful," he whispered. "When I saw you, I couldn't breathe."

She smiled and touched his cheek. "You look pretty great yourself."

"Baby, I've missed you so much." As he spoke, he drew her into his arms and kissed her. His lips trailed down her neck as his hands moved to her breasts. As he cupped each one, he felt her nipples grow hard under the smooth, silky fabric. Polly moaned, pressing against him, not surprised to feel his erection tickling her belly. "You know, if we take this any further, I won't be able to stop."

"I hope not," she whispered. "I've missed you too."

Polly's hands traveled downward until she found his fly, which she unzipped, releasing him, stroking him the way she knew he loved. "You have no idea how much I want you," she whispered, shocked as always by her boldness around him.

"Oh, yes I do," he said, reaching down under her skirt, hiking it up, hands on her hips as he slipped her panties down. "In those high heels, you're just the right height."

"For?" she asked, breathlessly waiting for what she knew was coming.

"For me to take these gorgeous legs, wrap 'em around me, and head for home."

Before she could say anything, he lifted her, hands grasping her ass as he plunged into her warm, wet depths, Polly's back against the paneled wall.

"Oh, oh, oh," she cried as she met his every move with her own. "Please, Kevin. Take me. Deeper, deeper," she moaned, crazy with desire.

Lost in a blazing climax, they almost missed the footsteps in the hall outside the room.

"Anyone there?" a voice called.

"Sounds like Aria," Polly whispered. "Should we call out?"

"Not unless you want her to find us like this," he said, thrusting one last time to make his point. He moved to shield her just as Aria flicked a switch and the sunporch was bathed in light.

"Jesus," Kevin whispered, withdrawing and pulling down Polly's skirt as Aria stepped into the room.

"Well, well, well, looks like I'm interrupting. Sorry." She lingered for a few seconds before stepping out and extinguishing the lights. "At least someone's having fun."

Polly buried her head on his chest, her face burning. "Oh no, what are we going to do?"

"Not a thing," he said, kissing her before he bent to retrieve her panties. "I'd suggest we try that again if I wasn't afraid my son was tearing up the place."

"Oh Kevin, this is so embarrassing."

"Who gives a shit? I don't."

As they walked arm in arm out of the sunporch, they burst into laughter. When they found Lynn, they were still chuckling. She was watching Jasper and Ben dance with Emma, but turned to look from Polly's wrinkled dress to Kevin's disheveled appearance "Good talk?"

"Not so much talking," he said, arm around Polly's waist.

Lynn smiled. "You two make me sick. Now I'm gonna dance with one of those gorgeous cowboys, and *you* can babysit!"

They never did talk or resolve anything. Kevin left at ten, but at Lynn's insistence, she and Polly stayed until just after midnight. At the stroke of twelve, Lynn was rewarded by a kiss from Tom Jacobi.

On the ride home, Lynn asked her if she and Kevin had decided anything, and Polly said, "No, just taking it slow."

"Yeah, right," Lynn said. "Don't forget, I saw you after your little stroll."

CHAPTER 60

The week went by in a blur of activity. With the new children at the Cottage, Polly, Lynn, and the others never stopped. Polly talked to Kevin in the evenings and sometimes at dropoff and pickup, but every time he asked to do something, she declined, afraid to have a repeat of the lasagna episode. Wednesday morning, he caught her at dropoff as Polly helped Dulcie Casey dress a cowgirl doll. He loved the gentle way she had with the children and wished Jasper could settle down and draw closer to the woman he loved.

"Hey," he said when she looked up.

She stood, giving him a crooked smile. "Mornin'."

"Don't 'spose you'd like to try again? Getting together, I mean."

"It's been crazy this week."

He gently took hold of her wrist. "Please, Polly, I'm dying here. I can't do this without you."

"He's been great so far this week. I hate to push it," she said, reluctantly slipping away from his warm touch.

"I could get a babysitter."

"I don't know. Let's see what the end of the week brings. That might make it worse, you know, if he thinks he doesn't have you because you're out with me."

"I saw Haley yesterday. She's given me some suggestions."

"Great, I'm happy for you. Oh!" she said, suddenly distracted by a tower of blocks cascading down on Christy Perez and Dulcie, the perpetrators Jasper and Ben. "I've got to get this. Have a great day."

He watched as she gently intervened and was heartened to see that his little devil listened to Polly all the while linking arms with his coconspirator.

"Monsters," Lynn whispered, coming to stand beside him.

"I'll say. Doesn't that warrant a time-out?"

"She'll handle it."

"I know," he said, his voice wistful.

"Give her time. Aside from the adjustment of Jasper and all, she was hurt pretty badly by her last boyfriend."

"That was a while ago, wasn't it?"

"Yup, but the heart carries wounds that have a way of cropping up at odd times."

"That's for sure."

Lynn grinned, patting his shoulder. "Have a good day, Kev."

*****

After nap and snack, Ben and Jasper were terrorizing everyone on the playground until Lynn told them to take a break on the bench. She and Willow were watching the kids while Polly cleaned up from snack. When Polly came out, she spied the benchwarmers. "Uh-oh, now what?"

"Marauding," Lynn said.

Willow laughed. "They've been extra naughty today."

"Testing, testing, testing," Polly said. "I can't tell who is the instigator."

"Both!" Lynn and Willow said simultaneously.

"Watch 'em on the monkey bars," Lynn said. "Jasper's been benched twice today for hanging off the top with one arm."

"Will do," Polly said. "You off?"

"In a few minutes. Gotta set up for tomorrow before I go."

"We can do that," Polly said. "You don't want to be late for your first day of yoga."

Lynn had signed up for a yoga class at the ranch spa, to "limber up for darling Tom!" Ranch employees could take spa classes for free, and she had also cajoled Polly into joining her for the Saturday class.

"It's fine. I've got time. Okay, guys," she called to Ben and Jasper. "You ready to play nicely." They nodded their heads, looking like innocent lambs. "Be good." She waved, and they jumped up.

Not three minutes after Lynn disappeared, she and Willow were pushing Dulcie and Fara on the swings when Polly looked over to spy Jasper and Ben at the top of the monkey bars, Jasper leaning out, holding on with one hand. As she called, "Jasper, get down," his buddy tickled him. "Oh Lord! Can you watch the girls, Willow?"

She started for the monkey bars just as Jasper screamed and fell to the ground. When she reached him, he was crying, his lip cut open. She scooped him up and called to Willow, "I'll get Lynn and take him inside, okay?"

As they gently cleaned Jasper's face, Lynn said, "That's bad. He's gonna need stitches."

They called Kevin's cell. No answer.

"I'll take him to Dr. Black," Polly said. She was still holding Jasper, who clung to her, whimpering. "I'm sorry about yoga."

"No worries. There's always next week. Now go." Lynn waved them out.

*****

Although a cardiologist by training, Chester Black was now the town's GP. Polly carried Jasper into the office and was ushered right in to see the man himself. "Hey, young fella," he said, smiling at Jasper, who cowered against Polly. "Ms. Granger, isn't it?" he asked.

"Yes, I work on Morgan's Run. At the day care."

"I've been hearing about you gals and the fine work you've been doing. Now, what happened here?"

"Fell off the monkey bars. Jasper, can you let Dr. Black look at your mouth?"

"No!" The toddler shook his head.

"How about me? Can I take a little peek? Won't hurt, I promise."

Jasper sat up and allowed her to remove the facecloth covering his mouth. The gash on his lower lip was still bleeding. Black studied it briefly and said, "Should have a stitch. Have his parents been notified?"

"Yes, I called after we pulled into your parking lot. His dad's on his way. He should be here soon."

"Well then, let me give you a clean wet cloth, and you can keep that on till he gets here. You two stay, and I'll get things ready. Okay?" He stepped out and closed the door.

"See, that wasn't so bad," she said, patting Jasper's back. In response, he leaned his head on her chest. Polly's heart melted. Despite all the tantrums, she already loved this scared little boy who had lost his mother, been kidnapped, and then moved across the country to live with strangers.

Ten minutes later, the door opened again, and Kevin stepped in. "Hey," he said softly. Polly looked down to find Jasper asleep.

"What happened?" Kevin whispered.

Polly filled him in quickly, ending with "Dr. Black'll be back soon."

"Already saw him and took care of the paperwork. He's with another patient and will be in shortly. What about you? You okay? Do you have to get back?"

"Pretty soon," she said, gazing down at the child sleeping in her arms. "But I hate to give him up."

"Yeah," he said softly. "That's a beautiful sight." He came closer and kissed her forehead. "Thanks for takin' care of him."

"Anytime," she said, leaning her head against his side as the door opened again.

"We ready?" Dr. Black asked. His nurse followed with a sterile tray.

"Hey, buddy," Kevin said as Polly tried to sit him up.

The minute Jasper opened his eyes, he pushed away from Polly and leapt into his father's arms.

"We need him on the table," Dr. Black said. "You're going to have to hold him very still. Peggy will help. Not easy, but I promise, we'll be quick."

"I'll wait outside," Polly said. Kevin gave her a grateful smile, then turned away to get Jasper settled on the table.

Polly sat in the waiting room, her bloodstained sweater soliciting a few queries as to whether she was all right. She and the two patients waiting could hear Jasper's screams, but, true to his word, Dr. Black was quick. Five minutes later, silence reigned. Soon after the receptionist called for the next patient to go in, Kevin emerged, Jasper in his arms, an ice pack over his mouth.

"How you doing, sweetie?" she asked, but Jasper grunted and refused to look at her. She gave Kevin a wan smile.

"He was a brave man. I'll take him home and get his things tomorrow."

"I'm going back. I'll drop them at your house on my way home."

"Look at you. I'll buy you a new sweater if that doesn't come out."

"It's fine."

"Don't 'spose you'd like to have dinner with us?"

"Can't. We're busy."

"Oh? Okay."

Noticing his expression, she added, "The Perez family asked us to dinner. They're having Gus Casey and his kids too."

"Another time, then?"

"Of course."

"I miss you, Polly."

"Me too," she said, reaching out to touch his arm. As she did, Jasper shoved it away.

"Jasper, no!"

"I'll see you later," Polly said. "See you tomorrow, Jasper."

"Thanks," Kevin said.

"My pleasure," she said. Polly smiled, then turned to walk to her car, her heart broken by Jasper's rejection.

*****

Jasper's backpack and lunch box in her arms, Polly knocked at Kevin's door, then checked the driveway and saw his truck was gone. She nestled the things between the storm and inner doors and walked to her car. *Better this way*, she thought, heading home.

CHAPTER 61

The next two days, Jasper avoided Polly. It felt as if their brief moments of closeness after his fall had been a dream. With his swollen lip, he looked like a prize fighter and had the pugnacious behavior to match. As they watched Kevin wrestle his son out of his jacket Friday morning, Lynn said, "I see many time-outs in his future today."

Polly laughed. "TGIF. Here comes his partner in crime."

Maggie Morgan flew in with her two. "Hey, ladies," she called. As Ben ran off to join his friend in the block corner, she approached them. "We, Ben, Emma, Ben, and I would love to have you for supper tonight. Jeb and Amy are coming with Toby. We asked Kevin, but he has a crew dinner. You free?"

"Always," Lynn said.

"We'd love to come," Polly said, "Can we bring something?"

"Just your incredible selves," Maggie said brightly. "We know he's a handful, but we are so grateful for the warm, wonderful place you've created here. Ben loves you both and loves coming every morning."

"We love him too," Polly said.

"And he's been great for Jasper," Lynn added. "The friendship has really helped him feel comfortable in his new home."

"They are wonderful buddies, aren't they?" Maggie said, smiling as she watched the two building a block tower. "Naughty, but so sweet."

"We love naughty boys, don't we, Poll?"

Polly nodded. "Absolutely."

"Well, I've gotta hightail it. Busy morning. We've got two border patrol guys coming to meet their mounts. One of them may take Archie."

"Oh, I'll miss him," Polly said.

"There'll be more coming," she said. "And Archie won't be going anywhere for at least six or seven months. Have a great day, and we'll see you about six?"

They watched her fly through the rooms, kiss Emma and Ben, then disappear. "She's amazing, isn't she?" Polly said.

"And gorgeous, even in jeans and boots."

"Especially in jeans and boots," Kevin said, coming up to say goodbye. When the two gave him a look, he said, "Hey, I can look, can't I? Gotta go. Sorry we won't see you tonight. I didn't even tell Jasper as he'd be so bummed to miss a night at Bennie's. Call you later?" he said to Polly.

"Of course."

Polly forced a smile as they watched him say goodbye to Jasper.

"Poor guy's in rough shape, isn't he?" Lynn said.

"Poor guy? What about me?"

Lynn grinned. "Well, there is that. Let's get this party started and take your mind off your love life."

"Ha-ha," Polly said, following her into the craft room.

*****

Kevin had just gotten Jasper to bed when his cell phone rang. "Kevin?" a woman's voice said.

"Ivy, hi."

"How's it going out there?"

"Pretty good. A few ups and downs, but the little guy has been through a lot."

"Yes, he has. I miss him."

"Come visit."

"Maybe in the summer. How're things with your girlfriend?"

"That's been a little challenging because for some reason, Jasper hasn't warmed to her."

"Give him time. He'll get there. I wonder… Naw, that couldn't matter."

"What're you talking about?"

"It's probably nothing, but I was calling to say I got the Christmas card you sent of him with his little nursery school friends. So adorable."

"He's made a really good buddy, Ben Morgan. He's the one with curly brown hair. They're monsters when they're together, but it's been really great for him."

"That's terrific news. I'm so happy for him. Listen, Kev, I'm looking at the card now. Who's the pretty woman with the long blonde hair?"

"That's Polly."

"Your girl?"

"Yup."

"She's beautiful. It's funny, though… She…she looks so much like a friend of Judith's, Esme."

"Yeah? Did Jasper know her?"

"Yes, but not well. The thing is… She's the one Judy went out with that last night. Jasper and I stood and waved goodbye to them. That's the last time he saw his mom."

"Jesus, how close a resemblance?"

"They could be twins, or at least sisters, except that your Polly looks healthy. Esme's a junkie."

They talked for a few more minutes, then said goodbye. Kevin grabbed a beer, sat on the sofa, and called Polly. He told her what Ivy had said about Esme and the resemblance.

"Poor baby. Do you really think that could be it?" she asked.

"I dunno. It's probably a lot of things, but it can't have helped. I'd really like to see you. What's your weekend like?"

"Quiet. It's supposed to be much warmer tomorrow. I'm walking Archie in the morning. Think Jasper might like to see the stables? If he's not too skittish, we could all walk Archie."

"That'd be great. What time?"

"Nine okay?"

"Nine it is."

"Night," she said, wanting to say more.

"Night. I love you, Polly. We are going to get past this."

"I know. I love you too."

CHAPTER 62

Kevin set Jasper's bowl of cereal in front of him and took the stool beside his high chair. "How'd you like to see some horses this morning, buddy?"

Jasper nodded. "Yup"

"Polly's gonna show us around the barn. She has a *really* big horse friend. His name is Archie."

Jasper frowned. "Don't want to."

"Okay, buddy, we need to talk. Does Polly look like someone you know?"

His son looked away, refusing to meet his eye.

"Does she look like Mommy's friend?"

Jasper shoved his bowl away and put his thumb in his mouth. As Kevin watched, a tear trickled down his chubby cheek.

Kevin unstrapped him and carried him to sit in his recliner. "Hey, buddy, what's wrong?"

"Took Mommy."

"You mean Mommy's friend Esme?"

He nodded.

"Well, Esme lives far, far away. She's not gonna take anyone. Polly might look a little like Mommy's friend, but she isn't. She doesn't know Esme. You understand?"

He nodded.

"Polly is my friend, just like Benny's your friend. Am I mean to Benny?"

Jasper shook his head.

"Course not, 'cause I know he's your friend. Polly's my friend, and I love her, just like I love you. No one's going take anyone away. Ever. Someday, maybe you and I might wanta have Polly be part of our family. Then we could all be together, all be friends, and take care of each other. Whaddya say?"

Jasper stared at him but said nothing.

"Anyway, I want you to be nice to my friend, just like I'm nice to Benny. Okay?"

Slight nod.

"Okay. Let's get you dressed and have some breakfast. Polly and those horses are waiting for us."

*****

Polly decided it might be wise to walk Archie a bit before Kevin and Jasper's arrival. She got to the stables at eight thirty and found Nick and Jeb just finishing the stalls. All the horses were out. "Morning!" she said brightly.

"Hey, Poll," Nick said. "You takin' Archie out?"

"If it's okay?"

"Morning," Jeb said, tipping his hat as he rolled a full wheelbarrow by her.

"Would it be okay with you guys if Kevin brought Jasper down to see the horses?"

"Fine by us. It's a pretty slow day. Couple of lessons and that's it."

"How'd everything go with the border patrol guys?"

Nick grinned. "Fine, except Archie's rider was a little freaked out by his size."

"Dino-horse is tied out back," Jeb said, stowing the now-empty wheelbarrow and grabbing a bale of sawdust.

"Thanks. I thought we'd take a short walk before the guys get here. I'll head down the camp road."

"We'll send 'em your way," Nick said.

She and Archie looped around the outskirts of the camp and were halfway back to the stables when she spied Kevin and Jasper walking toward them. He was holding Jasper's hand. Polly waved, then patted Archie's flank. The horse was calm this morning and the sight of the newcomers did not seem to faze him. Suddenly, before Kevin could grab him, Jasper wriggled loose and started running toward them, arms outstretched. Polly thought he was running to Archie, then realized he was running to her.

"Polly! We came!"

Archie was calm, but just in case, she dropped the lead and stepped away. Before she knew what was happening, Jasper flung himself into her arms. Archie stood calmly beside them as Polly twirled him around, tears streaming down her face.

"Now that's what I call a good morning," Kevin said, grinning from ear to ear as he took hold of Archie's halter. He came closer, and his arms circled them both as he kissed her. "Hey, baby. It's sure good to see you."

"You too," she said, smiling through her tears.

They walked Archie along part of the Loop Trail, then spent an hour at the stables. Jasper chattered as Nick and Jeb brought him from horse to horse, sometimes setting him on their backs. As clients arrived for lessons, Polly suggested that it might be time to go. When they were saying goodbye, Kevin and Jasper ahead of her, Nick caught her arm. "Hey, Poll, looks like things are going better."

She beamed. "You have no idea. Thanks for this, and please thank Jeb too."

When she stepped out of the barn, Kevin was buckling Jasper into his car seat. "So guys, where're you off to now?"

"Play date at Benny's, and I just got a call from Harley, so I'm headed out there after I drop Jasper off."

Polly's face fell. "Oh okay. Then I guess I'll see you around."

"Yes, you will," he said, drawing her into his arms. "We're having dinner."

"Oh? Are you cooking?"

"Nope."

"Jasper, are you cooking?"

"No!" he said, throwing back his head and giggling.

"Willow's coming over to have supper with Jasper, and you and I are going out."

She smiled. "Casual?"

"I made a reservation at the Red Mesa, but if that's not what you want, we can go anywhere. Bulldog? Gracie's?"

"The Red Mesa sounds lovely. I've never been there."

"Me neither. 'Sposed to be nice."

"And fancy."

"I can do fancy. Pick you up at seven?"

"I'll be ready."

CHAPTER 63

All through dinner, Polly thought she was dreaming. They sat eating and drinking in the Red Mesa's walled terrace garden. "This is the most romantic place on earth," she said as they shared a delicate fruit tart. They were surrounded by walls of flowers and gardens in full bloom. The small secret space held one table, and its occupants enjoyed complete privacy.

"Not quite," he said. "Have I told you how beautiful you look tonight?"

Polly blushed. "About ten times, but I still like hearing it."

"I thought nothing could top your New Year's Eve dress." Tonight, she wore a sleeveless linen dress in pale pink, a delicate silver necklace her only adornment.

"I think you have stars in your eyes. This is a fairly ordinary dress."

"Nothing's ordinary when it's on you, baby."

"Well, you're looking pretty extraordinary yourself," she said. "What did you mean just now about not quite? What place do you know that's more romantic than this?"

To her surprise, he stood and reached out his hand. "I thought you'd never ask." He led her to the opposite side of the garden and opened French doors. Polly found herself in a candlelit room with a four-poster bed, its white eyelet cover strewn with red rose petals. Wide-eyed, she asked, "How did you…?"

"Harley told me about this place. Pretty cool, isn't it?"

"But, we can't stay. What about Jasper?"

"Willow offered to stay the night, but I promised her I'd be back by one. It's ours till midnight." He crossed the room and brought back an exquisite cut-crystal vase of red roses. "I know this isn't your grandmother's, but I hope it will bring you new memories. Merry Christmas, baby."

"Oh, Kevin, it's beautiful, but my gifts for you and Jasper are at home."

"There's plenty of time later," he said, taking the vase and setting it on a nearby table.

She smiled. "I feel like Cinderella."

"Well, I don't have a glass slipper, but I do have something, and it's been straining my pocket all night."

"Is that the something that gives me pleasure beyond my wildest imagination?"

He grinned. "I love that you're thinking like that, sweetheart, but it's not that. Although that something needs you bad."

He stepped back, holding her hands, then knelt down. "Polly Granger, I cannot imagine living another day of my life without you. I love you more than anything in the world, and I asking… I'm asking—"

"Yes!"

"I was going to say, will you marry me?"

Polly threw herself into his arms, knocking them both over. "Yes, yes, yes."

"You know, we have a great bed right there, but if we don't get up soon, I'm gonna ravish my fiancée right here on this rug."

"Yes!" she said as she unzipped his pants and released him.

In one fluid motion, he slipped off her panties and slipped inside her moist depths. "Oh, baby."

Eventually, they found their way to the bed, where he turned her gently and took hold of her beautiful round ass. "What do you think?"

"Yes, yes, yes," she murmured.

Polly gasped as he took her from behind. Kevin drew back. "Did I hurt you, baby?"

"No, please, please, Kevin. I love you. Go deep, so deep, so deep."

After astonishing mutual orgasms, they lay nestled together. Kevin kissed the back of her neck as he stroked her breasts. "Mmm… You've found one of my hot spots," she whispered, moving her ass in a circle, squeezing him deep, grinning as she felt him grow hard inside her.

"Baby, are you trying to kill me? I'm an old guy, you know."

"Don't play the age card with me, Kevin Larrabee," she said. "You're my fiancé now. You've gotta keep up."

They took it slow this time. Their climax was tremulous and sublime. Afterward, they fell asleep. When they woke, it was close to midnight. Reluctantly, he slipped out of her and gently helped her to dress. Then he laid her back on the bed and began retrieving his own clothes, which were strewn about the room. Polly watched, loving every inch of the strong, hard body that loved her so completely and so well.

Finally, he came to sit beside her and kissed the tip of her nose. "Hey, my wild, wanton baby, you didn't let me finish back there," he said, bringing the small velvet box from behind his back and opening it.

"Oh, Kevin, it's beautiful," she said, gazing down as he slipped the ring onto her finger. It was a lovely antique setting, a single diamond surrounded by tiny sapphires.

"Not half as beautiful as you, my love. And nothing ever will be."

Please read on for sample pages of **Song of the Spirit**, *a fast-paced, breathtaking tale of courage and romance.* **Song of the Spirit**'s *unforgettable characters intersect with historical events of the day, including the devastation of the Wounded Knee massacre.*

In the late 1800s, post-Civil War, two young Cheyenne sisters are wrenched from a loving family, kidnapped, and incarcerated at Rose Academy, a harsh Indian boarding school established to assimilate young Native people, teach them English, and eradicate their knowledge of traditional ways, considered inferior to the ways of the Washita (whites).

Forbidden to speak their native language, the sisters are whipped and punished; however, the school's harsh life fails to break their spirit. The eldest, Wind Flower, on the cusp of womanhood, excels academically, while continually planning their escape. Time and again, she runs away and is hunted down and returned to Rose Academy. There, she watches her beloved little sister's alarming transformation into a proper Washita girl. At the same time, Wind Flower finds love with a young Sioux renamed Caleb Green by his captors. Will these three courageous young people find freedom, or lose themselves and their way of life to the relentless cruelty of the Washita world?

Song of the Spirit
Chapter 1

Winnowing fingers of sunlight danced above them as the pair made their way through the forest. They'd been well taught by their elders to move like shadows in deep woods of silence. As they walked, scanning the ground, the older girl kept a watchful eye on her companion, never straying more than a few yards from her. It was the first year they'd been allowed to forage apart from the others, and she recognized this freedom was also a test of her responsibility.

Suddenly, the little one stopped, bending over to thrust her sharp wooden tool into the earth, grunting as she struggled with the task. Immediately, the older girl moved to her side. "Take care, little Dove. The roots are delicate, and Na'go needs them whole. Don't cut too sharply with your dibble, or there'll be nothing left of them."

She spoke softly, sensing that the child would greet her words with anger, yet unable to stop herself. The roots of the red turnip—much scarcer than its white cousin and a favorite of their people—were too precious to end up in shreds. Harvested intact, the roots could be used as the base of a delicious soup—perfect for the feasting in four days. In shreds, the roots wouldn't last the night before rotting.

As the older girl watched, her sister's chubby hands worried at the root, alternately pulling and chopping at it. Her face was all determination as she mined the tiny patch of tubers. "Go away, Wind Flower! I know how to do it. Na'go showed me!" she sputtered, her face the color of the root.

"I know, little one. I just—"

"And don't call me little one—my name is Laughing Dove!" she said chin thrust out, eyes blazing up at her sister. "I'm not little. I'm not! Father says I'll be much taller than you when I'm grown."

Recognizing the futility of further conversation, Wind Flower wandered off a little, hoping, albeit belatedly, to give her sister an unspoken message of trust. Glancing back, she saw Laughing Dove's shoulders relax. She smiled, full of love for the seven-year-old—the only one of her siblings still alive. These days, life for the Cheyenne was full of sorrow, but out in the woods, away from the reservation and the soldiers' prying eyes, Wind Flower felt happy and free. Free as her people must have felt years ago. Before the coming of the Washita.

The soldiers had permitted this gathering for the renewal of arrows and had not followed or pried into the sacred rite. They were busy elsewhere. Fighting still raged on the Plains, and the army had little time for the ragged band of Cheyenne and Arapaho they had corralled onto the reservation. It was the year 1887 by the white man's reckoning, and Wind Flower was thirteen.

Before her birth, there had been Sand Creek, the massacre by the evil White Hair's army. The old ones still spoke of Black Kettle and White Hair, who was killed at Greasy Grass. Wind Flower, two at the time of Greasy Grass, had often listened to whispered words of the battle the Washita called Little Big Horn. Whispered words of the man Custer and his defeat, hushed remembrances of a life that had all but vanished for the Cheyenne. The reservation on the Tongue River was the only home Wind Flower remembered. Still, she longed for the past her parents spoke of now in sorrowful whispers, late at night while their children slept.

When Wind Flower was small, Little Wolf had led the people to the Tongue River. Since then, the tribe had lived peaceably with their white jailers, but stories drifted back from the Plains where the Sioux fought on.

Of the journey to Tongue River, Wind Flower remembered little save for the intense cold and the wailing that seemed to envelop the tribe, blanketing them in sorrow and grief. The Great Spirit took her two brothers before the march began, and another sister, Pale Deer, died during the winter spent in the frozen caves of Lost Chokeberry Creek.

Over the years, Wind Flower had heard many stories of the events that led the Cheyenne to the land of the Tongue. Stories of the surrender at Fort Robinson with Crazy Horse and many of his Oglala Sioux with them. Stories of the Washita's betrayal and breaking of the treaty agreement, a betrayal that sent them to live in sickness and squalor with their Southern Cheyenne brothers. Stories telling of the fevers, chills, and aching of the bones that had taken her brothers and many more until Little Wolf dared to break away and push northward. Now, they lived under the white man's thumb, caged like animals but in relative peace, with less sickness and death than there'd been in the South.

"Someday," said Na'go, her mother. "Someday, we may be able to wrench the fire water from the hands of our warriors and their strength will return. Then we can break away to live in freedom once more." Na'go sighed when she spoke, knowing the elusive nature of freedom now that the Washita were here to stay.

Finding another patch of turnip, not the sweet red turnip but its more plentiful cousin, Wind Flower stooped and sank her dibble into the surrounding earth, teasing out the large white roots. She worked the smooth wooden spade carefully, shaking the dirt from the unblemished roots as she tucked them into her bag before moving on. Thus they continued until the sun reached its uppermost point. It was Laughing Dove who began complaining.

Dove, so like their mother with her dark eyes, long braids, and chubby figure, had trudged along behind her older sister, puffing noisily as the sun grew hotter, but now she'd reached her limit. There was no help for it. They would have to stop and rest, at least for a little while.

"Flower, I can't walk anymore," she whimpered, her voice echoing through the silence of the forest. The others were out of sight and hearing. To Dove, the woods, so cool and welcoming when they'd started out, now seemed full of unseen terrors.

Laughing Dove was afraid of everything, even the Wise Ones. Her sister knew she would soon be crying, imagining wild beasts all around them. "All right, my sister, we'll stop here and rest, but only for a little while." They'd reached a clearing, and Wind Flower set down her bag on the soft moss at the edge of the path, beckoning to her sister. "Come sit beside me, and I'll sing."

As an infant, Laughing Dove had napped little and cried incessantly, no matter who held and coddled her. She would drink quietly at her mother's breast, but the rest of the time, she howled. One day when her na'go was too busy to hold her, she was handed to her older sister.

Wind Flower took the tiny squalling baby and walked to the edge of camp, singing and rocking her. Round and plump even then, Laughing Dove's chubby, soft arms and tiny hands poked out of the blanket, reaching up to her sister's braids. Wind Flower continued singing and rocking, and before long, the baby quieted. The perpetual crying had ceased as Laughing Dove lay gazing adoringly at her sister.

Wind Flower's singing had always been a source of cruel teasing among her people. While the other women's voices reached to the skies, her voice sank to the earth, like a stone dropping from a high cliff. Before that morning, Na'go would motion for silence whenever her eldest daughter burst into song, but never again. As long as she held her tiny sister, Wind Flower was never silenced.

To this day, Laughing Dove could always be comforted by her sister's songs, and Wind Flower's kindred were forever grateful. A croaking girl's songs were always preferable to the screams of an unhappy child. Wind Flower felt needed. Upon her little sister, she could pour all the love she felt, all the love that her kindred had no time for anymore. As their world disappeared, wrenched away by the avarice of the Washita, her parents and elders had closed their hearts. Survival consumed every waking moment; there was no time for love.

Now the warm sunlight filtering down through the trees and her sister's singing lulled Laughing Dove to sleep. As her sister's breathing became regular, Wind Flower leaned down to kiss her cheek, brushing damp curls from her face. Perhaps Dove should have stayed behind, she mused, thinking of the long walk ahead of them. Back to the camp with over two hundred tipis arched in a huge crescent, curving toward the mountains beyond the plain. "Sleep, my little one," she whispered. "You'll need it."

Wind Flower leaned back, intending only to rest her eyes, but unexpected weariness overtook her. Before she knew it, she too was asleep—a deep, dangerous sleep full of dreams and remembrances. A sleep so deep that she failed to hear the horses. By the time the white man's voice broke into her dreams, it was too late. Too late to run, too late to hide.

CHAPTER 2

Wind Flower found herself in a familiar dream. Lost in the woods, she spied Ni'hu, her father, through the trees, calling, beckoning for her. Running to him, she cried, begging him to hold her. As strong, gentle arms enfolded her, Ni'hu whispered, "Be still, my daughter—you're safe." Suddenly, a shadowy figure stepped into the clearing—a Washita, his blue eyes blazing into hers. "Come, daughter." The Washita's eyes beseeched her to follow. They were her own eyes gazing back at her. Ni'hu held tight, and she was safe, but the Washita stayed too, close by, watching, waiting.

Suddenly, Corn Woman's face replaced that of the Washita. Corn Woman, tall and proud with her long, black braids tinged with gray. It was Corn Woman and her troubles that had brought the people together for the Renewal of the Sacred Arrows. Her shame had to be healed, and her brother, Bear Claw, had pledged the arrow renewal to bring the tribe back into favor—his sister's disgrace had touched them all.

Corn Woman struck Small Willow, her daughter, and soon after, the young girl killed herself in shame. For this, Corn Woman had been banished from the tribe forever. But her leaving was not enough—bad luck hung over the tribe like a black cloud, smothering what little good fortune remained.

The Cheyenne had suffered too much misfortune, and now Bear Claw hoped to bring back the luck. The ceremony, coming as it did at the height of the hunting season, promised prosperity and hope for all. The Sweet Medicine Chief would guide the Cheyenne on their journey, his powerful wisdom and knowledge delivering them out of the darkness.

Once the ceremony began, all the women and children would be confined to the tipis for four days and nights. Wind Flower recognized the importance of the arrow renewal, but she dreaded the confinement. Today, the air had smelled especially sweet. In her dream, she breathed deeply, gulping up the sweet crisp air, hoping to hold on to a little to take with her into the dark stuffy tipi. As she breathed in, half-asleep, half-awake, the air suddenly changed, growing thicker, and she began to choke.

"Hey, Cooky. What we got here? A couple of little squaws! Musta wandered off the reservation!" He'd already grabbed Laughing Dove. She screamed, struggling to free herself as the horses pawed the ground, circling them. Choking dust surrounded Wind Flower as she struggled to her feet. The man kept one arm around Laughing Dove's waist while he fought off the kicks and scratches of her older sister.

"Jesus, Cooky! Git off yer horse and help me. We got a regular wildcat here!"

Jumping from his horse, Cooky grabbed Wind Flower's arm and pulled her away. "Well, now, little missy. Ain't no call to carry on like that! We ain't gonna hurt ya. Gonna help, don't ya know? You'll be a dern sight better off where we's headed than you are now, I reckon. Now settle down, you hear?" His breath reeked of tobacco and whiskey, and his rough beard brushed against her cheek as he held her against him.

Laughing Dove called out, her wails echoing through the forest. Wind Flower kicked and scratched, desperately trying to free herself. "Ouch! Christ Almighty, Les—the little hellcat bit me!" He raised his hand, then brought it down full force, knocking her to the ground.

Sometime later, Wind Flower woke to the jostling of the horse and a sharp, stabbing pain in the small of her back from the saddle horn pressed up against her. They rode in silence on a well-worn trail across open ground. The land was unfamiliar to Wind Flower. She attempted to sit up but was pushed down roughly with a "Not so fast, my little bobcat. After yer clawing, you kin suffer fer a bit."

Twisting her neck, she vainly tried to catch a glimpse of her sister, but the other man rode alongside Cooky, and she was unable to see over or around the horse. No sound came from the other riders save for the clopping of hooves on the hard, dusty ground of the trail. Closing her eyes, she beseeched the Wise Ones Above to help them.

As it grew dark, the men began searching for a place to camp for the night. "We'll never make the train tonight, Cooky. Better to sleep here and make an early start."

At his words, Wind Flower woke with a start, her head fuzzy and sore. Cooky dragged her down, then shoved her toward the others. Finally, she spied her sister and discovered the reason for her silence. Laughing Dove had been gagged with the man's grimy bandana, now soaked with her tears. Wind Flower tried to go to her, but Cooky yanked her back. "Oh no you don't. Get us some wood, and hurry up."

When she pretended not to understand, he grabbed a fistful of twigs, gesturing. "Wood, you stupid squaw. Wood. And hurry up, or your sister gets it," he added, pointing a hunting knife at Laughing Dove, who cowered on the ground, eyes wild with fear. Wind Flower's gaze reached out to the frightened child, reassuring her before she turned to hurry off for wood.

Wind Flower understood the men perfectly, but Laughing Dove knew not a word of English, and with every word, her fear escalated. Her older sister decided to feign ignorance as well, perhaps learning more of their plans if they thought she didn't understand their talk. Jack Wilkins, a scout who had lived with the tribe for a time, had taught Wind Flower the white man's tongue. Jack, or Fire Hair, as the Cheyenne called the tall, gentle man with the head of flaming red hair, had lived for several moons in Lone Turtle's tipi, but then he had been called away East. It had been twelve moons since they'd last seen him.

Jack said Wind Flower was a fast learner and urged her parents to enroll her in the government school. "She'd outshine them all," Jack had told them, but Strong Arrow and Smooth Water wouldn't hear of it.

Hurrying to gather as many twigs and branches as she could, Wind Flower rushed back, frantic with worry and longing to comfort her sister.

Where were they taking them? There had been so many stories circulating among her people, tales of children abducted and sold into slavery in Mexico, but these men were not Mexicans. Who were they? Her kindred always spoke of the white man and his devilish ways in hushed tones, breaking off the talk when children appeared. She felt so ignorant, so unprepared.

Dropping the twigs in front of the man called Les, she moved toward her sister. "Not yet," he snarled pulling her back. "Fire first, then the kid." He used the Cheyenne word for fire, then repeated it. "Fire."

Wind Flower was experienced in fire starting, a chore that had been hers alone for many moons, and she soon had a small crackling fire blazing. The men brought food and cooking utensils from their saddlebags.

As they prepared dinner, she began inching her way toward Laughing Dove until she sat at her sister's side. She slid her arm around the trembling child, and Laughing Dove collapsed against her, sobbing. As the men appeared to take no notice of them, Wind Flower quietly slipped off the gag, and the muffled sobs became more audible.

Their captors turned, and Cooky yelled, "Hey," but the other man said, "If she can shut up, it can stay off. If not, back on it goes. Understand?" He gestured with his hands and Wind Flower nodded, whispering to her sister, beseeching her to be silent. After several great sighs and heavings of breath, her weeping ceased, and she lay shivering in her sister's arms.

As he pulled a tin pot from the stove, Cooky motioned to them. "Come, eat." They were each given a bowl of something called hash that burned their throats and tasted horrible. The girls tried to eat for fear of angering their captors, but the hash simply would not go down.

Finally, the men allowed them to retreat back from the fire to where their root bags lay forgotten on the ground. Wind Flower reached into hers for a turnip, intending to share it with Laughing Dove, but the cocking of a pistol stopped her.

"Not so fast." Cooky's gun was aimed at her heart, his eyes, cold and empty, glaring down at her. Killer's eyes.

"Put it down, Cooky." Les pushed his partner's hand away, then advanced toward the pair huddled on the ground. In their tongue, he asked, "What's in the bag?"

In reply, Wind Flower spilled the contents onto her skirt. When he spied the small stash of roots and berries, Les laughed. "Yep, Cooky, ya better shoot 'em! That there's a dangerous bunch of loot they got theirselves." Cookie scowled, turning back toward the fire, ignoring Les, who laughed until tears ran down his cheeks.

The girls chewed small pieces of turnip, comforted by the familiar taste after the putrid hash. They huddled together on a blanket the men had thrown them, until Les said, "Time to sleep, little ones. Don't you be scared, now. We's taking you to school. Understand? School? Not gonna scalp you or kill you. So you can rest easy."

In spite of her fears, sleep soon overtook Wind Flower, lulled as she was by the even, steady breathing of her sister beside her. Laughing Dove had fallen asleep with the turnip still in her mouth. Fallen asleep, midchew.

The man's words made no sense to Wind Flower. What did he mean about school? Was he taking them back to the reservation school? If so, why had they grabbed them in the first place?

About the Author

M. Lee Prescott is the author of dozens of works of fiction for adults, young adults, and children, among them *Prepped to Kill, Gadfly, Lost in Spindle City* and *Poof!* **(Ricky Steele Mysteries),** *A Friend of Silence, In the Name of Silence* and *The Silence of Memory* **(Roger and Bess Mysteries),** *Jigsaw,* and *Song of the Spirit,* and her newest contemporary romance series, *Morgan's Run,* of which *Polly's Heart* is the seventh! Three of her nonfiction titles have been published by Heinemann, and she has published numerous articles in the field of literacy education. Lee is a professor of education at a small New England liberal arts college, where she teaches reading and writing pedagogy. Her current research focuses on mindfulness and connections to reading and writing. She regularly teaches abroad, most recently in Singapore.

Lee has lived in southern California (loved those Laguna nights!), Chapel Hill, North Carolina, and various spots in Massachusetts and Rhode Island. Currently, she resides in Massachusetts on a beautiful river, where she canoes, swims, and watches an incredible variety of wildlife pass by. She is the mother of two grown sons and spends lots of time with them, their beautiful wives, and her beloved grandchildren. When not teaching or writing, Lee's passions revolve around family, yoga (Kripalu is a second home), swimming, sharing mindfulness with children and adults, and walking.

Lee loves to hear from readers. Email her at <u>mleeprescott@gmail.com</u>, and visit her website to hear the latest and sign up for her newsletters!

A Note from the Author

I am thrilled to bring you Polly and Kevin's sweet and sensual love story! This marks the seventh of the ***Morgan's Run*** books, with more coming soon. Thank you so much for reading it. These beloved characters will be around as the series continues to grow. The *Morgan's Run* books are set in the gorgeous American Southwest, an area of the country that is dear to my heart not only because it is home to my youngest son and family, but also because its beauty is so extraordinary and so startlingly different from that of my New England home. What a backdrop for romance and adventure!

If you like ***Polly's Heart*** and would be willing to write an Amazon review, I would be very grateful. If you would like to sign up for future book releases and occasional notices about my books, please visit my <u>Author Website</u> and sign up for my newsletter. I promise I will not share your address, nor will I flood you with emails. Do visit my site to read more about my books and hear what's next.

Finally, this book has been revised, proofed, and edited many, many times, but my intrepid assistants and I are human, so if you spot a typo, please email me at <u>mleeprescott@gmail.com,</u> and I will fix it. If you'd like to know more about my other books, please scroll ahead to the next section.

Warm wishes,

M. Lee

OTHER BOOKS BY M. LEE PRESCOTT

The Ricky Steele Mysteries

Book 1: *Prepped to Kill*

Book 2: *Gadfly*

Book 3: *Lost in Spindle City*

Book 4: *Poof!*

Also, featuring Ricky Steele:

Jigsaw

Roger and Bess Mysteries

Book 1: *A Friend of Silence*

Book 2: *In the Name of Silence*

Book 3: *The Silence of Memory*

Contemporary Romances
Well-Loved Romances

Widow's Island

Hestor's Way

Morgan's Run Romances

Book 1: *Emma's Dream*

Book 2: *Lang's Return*

Book 3: *Jeb's Promise*

Book 4: *Rose's Choice*

Book 5: *Hope's Wonder*

Book 6: *Ruthie's Love*

Book 7: *Polly's Heart*

Young Adult Historical Romance

Song of the Spirit

www.ingramcontent.com/pod-product-compliance
Lightning Source LLC
Chambersburg PA
CBHW061016120726
47910CB00006B/1970